EARTH:
THE SALVAGE
GAME

EARTH: THE SALVAGE GAME

The Death of Thera

LEO HELLER

authorHOUSE®

AuthorHouse™ LLC
1663 Liberty Drive
Bloomington, IN 47403
www.authorhouse.com
Phone: 1-800-839-8640

Published by AuthorHouse   10/19/2013

ISBN: 978-1-4918-2773-4 (sc)
ISBN: 978-1-4918-2635-5 (e)

Library of Congress Control Number: 2013918488

Introduction

Every legend and every myth has an element of truth somewhere within it. Often the story has been so distorted with the endless re-tellings that the factual part is so enveloped in falsehoods that it's nearly impossible to tell where the fabrications end and the truth begins.

Though still bearing the derogatory label, the myth was originally rooted in actual persons and actual events, but like the tales of an old story-teller I once knew, the facts often get distorted to fit the agenda of the teller of the tale.

Nineteenth and twentieth century scientists were quick to dismiss the claims of any lay person who wasn't graced with a university diploma, or, with anything they hadn't personally verified, or, for that matter, anything which seemed to fall outside the realm of the finite physical universe as they understood it.

Much as the Orthodox Christians had done in the wake of the Roman Empire's demise, the Orthodox Scientific Community as much as said, "These are the facts, and anything that falls outside the accepted facts is superstitious hokum, and therefore heresy." I don't know that the above sentence is printed anywhere, but all one has to do is step on the toes of the scientific community, and like any of the heretical Christian sects of the first millennium after the death of Jesus, if you don't accept the Orthodox view, you are a heretic and therefore an enemy of the state, subject to derision, censure, imprisonment, and maybe even death.

If our story turns out as I hope it does, then much of what is today accepted as scientific fact will one day fall into that discredited 'myth' category, and truth will be disseminated to the people, regardless of how preposterous it may have seemed to twentieth century scientists.

After all, the twentieth century brought us two world wars, insane despots the likes of Hitler, Stalin, Mao, Pol Pot, George Bush, Bill Clinton, and Barack Obama; the legitimization of the pseudoscience of psychiatry, and a financial system run completely amok.

If Enlightenment is ever truly achieved, the twentieth century will, in retrospect, appear to be an Age as Dark as the thirteenth.

With the previous paragraph now in our consideration, I know we have all heard stories of Bigfoot, Sasquatch, Yeti, Grassman, and the Skunk Ape. Though no evidence has ever been 'officially' recorded, there have been thousands of sightings by un-diploma'd individuals for nearly all of recorded history. And their beginnings were told in the oldest known written document of Ancient Sumer, The Epic of Gilgamesh.

Some of you may have actually seen one of these creatures, while others of you may believe that since science hasn't provided the proof to the public, they must not exist, and therefore all sightings are pure superstition by ignorant people.

By that same token, you may be completely convinced that an underwater hominid society, which are laughingly called 'mermaids', is a fantasy created by an over-imaginative superstitious populace, but yet they, too, have been sighted throughout recorded history by the Greeks, Chinese, Phoenicians, Spanish, English, and even the residents of a long-evaporated coastal culture in the deserts of Egypt. Twentieth century science dismisses this as childish foolishness, and perhaps you, as have I, thought it not worth considering.

And just as I begin to think I am a learned man, I realize I yet know almost nothing. And such was the situation when I learned of what happened just a few short years ago.

*　*　*

It was a chilly day in April, 2004 when a trio of scientists was investigating a mass whale beaching off the Washington coast. When they arrived, there was a group of people in hazmat suits already on site, working in an area that was roped off as "Restricted".

This seemingly clandestine and possibly dangerous situation was not why the scientists had arrived. They were there to investigate the beaching of the whales, and were aware, just a few years earlier, that the US Navy was using sonic waves that frightened whales into shallow waters, where their internal organs collapsed from their own body weight. A whale must remain floating in water to prevent his own weight from crushing himself.

But on this day, the scientists noted that every single whale on the beach had blood running from its ears, and the trio proceeded to take as many tissue samples as they could carry.

Unbeknownst to the investigators, two young boys had first spotted the beached whales earlier that morning and had taken video on a cell phone camera, something no one expected young boys to possess in 2004.

The Navy intimidated the boys and their families into silence, and into recanting the story they had originally told. Because of pressure from naval officers, the boys admitted that what they had seen was a decayed seal. Fortunately, the boys never mentioned the cell phone camera.

But when the video was finally seen, some months later, by the scientists, it was obvious that what they had videoed was not only *not* a seal, it wasn't decayed, and it damn sure wasn't dead.

When they returned to the lab to analyze the whale tissue samples, they discovered that every sample contained signs of blunt force trauma. And while they suspected the Navy in this mass beaching, they expected to see crushed internal organs, not blunt force trauma. This was something new.

Knowing that sonic waves from the Navy was a probable cause for this event, they sailed out to retrieve an underwater recording device, and returned to the lab to listen to the recordings of the previous few days. They listened in disbelief to the sounds picked up by the device just prior to the beaching.

There was a long low groan just prior to a huge sonic blast that sent all the marine mammals screeching in pain. Trying to escape this blast was what drove the whales ashore, and caused blood to run from their ears. The sonic weapon had also caused the blunt force trauma. While reviewing the recordings, they located a highly articulate group of sounds which, try as they might, they could not identify, but realized it was much more complex than dolphin communication. They thought perhaps that they had located a new subspecies of dolphin.

Shortly after the Washington State beaching, there were numerous mass beachings all over the planet, which the scientists followed in an effort to gather enough evidence to get an injunction against the Navy to stop them from murdering the whales. They still had no idea about the video, or what the mysterious men in the hazmat suits were doing, or that they had taken a live creature to a naval facility in Beaufort, South Carolina.

While cruising the southern oceans following the wave of beachings, they got a call to come to South Africa to view a strange anomaly. When they arrived, they believed they had been called in error. A great white shark, even one as big as this, was no anomaly. It was only then that they were informed that it wasn't the shark that was the anomaly . . . . it was what was inside it.

After searching through the smelly contents of the shark's stomach, and identifying everything that was readily identifiable, they took what was left to a local lab, and applied for permission from the South African Government to remove the specimens to their lab in the United States. And then they began to wait . . . . and wait . . . . and wait . . . . while they did the best research they could in the local laboratory.

They had in their possession, about 30 percent of a body of some creature that they hadn't been able to identify. As they examined what they had, they gradually ruled out any known species of marine mammal. They thought at first perhaps it was a manatee, but a manatee has no tail bones, and this creature's tail had bones like an elongated, flattened foot.

And then they realized they had identified humanoid *fingers*.

While still patiently waiting for permission to remove the remains to the US, their lab and all their findings were confiscated in an early morning police raid. All the remains and all the research were gone . . . forever. They did, however, get a report back on a DNA test they had requested.

It said, "The DNA you forwarded to us must have been contaminated and is therefore deemed worthless. All the markers indicate that it is *human*."

Realizing that their own government was complicit in this confiscation and cover-up, they soon left their positions in the NOAA, but independently continued their research. It was then that they found the Baltic Sea fisherman who had discovered, many times, bone spears in fish he had recently netted, and was once fortunate enough to get a photo . . . . of what, he wasn't quite sure.

Not long after, they found a video of an Adriatic Sea fishing venture in which one of these creatures was hauled up in a net and briefly appeared on the video before it escaped the net and leapt back into the sea.

And of course, there was the cell phone video shot by the two boys at the original beaching, which was simply inconceivable.

The boys had videoed a webbed hand, barely protruding from beneath a mass of seaweed. It suddenly began to clench its fingers, and as one boy filmed while the other touched the seaweed, the creature sprang to life.

In the few seconds before absolute panic consumed the boys, it was plain to see, the bony ridge in the skull, the webbed fingers, long arms, a fluke for feet, and a definitively hominid face . . . . just like the Adriatic Sea netting.

In this and subsequent volumes, I hope to show you that these creatures are one branch of the family of descendants of a god named Poseidon and a human female named Cleito.

*   *   *

In a seemingly unrelated vein, there is a common consensus in the 'scientific' community that "everyone knows you only live once." The healthcare industry in the United States profits untold sums of money from that consensus. After all, if you only live once, you must do everything in your power to save your body; but if a person truly understands he is an immortal being trapped inside a finite, mortal human body, his irrational protection of his body becomes passé.

This digs directly into the pockets of Big Pharma and Big Banking, so the myth of one-body/one-life is disseminated as fact.

I hope to show, through my own previous experience, that I have found the 'one-life' theory to be highly erroneous, and that my experiences have a direct connection to Sasquatch and, for lack of a better term, *Mermaids*.

Synopsis of Lunacy and Lobotomy in the Lead Belt

When we first met Charles in the previous volume, he had spent the last 40 years hoping that his son was still alive and that he may, after all this time, (at the very least), discover the truth. And the truth he discovered was one he, in his wildest dreams, would have never imagined.

Shortly after meeting the daughter of the man he held responsible for his son's disappearance, he found himself in the bottom of the Doe Run Lead Mine, surrounded by beautiful bald aliens.

Once he was introduced to the fountain of youth contained within himself, he and his new lover began a campaign to provide an abundance of green energy for the local residents, and had established a 300 acre naturist resort in Madison County.

All was proceeding well until the aliens decided that politicians, once the evil intentions had been erased from their minds, would, on their own, reverse the dwindling spiral that was spinning our nation and planet out of control. What they hadn't planned for, however, was the depth of debauchery to which the secret Emperor of Earth would sink, and the effect that would have on the only political ally they had: The President of the United States.

I, who had planned only on being the narrator of this tale, was soon dragged kicking and screaming into the middle of it. But in the process, I found the soul mate for whom I had searched for centuries.

After she and I had abducted the Evil Emperor in order to bring him to justice, our craft lost power and we were forced to land on an uncharted island in the South Pacific . . . . an island inhabited by starving cannibals . . . . When we left the story, the Emperor had escaped his electronic restraints, and had knocked my inamorata, bleeding and unconscious, to the floor.

But before we pick up where we left Lunacy and Lobotomy, it's time to fill in a few of the gaps and learn a little more about some of these folks. As you may recall, after undergoing de-implantation, I began having these strange recollections of a past I couldn't explain in polite company. But by the very fact that you are astute enough to hold this volume in your hand, I believe that I can explain to you how the past we shared thousands of years ago brought us back together in a tiny ghost town in Southeast Missouri.

The Characters:

Charles Dietzburg:	World War II veteran, truck driver, father of Sam. I first met him in Belize tens of thousands of years ago.
Veronica Schulte:	Daughter of Horatio Schulte, the psychiatrist who had medicated Sam into an inanimate biological lump. In a past life, she was once my little sister.
Sam/Charlie Jr.:	Son of Charles, who escaped from the psych hospital into the caves under Delassus. Befriended by and eventual husband of Marie Wallingford.
Marie:	Fellow escapee from the hospital, living in the caves. Wife of Sam.
Homer:	Former hospital orderly, whose wife was murdered by a staff psychiatrist when she discovered his illegal activity. Homer had been my grandfather when we first came to Earth a thousand centuries earlier.

Cleo/Karpokula:
: The beautiful bald alien who brought the technology to Earth to save it from itself. Originally came to Earth with her lover, my grandfather, my sister and me.

Billy:
: Tongue-less old man who also escaped the psych hospital as a boy and spent his life living with my great aunt. Once Cleo's boyfriend, Dobber.

Janey:
: Former lover of Charles before he was shipped overseas in WW II. Co-worker of Roy, the septic system installer.

Constance:
: Marie and Sam's daughter

Toni:
: Former employee/spy at psych hospital, who was, in a former life, the twin sister of Marie.

Leo:
: Narrator and unwilling participant in the journey. In the process, he found the soul mate he knew existed somewhere; a beautiful bald alien named Cleo.

Roy:
: Septic System installer, co-worker and pretended brother of Janey

GENESIS

＊

Northern Mexico 98,000 B.C.

I was eight years old the summer we landed in what you call the Chihuahuan Desert. My grandfather had been here many times in the past, dumping his trash here for years. In fact, he wasn't alone. Many of our people had been dumping here. He said no one could remember how long or why we ever made this our dump.

"Grandfather," I asked, "Is it like this everywhere?" I paid close attention to the flora, particularly the ocotillo and agave. "We have plants like that back home, don't we Grandfather?"

"Yes, Solan." He always seemed too busy to talk to me unless I was in trouble. I wanted to tell him that I would be in trouble less often if he spoke to me more often, but I didn't think it would do any good. He was always so preoccupied that I felt like I was mostly in the way. I didn't know the word or the emotion at the time, but he was patronizing me. Many years later I understood his impatience as adult responsibilities overtook my life, and I, too, became a patronizer of children.

"Why do we dump our trash here and not just kick it out through the hatch?" I asked, failing to grasp his annoyance with me. Every other time we'd been here we just kicked it out while still in the air. I wondered why we landed this time.

"What . . . why . . . . huh? What did you say? Can't you see I'm busy, Solan? Our lives here depend on me right now, and I can't be answering your annoying questions all the time." Of course, by the time I realized I was getting on his nerves, it was too late. I'd made him mad again, something I seemed to do more and more these days.

I left the bridge and trudged back to my cabin, burying my head under my blankets in a deep funk. After about an hour of feeling sorry for myself, I dug my little body out of the quilts and went down to the mess hall. Dobber, the first (and only) mate, was sitting alone drinking a cup of coffee and eating a sweet roll. "What's up, Solly?" he asked; always cheerful and always glad to see me.

"Grandfather's mad at me again," I moaned, trying to gain his sympathy.

"Oh, he's not mad at you. He's got a lot on his mind lately, now that we can't go home . . . ." He cut himself off in midsentence.

"Whaddya mean, can't go home?" Now I was worried.

"Uh . . . uh . . . . I mean not for a couple weeks, maybe even a month," he lied. "Till things settle down at home." I knew he was lying but didn't have the skills to draw him out and make him tell me the truth. "C'mon, kid. I've got about 20 minutes before I have to go back to the bridge. Let's go play some Deathstar. Maybe that'll cheer you up."

"O.K." I pouted. I could never understand why adults always tried to bribe you to take your mind off the fact that they were the reason why you were unhappy in the first place. I moped my way down to the arcade to make Dobber a little more uncomfortable, hiding the fact that I'd much rather be playing Deathstar than burying my head under the blankets.

Even though he was adept at masking it, Dobber let me win three games in a row. I confess it did cheer me up and alleviated a little of my self-pity. But by the third loss, I knew he was sandbagging, and I grew bored with it.

"I gotta get back to the bridge, Solly. Good Games. You're getting' better all the time."

"Yeah, yeah," I patronized him back.

"Why don't you go find Princess? Maybe she wants to play."

"Oh, I don't wanna play with her. Stupid girls just wanna play with stupid dolls and have stupid tea parties." My moroseness was quickly returning. "I wish Grandfather would talk to me. I wanna know when we can go home. I wanna see my mom and dad."

"Well," he hesitated. "I'll talk to him. See what he says." He tousled my hair, and I quickly brushed him off. My ennui was getting the best of me. "Go read a book or watch a movie. I've gotta get back to work."

"Yeah, yeah," I mumbled again. I'd read enough books and seen enough movies to hold me for another year. I wanted to know what was going on and why everyone was keeping me in the dark.

As Dobber disappeared down the corridor, I thought to myself, *To Hell with the books and movies. If they won't tell me, I'll find out on my own!* and followed him surreptitiously down the corridor. As he opened the door to the bridge, I ducked in an alcove and hid until he was securely inside. I then tiptoed down to the bridge door and pressed my ear against it. There was a window high in the door, but I wasn't tall enough to see through it.

"Caesar," I heard Dobber say, "You've got to talk to Solly. This mystery is driving him crazy. He wants to go home and I don't know what to tell him."

"Don't tell him anything. He's too young to understand." He hesitated for a moment, then added, "I'll tell him when *I* think he's old enough."

"Well, with the questions he's been asking; the questions *you* haven't been listening to, I think he's old enough to understand. Just make it comprehensible to him." I knew I needed to see through the window, so I ran down to the storage room to find a step stool.

When I returned with the stool and stepped carefully upon it, I heard Grandfather raise his voice. "That's MY decision, Dobber, not yours! Is that clear?"

"Yeah, I get it that *you* think so, but these aren't ordinary circumstances, and you're not really in a position to pull rank. I have no desire to cause you any additional trouble, but if you think you can put me in the brig for insubordination, you're doing nothing but pissing in the wind. We need each other now more than ever!" By the change in pitch of Dobber's voice, even I could tell he was agitated. He *never* talked to Grandfather like that. He turned around and I quickly ducked out of sight, but only for a second.

What happened next, I never expected. Would Grandfather punch him in the nose? Put him in the brig? Maybe just give him a good cussing? Nope, none of the above. My grandfather plopped down on the floor and began sobbing. I couldn't believe my ears. I pressed my ear closer to the door to be sure it wasn't Dobber that was crying . . . . It wasn't.

Grandfather tried to speak, but the sobs jerked his body and words came out as gibberish. I couldn't understand anything he said, and I felt a sudden rush of sympathy for him, when before I felt mostly fear, and tears began to well from my eyes as well. When he could finally speak, I was still only getting a few words between the sobs. "No . . . . radio contact . . . . for weeks . . . . been sending . . . . a . . . . signal . . . . continuously . . . . but nothing . . . ."

"I know," Dobber was solemn. "I know Caesar. I've known all along. We both thought the other ship would make it, but we have to assume they're lost, so we need every man jack we can muster if we plan to survive. It doesn't matter if he IS eight years old. He needs to know the truth. And the sooner we can train him to help, the better off we'll be." After a few moments of silence, he added, "They *are* the future of our race, Caesar."

"Sixty . . . . billion . . . . people? And . . . . five . . . . survivors? It simply cannot be!" My grandfather wailed.

"C'mon, Caesar. Get a grip. You've been through hundreds of tough battles. Commanded thousands of men. This is just another battle. The future of our race depends on what we do here and now. Pull you shit together old man. The rest of us need you." Dobber smiled at my grandfather, and he mustered a weak smile in return.

"You're right . . . . I know. I'm just . . . . overwhelmed . . . . don't know where to start." I could barely hear his words.

"Start by facing the reality. Not what you wish it was, but what it REALLY is. We're all alone. No one is going to come rescue us."

"Go get Solly," my grandfather acquiesced. "And Dobber?"

"Yes?"

"Thank you."

EXODUS

When Grandfather stood up, I quickly ducked down and got off the step stool. "Damn!" I nearly said out loud. I was certain he had seen me. I ran as quickly as possible down the corridor and ducked into the utility closet. Holding my breath as much as I could, I was sure they hadn't found me. Then, nearly silent footfalls stopped near the closet door.

"Wonder where he went," I heard Dobber say.

"Well, it must not have been Solly," Grandfather answered. I was too young to appreciate sarcasm. The only other two people with us were Princess and Cleopatra. In my young mind, I wanted to believe the men believed it wasn't me. When I heard the quiet footfalls diminish, I cautiously opened the door. Two heads popped around the corner.

"Hello Solly," both said simultaneously.

I leapt backwards and tumbled into brooms, mops, buckets, steps stools and cleaning supplies. I fell to the floor with a crash and then an avalanche of handles cascaded down upon my head. The smell of ammonia began to fill the room as the liquid leaked from cracked bottles.

The two men broke out into laughter as I fumbled my way out from under the debris. My ire was getting the best of me, but the madder I got, the more they laughed. The more they laughed, the more infuriated I became. They reached for my hands, but I slapped them away. "It's not funny!" I shrieked.

"I'm sure it's not . . . . at least from that perspective," Dobber grinned. "But from this one, it's hilarious!"

"C'mon, Solan. Let us help you up. We're not laughing at you, we're laughing with you." Grandfather tried to lighten my irritation.

"I'm not laughing!" I shouted. "How can you be laughing WITH me?!"

"Sorry, Solly," Dobber interjected. "Let us help you up." They reached out together, took me by the hands and pulled me to my feet. C'mon. Let's go get you cleaned up and then get some milk and cookies. Maybe your blood sugar is low."

"I don't want any milk and cookies!" I lied.

"Well, I do," Dobber replied. I knew he was lying too, because he just had his break not twenty minutes earlier.

"What about the radio?" Grandfather asked.

"Well if you think somebody is going to call, go set the recorder. But I think it's a waste of time. How long you been listening to that damn silence?"

Grandfather stared at the floor, trying to mask his shame, then headed toward the mess hall. The call of the Apollo would go unheard because of me.

When we reached the cafeteria, Princess and Cleopatra were already there, and Grandfather noticeably shuddered. Spilling the truth was going to be hard enough in front of me. He hadn't anticipated my little sister being there as well. Dobber put his arm around Grandfather and whispered, "You can do it. Cleo and I will help." My curiosity was eating me alive, but Princess was oblivious.

The ladies were playing checkers, and like Dobber had done with me earlier, Cleo was letting Princess win. She cast a grin in Dobber's direction, and I noticed a subtle shift of body language in my Deathstar challenger. Cleopatra was gorgeous . . . . even to my eight year old eyes. I loved her more than I loved my own mother. I was suddenly saddened when my thoughts turned to my mother, the woman whose attention I so desperately craved and yet never seemed to receive. I sorely wished I could have made her love me like I loved her, and wondered where she now might be. I felt I hadn't done enough to deserve her affection, and wished I had been what she wanted me to be. Gradually, pangs of guilt for loving Cleo more than I loved my own mother crept up on me. Was that what growing up felt like? I wasn't sure I liked it. Life can sure be confusing.

"Princess," Grandfather interrupted my reverie. "We have something to tell you and Solan."

"Just a minute, Grandfather. I'm about to beat Cleo at checkers." Her childish comment made me feel much older and more mature than my six-year-old sister.

Cleo made a sacrificial move that allowed Princess to quickly eliminate her from the board. My sister squealed with delight at her victory. God, but six-year-olds can be so immature!

"Princess!" my grandfather said more forcefully this time. "Come here NOW. We need to tell you something!"

My little sister begrudgingly came and sat beside me. She pinched me on the arm when she sat down. "What did you do this time, Solan?" She was certain I was the reason for the lecture. I slapped her hand away.

"Grandchildren," he began, in a speaking style that was anachronistic, even for his generation. Nobody talks like that anymore; and his mannerisms were the reason why we called him 'Grandfather' and not a less-formal name like 'Grandpa' or 'Paw-Paw'.

"Grandchildren," he said again. "This is our new home. We can't go home ever again."

Princess was quiet for a moment, then asked, "Ever?"

"Ever."

"Where's Mom and Dad? I want my mommy and daddy!" she began to wail.

Grandfather looked at Dobber and Cleo. They nodded approval at him. "They're both dead, children." He paused as the words sank in. "I'm sorry but it's true."

"Can't the doctors bring them back to life?" my sister pleaded.

"No, honey. There are no doctors to bring them back. They've all been totally vaporized. No one can come back from being vaporized." She didn't know what that meant, but I did. I learned it playing Deathstar. You don't learn about vaporization from playing checkers.

"But WHY?"

"There was a war." It was Cleopatra who spoke up to take some of the burden off my grandfather. "Thera is completely gone. There is no home, no towns, no roads, no cars, no ships, and no people. There's nothing left at all."

"I don't believe you!!!" she screamed and went running to her room. Cleo started after her when my grandfather interrupted.

"Don't. Please Cleo, I beg you. Let her be for a while. If she doesn't come out in a half-hour, you can go check on her." He looked at me for a few moments, then his soft eyes asked, but no words were spoken.

"Yes, Grandfather. Please tell me the truth. I suddenly felt REALLY grown up.

'You know there was a war?"

"Yes, Grandfather, I know."

"Thera is completely gone. We were attacked from three other planets. It's a really long story why, but our government betrayed us . . . . a little at a time. Some people complained, but like a frog in a pot of water brought to a slow boil, we stayed quiet until the damage was so profound there was no saving us."

"Who attacked us?" I asked. The frog analogy was lost on me. I didn't even know what a frog was.

Dobber looked like he was about to answer when my grandfather nodded his head, silently granting his permission for Dobber to answer, "Nicha, Qari, and Oxecmi." He waited for me to say something, but I didn't. "Have you heard of them?"

"Maybe," I answered. I'm sure I heard the names, but I never had any reason to pay attention. "We really can't go home?"

Three heads shook in unison and eventually my grandfather whispered, "No, we can't. This is now our home. If we survive at all, we survive *here*."

EDUCATION

P rincess came out of her room to look for me. Most of the time she did nothing but antagonize me, but now things were different. "Solan?" She looked so small and pitiful that, for the first time in my life, I felt sorry for her.

"What, Princess?"

"Is it true? We really can't go home? We'll never see Mommy and Daddy again?"

"I guess so. Dobber let it slip by accident. He didn't mean to say anything, but I knew something was wrong. Grandfather got really mad at first and then he got really sad when Dobber wanted to tell me. You know Grandfather. He might keep a secret, but he'd never tell a lie. Not even to a kid. Mom used to get really mad at him sometimes when he'd tell me something she wanted to keep secret." Princess began to cry again, and tears welled up in my eyes too. She hugged me for the first time that I could remember. I held her close hoping that the hug might offer her some comfort.

"Do you think Cleo would like to be our Mama?" Her question nearly knocked me off my feet, it was the last question I would have expected. "I really like her. She's really, really nice to me." Princess needed a stable point like Cleo to cling to. She knew I wasn't big enough to take care of her.

"Maybe so. I think we're the only ones left." I didn't realize that Grandfather's time away from the radio made my statement painfully true. Perhaps if he'd heard the call, we might have located some of them. But unbeknownst to the five of us at the time, our sister ship missed Earth entirely.

Princess' eyes lit up and I followed her gaze to see Cleo enter the room. I didn't know the word at the time, but Cleo had a *charisma* that attracted people to her. I always had a funny feeling when in her presence. I couldn't describe it then, and can barely do it now. I hoped that Princess would grow up to be like her. Sometimes I wanted to be like her. Her natural serenity pervaded every room she occupied and helped to calm those who were prone to bouts of anxiety.

After some discussion, Princess announced that they were going to see a 'chick-flick' and that I wasn't invited to come. I felt no small sense of betrayal as they headed toward the onboard theater, but announced, "Good. I want to be with the men anyway. Not silly girls." Those stupid chick-flicks always made the girls cry and I needed to be strong. I couldn't be a cry-baby. Besides, I was too old to be a bawl-bag. Crying is for little kids . . . . and girls . . . . I kept telling myself . . . . trying to ignore Grandfather's tears from earlier today.

I walked back to the bridge. I needed to be with MEN. We would find a way to survive. Grandfather, Dobber and me. And we'd take care of the girls.

*　　*　　*

When I walked in, Grandfather was still trying to make radio contact . . . . with anybody or anything. Dobber was studying some maps on the video screen. "What ya doing, Dobber? I hoped I could help.

"Looking for someplace we might go beside here. There's almost no water here. Pretty country but we need somewhere with water."

"And firewood," Grandfather added.

"What's that?" I asked

"Trees," Dobber answered.

"For shade?"

"No. To cut down and burn," Grandfather replied.

"You're going to cut down a tree?" I was incredulous! It simply wasn't done back home. There were only a few I'd ever seen up close, and you would be sent to prison immediately for cutting down a tree. The only time I'd ever seen it done was after a big storm came through our town and took down all of our trees. They were cut up with lasers and hauled off. That was the last time I'd seen trees on Thera. I'd seen a few here, on this planet . . . . from way up high, but not up close. I'd seen some on TV when they were talking about the war . . . . Now I remembered hearing about Nicha . . . . something about sending our trees to Nicha. Seemed impossible sending trees, since they were so attached to the ground.

"Yes, there are lots of trees here. We'll have to burn them for heat and for cooking eventually." Grandfather seemed lost in these thoughts . . . . talking . . . . but to no one in particular . . . . maybe just to himself.

"Solan," Dobber looked at me in his most serious expression. "When we run out of fuel, as we will soon, we'll have to abandon the ship. We'll have to move outside. When the ventilation systems no longer work, the ship will become like an oven in the summer heat. We can stay close by it, and maybe find a way to heat it in the winter, unless we find a place that's warm year-round." He stopped abruptly and turned to my grandfather. "This place has got to have a climate that's warm all year, doesn't it?"

"Sure. Near its equator."

"Got enough fuel to get there?"

"Doubt it. We have to use the planetary engines, and I didn't have time to fuel them before we left. We could travel space indefinitely, but not locally. How about the food supply?"

"A week. Maybe two if we're careful."

That's when I really got scared. Why had my grandfather kept this from me?

"We're gonna need your grandpa," Dobber was dead serious now. . . . . something he wasn't particularly known for. "He knows how to survive in the wild. Something none of us know how to do."

"Nice to be needed, but I could do without the circumstance."

"When your grandpa was a boy, Thera was covered in trees. He grew up in the forests. He hunted and fished. Electricity hadn't even been invented yet."

"No TV? No Movies? No lights? And they let you kill animals?" I couldn't believe my ears.

"That's right," Grandfather answered. "No cars, no space travel, no trains, no planes. And . . . . there were animals and trees everywhere! Not just in zoos and museums."

For the first time in my life, I started to see my grandfather as a very wise man, not just some old geezer that smelled funny. Someone who had been everywhere and done everything. Not just a grouch who was always telling me to get out of the way. He was the man I hoped I could be. "How old *are* you, Grandfather?"

He didn't answer for a few minutes and I wondered if he had even heard me. I started to ask him again, but he interrupted, "Solan, I'm not really your grandfather."

Dobber and I looked at him sideways.

"I'm your great-great-great-great grandfather."

Dobber did some quick math in his head. "That would make you almost 250 years old!"

"Two hundred and sixty-one to be exact."

"Wow! That's really, really old!"

"Gee, thanks, Solan. You sure know how to hurt an old man," he grinned for the first time in nearly three weeks. I was beginning to understand sarcasm. Maybe now that he wasn't keeping a secret, he wouldn't be so grouchy.

"It's because of my age; combined with the wisdom of Dobber and Cleo that we are here. If it had been up to your parents and grandparents, you'd have died with them. They didn't believe me, even though I'd been telling them for decades what was happening. They, like the rest of the frogs, sat comfortably in the water until they were cooked alive." I didn't realize at the time that the "cooked alive" phrase was literal.

"Mom said you were just an old man who worried too much." I wished I hadn't said it as soon as the words were out of my mouth.

"Let the obvious speak for itself," Dobber interjected. I looked at him stupidly. "Who's alive and who's not, Solan? It suddenly sank into my eight-year old skull, which seemed to be maturing at the rate of one year per minute this afternoon.

"Why did those planets attack us, Grandfather?"

"It's a really long story, but I'll try to make it understandable. Do you remember our former president, Clint Billion?"

"Yeah, we learned about him in school. He was president before I was born."

"Yes, sometimes I forget how young you are, and how old I am. I can remember 56 presidents during my life."

"Oh my God! You really are old!" Stuck my foot in my mouth again!

"Well, a hundred years ago, we had a big economic depression . . ."

"What's that mean?"

"The banks went broke. There was no money. People were starving. There were no jobs. I guess that's the easiest way to explain it.

"After the depression, the Government," he went on, "put rules into place to keep people from doing stupid things with money. I know it's hard to grasp, but people sometimes do stupid things, and money can make people crazy. Clint Billion abolished all the rules that had been put into place many decades ago. This allowed people to do some of the same stupid things all over again . . . . and sure enough . . . . they did."

"Why would he do that? I thought our presidents were brilliant leaders!"

"Because it helped him and some of his buddies get unbelievably rich! He didn't care what happened to Thera. He and his buddies got the money and that's all that mattered to him.

"On top of that, he changed the laws and let big companies move all the jobs to Nicha and Oxecmi, where the workers only got 10% of the pay that Therans got. That means they only earned one dollar for every ten dollars that a Theran made for doing the same job."

"So who got the other nine dollars?"

"The bosses at the big companies. Nine dollars doesn't sound like much, but when you multiply it by millions and millions of workers working millions and millions of hours, the bosses got so rich, it's more money than an eight-year old can imagine. It's more money than most adults can imagine."

"What happened to the Therans who used to have the jobs?"

"They collected money from the government for a while, but then the government went broke, because there was no one working to pay the taxes that provided the government with money. So they started borrowing money from Nicha and Qari. Qari got all its money because it owned all the fuel in the planetary confederacy. The fuel that provided the energy to create electricity and drive all our cars and space ships. So the government was borrowing money from the planets that it was buying everything from.

"Soon, Nicha, Qari, and Oxecmi had all the money. Oxecmi got all its money from drugs, but that's another story. The governments of the three planets told the government of Thera that they were calling in their loans and wanted the money back. If we couldn't pay them, they'd take over the planet and divide it amongst the three of them."

"Then why did they vaporize us?"

"Be patient, Solly, and listen closely." It was Dobber who encouraged my silent attention.

"Thera, which once had been a major military might among all the planets in our confederacy, thought they could easily wipe out the other three planets. We had a different president at that time. A really stupid man. Clint Billion was evil, but he was smart. Not as smart as he thought he was, but he was a genius compared to his successor, Gus Borghe. Borghe attacked the three planets, but they promptly cut off all our loans and we didn't have the money to afford a war. Borghe was able to borrow more money for a while from other planets, but after a couple years, they realized that they, too, were throwing good money after bad, and they cut him off.

"Thera was doomed and although its own people didn't realize it, the rest of the planets in the confederacy knew it. Qari began smuggling in bombs to create chaos among the people. Oxecmi was smuggling in drugs to destroy the will of the people. Even the Theran doctors were supporting the Oxecmi drug cartel, because they were all paid large sums of money to get the population hooked on drugs. It didn't do them any good, because they all died as well when Thera was vaporized.

"Borghe threatened the Nichans and Qaris, and told them if they didn't loan Thera more money, he was going to attack. He made a few puny attacks, then got on TV and declared 'Mission Accomplished'. The Nichans took out two cities in retaliation. Our government was completely unaware of Nicha's true power.

"Borghe made one more attack. It was Thera's last. Nicha had a secret weapon they called a 'planet buster'. And it was. When Borghe launched his second attack, that's when I got you and your sister off the planet. There were others I'd been in communication with, and we synchronized out departures to leave at the same time. I've been trying to locate them ever since, but to no avail . . . ."

"It's a little more complicated than that," Dobber interjected.

"Yes," Grandfather answered, "but not much . . . and who was the one who told me to make it understandable to Solan? I had to make it comprehensible to him, not an economics professor." More sarcasm. I was starting to catch on.

"Why did the doctors help the Oxecmis, Grandfather? That seems crazy!"

"It is!" Both adults chimed in, then Grandfather went on, "But they were enticed by the drug companies to promote hundreds and hundreds of drugs for made-up diseases. They targeted people who had some small ailment, gave it a fancy name, and created a drug for it. But the drugs all made the people fatter and lazier and more and more dependent on the doctors and the drugs until most of the population of Thera was hooked.

"When a person has an addiction, the only thing they think about is feeding that addiction. The world can be in flames around them, but their need to feed the addiction is so great, they don't even notice the fire. And almost the whole planet was addicted."

"Mom and Dad too?" I didn't really want to know the answer, but the question was out.

"Yes, Solan, I'm afraid so. They tried to get you and Princess on the drugs too, but I raised so much Hell that they gave up . . . . as long as I kept the two of you occupied and out of their way." He paused for a long moment, then cautiously added. "That's the reason why we've spent so much time together these past few years. It wasn't because I was trying to steal you away . . . . I was trying to save your lives."

I had to absorb that over time, but my curiosity was burning on another subject, I suppose as an indicator of the resiliency of children. "Grandfather?" I was afraid to ask, but curiosity defeated fear for the moment. "How did you get to be so old? I thought most people only lived to 80 or 90?"

"That, my boy," he grinned as he rubbed my scalp, "Is a story for another day. Right now we've got to figure out how to survive. There might be more of us arriving, but we have to have a contingency plan . . . . in case they're not."

No one else was coming. We were the last five Therans in this quarter of the Universe.

SOUTHWEST MISSOURI STATE UNIVERSITY

September 2010

"**T**his has got to be a hoax." Lois announced flatly.

"It can't be," I protested. It's been in the University Archives since the late 1800's."

"I don't care where it's *supposed* to have been for the last 150 years. It's a hoax! You and your stupid conspiracy theories!" It was an old argument that we continually rehashed. "Some student or some faculty prankster has hidden this in the archives waiting for some dupe like you to find it!"

"A scientist reviews all the data before rendering an opinion. You sound more like a religious fanatic that a scientist." I knew I'd stepped in it again. I'd be sleeping on the couch for a week. Her continual annoyance with me had had, in the beginning, the desired effect on me. I'd give in and shut up in order to keep the peace. But that tactic only works so long, and I was quickly tiring of it. "You're so sure it's a hoax . . . . prove it."

"I will. And when I do, how do you want your crow? Broiled or barbecued?" Her hubris only steeled my resolve.

"I'll make that decision after the case has been proven. But you might want to be pondering that same question yourself." I hated to admit it, because the very admission doomed the relationship, but I knew, deep inside me, that it had grown so one-sided, like a damaged ship listing to port, it was only a matter of time before it capsized. And there would be a 100% casualty rate.

"How do you explain," I continued to press my point (or dig my hole—depending on how you looked at it), "that this could only be read by a software program that Professor Kurtz devised by reverse-engineering it from the recording in 2007?"

"I explain it this way! It's a damn hoax. Somebody planted it! And you and that idiot, Professor Kurtz!" Badmouthing me was one thing, attacking my mentor was another matter entirely.

"Well, then," I interrupted her diatribe, "how do you explain that Kurtz first showed it to me in 1977? It took 30 years after that to develop the technology to read the damn thing?! And it had been in the University Archives for a century before that!"

"You're not listening . . . . as usual." She loved to get in the condescending remark. Ignore the argument and attack the character of the opponent. "The wheel was still square in 1977. And you and Professor Kurtz! What a joke! Everybody knows how ridiculous the two of you are! It's a goddamn hoax. Looking for a pair of fools like you and Kurtz. It found you."

There it was. "Everybody knows". The phrase used by an anti-social personality to spread the threat everywhere. It was a tactic employed by the most evil persons throughout history. "So, Lois, if we went out in the street and took a random poll, *everybody* we talked to would 'know' that Kurtz and I are ridiculous?"

I knew the question had hit its mark by her failure to respond. And I knew, with certainty, that this conversation was finished. Never wrestle with a pig. You'll both get dirty and the pig likes it. Did I just call her a 'pig'? That was one more nail in our coffin. "I'm taking the recording back to the Archives," I announced.

"See that you do," she ordered, suspecting that I intended to do what I had been warned by the University NOT to do.

This time she was right.

THE TROPICS

I'd never seen so many trees in my life! They were everywhere! "Dobber!" I shouted, "How will we ever land in all those trees?"

"No problem, Solly. Just watch." Within a few minutes, he and my grandfather must have picked what they deemed to be a suitable location.

We hovered for a second when Grandfather announced, "Now Dobber!" The trees below us turned from green to orange to black to GONE in about 30 seconds. The clearing wasn't huge, but it was definitely large enough for our ship to land. We settled gracefully down to the ground.

"Thank the Gods!" Grandfather exclaimed. "We're still 800 miles from the equator but this climate will be warm year round. The fuel is entirely gone, though. This is as far as we go. We're on a wide isthmus, with oceans on either side of us. Judging by the flora, this will be a high rainfall area." No one said anything for a moment, we were so awestruck. "Just one problem . . . . or maybe trillions of problems."

"What's that?" Cleo asked. I hadn't noticed her entrance.

"Insects."

"What are insects, Grandfather?" Princess peeked around Cleo's bare legs.

"They are tiny little creatures. They may make up the bulk of all living animals on this planet. They have voracious appetites. They eat everything they can. And sometimes what they like to eat are *US*. They'd all been eliminated on Thera. That's one of the reasons why we had to import all our food and all our trees were dying. Somebody once thought it was a good idea to be rid of them. Big mistake.

"The solar panels will keep us in power for a while. If anything should happen to me, you must remember to keep your lasers charged up enough to keep the trees from growing back over the ship and shading the solar panels. Trees grow very quickly here, and in a few months, without continual trimming, we'll be in the shade. And then we have no power; not even enough to charge the lasers to do the trimming. Solly, that job will belong to you and Dobber."

A sudden pride welled up inside me. I'd been given a job to help! Now I wasn't just a pesky kid underfoot all the time. I was a member of the team!

"Grandfather?" Princess almost whispered, still partially hiding behind Cleo. "Are there other people here?"

He didn't answer right away and seemed to me to be choosing his words carefully. Not to frighten my sister, I suspected. "There are . . . . people. At least I suppose there are. This has been a dumping ground, not only for trash and garbage, but also for . . . . uhmm . . . . 'undesirables'. If they have survived here, they probably will not be very . . . ." He searched for a word, then settled on, ". . . . civilized."

I peered out of the nearest porthole, totally dumbstruck by what I saw. The forest was absolutely amazing. My young eyes had never seen anything like it before. Trees, trees, everywhere! Tall trees, short trees, really, really TALL trees! "Where's all the animals?" I asked of no one in particular. "I thought there would be animals everywhere!"

"Vaporizing the trees probably scared them deeper in the forest." It was Cleo who spoke first.

"Can we go outside?" Excitement was spilling out of my body.

"Not yet," Grandfather ordered. "Dobber and I will make a preliminary reconnaissance mission and be right back."

"What does that mean?" Princess whispered to Cleo.

"They're going to go outside to see what's out there." Cleo answered. She then whispered to herself, "I wonder if these language lessons are even necessary any more."

"No . . . . WE won't, Caesar," Dobber announced flatly. "Both of us are not making the first scout. I will go alone. If something happens out there, one of us has to be here with the kids. They need you more than they need me."

As much as he wanted to argue, Grandfather knew that Dobber was right. It was downright foolish for both of them to leave the ship at the same time.

"Is the atmosphere safe?" Cleo seemed nervous for the first time since I'd known her. At the moment I hadn't grasped her concern for Dobber's safety. She was always calm and in control, never prone to emotional rants like my mother had been. I remembered Mom hadn't been that way when I was younger. The older I got the more unstable my mother seemed to be. Maybe it was the drugs . . . .

"Yes, the atmosphere is perfectly safe, though I can't say the same for the environment," Grandfather answered. "The oxygen content will be much higher than what we are accustomed to on Thera. You will feel lighter and more energized." He paused for a moment and looked out the porthole as Dobber prepared to go outside. "Solan," he added, "There are many things out there which can eat you . . . . things much larger than insects. There are cats bigger than anything you've ever seen. Some of them with teeth in excess of 6 inches long. You wouldn't stand a chance without a weapon. You must stay with an adult at all times.

"And Cleo, all of us will feel better here than we ever have. When we lost our trees on Thera and had to import all our oxygen from Nicha, the government gradually, over a period of several years, lowered and lowered the oxygen content to the minimum that would sustain life. It created an additional sense of lethargy in the populace, which made us an even easier target. You will feel a keen sense of rejuvenation here."

Dobber put on his helmet and goggles, and although it seems silly now, he felt they were absolutely necessary at the time. He had two weapons, one that was a laser sword, the one we would use to trim the trees back over the ship. The other fired a laser beam straight ahead that could penetrate a foot of steel. Surely no wild animal could stand up to that.

21

As the hatch opened, the heat and humidity struck us in the face. The air smelled wonderful . . . but I can't describe it. It was like a perfume, but it didn't burn my nostrils like the ones back home did. I never noticed Cleo wearing a perfume. Maybe that's why I like being around her? She didn't have a chemical scent to her. The humidity did make it a little strenuous to breathe, but in my mind, the jungle was a large magnet, and I was helpless as a paper clip.

It had, in that moment, lured me into a life that I never, in my wildest dreams, could have imagined with my overprotected, Theran childish imagination.

Dobber returned in about ten minutes as the four of us waited anxiously in the hatch opening. He called to us repeatedly during his excursion to announce that he remained uneaten. "All seems to be well. I saw a few monkeys up high in the tree tops. The mosquitoes are a menace, but beside that, all is quiet."

The five of us spent our most sleepless night ever. Caffeine was a poor stimulant in comparison to the anticipation, fear, and excitement that kept us up most of the night. Princess finally fell asleep with her head in Cleo's lap. Dobber and I played Deathstar till I fell asleep at the controls and collapsed to the floor. Grandfather reviewed his charts and maps till eye fatigue temporarily blinded him.

I awoke to daylight streaming in the starboard portholes. Cleo and Dobber were nowhere to be seen. Curiosity consumed me, so I went to the nearest window to see what I might see.

"Grandfather!" I shrieked. "Come . . . . come quick . . . . look outside!"

Dobber and Cleo must have heard me, for they came running down the corridor, Cleo dressed only in a shirt and Dobber without his. Their embarrassment was completely unrecognized by me, as my entire focus was the scene outside. Even Sleepyhead Princess came to look out the porthole.

There must have been a thousand of them. They all were naked and all on their hands and knees, bowing toward the ship. I ran to the port side, and there seemed to be a thousand more.

"Who are they??" Princess asked of no one in particular.

"The 'undesirables'," Grandfather stated matter-of-factly. "And they believe we are the Gods!"

THE TROPICS-PART II

"**G**randfather?" I was awestruck. "Now what do we do?"

"Look God-like!" It seemed to me like a thoroughly ridiculous answer.

"Stay inside," Cleopatra snatched Princess and me by the hands and led us to the window.

"Dobber . . . ." Grandfather demanded. "Run back to my quarters and get my bathrobe!

"Cleo! Quick! Get me some sheets of gold, green and red paper. Cut them into feather shapes and stick them into the top of my helmet!"

"Your what?" Dobber was already far behind in Grandfather's scheme.

"Bathrobe! And hurry! Solan! Pull the sheets off your bed and roll them up like a big snake. Bring them to me! Quickly!"

Dobber shook his head in disbelief, but ran down the corridor to Grandfather's room. The old man then put on his helmet and goggles. He held his arms out as Dobber returned. The first mate slid the robe over his arms, but backwards. He tied it at the waist, picked up his laser saber and handed it to my now ridiculous-looking grandfather.

Cleo ran back to my grandfather with the colored paper as I ran to get my sheets. I had no idea what he was up to.

When I got back to the group, Cleo was stuffing the artificial feathers in the band of his goggles. Dobber took the rolled-up

23

sheets and stuffed one end of the roll into the back of the older man's pants.

"How do I look?" Grandfather asked.

"Like a complete idiot." Dobber deadpanned.

"Good! That's what I was going for!"

Much to my amazement, he stepped out the doorway and onto the narrow deck outside the ship. He started speaking to them in a language that sounded to me like complete gibberish. I couldn't understand a single word he said. He went on for a minute or so, then, two-handing the saber in a sweeping motion, and from a distance of more than a hundred feet, cut off branches of some of the taller trees. They toppled to the ground near a few of the naked natives, though none were struck. They jumped back in fear and congregated close together. My grandfather made another sweeping gesture with the saber, but this time didn't activate the light beam. They pushed back in fear a second time, though no branches fell after the second sweep. When my grandfather stepped backward through the door, he removed his helmet, and his face was drenched in sweat.

"Did it work?" he asked Dobber as he wiped the perspiration of heat and fear off his brow.

"Like a freakin' charm!"

"Great! Maybe they'll leave us be."

"What did you say to them and what language was that?"

"It was Hyanthian, a language that's been dead on Thera for two thousand years. Only scholars of the language can still speak it, and most of those of my generation who could are long dead. I told them I was Quetzalcoatl and they'd better do what I said or I'd slice them up and eat them for lunch!"

Dobber and Cleo just shook their heads and laughed. Princess and I sat in astonished silence. Finally my sister asked, "Grandfather, why did you have to be so mean to them?"

"They understand strength and strength only. If I had approached them in a friendly manner, they would have viewed that as weakness and likely would have attacked. They were the original peoples of Thera, but that is a tale for another day."

The naked people all eased carefully and silently back into the forest, never taking their eyes off us until they were well masked in the forest blackness. We all heaved a collective sigh of relief and stood silent for a few moments while we pondered what was next. At least that's what I was doing.

Cleo broke the silence by asking, "Who wants breakfast?" The vote was unanimous. Grandfather added a suggestion after our vote, "Maybe some of us would like to put some clothes on?" nodding at Cleo's bare legs and Dobber's equally bare chest. It was only when they turned toward their bedroom that I noticed that Cleo's shirt didn't cover her bottom. My heart pounded in my chest as the sight of her beautiful bare derriere was etched forever in my mind.

While the two younger adults went to add a few garments to their attire, Princess, who hardly ever spoke to him, suddenly asked our grandfather, "What's a Quetzalcoatl?"

"Not a 'what', but a 'who'," the old man stated. "He was a Wyvern lord who terrorized the Hyanthians many thousands of years ago. The Hyanthians, who were a peaceful race, were terrorized by the Wyverns. The Wyverns were not quite human, though they walked on two legs and had human-like heads. They were descendants of both birds and reptiles, and had feathers on their heads, yet had scaly bodies and snake-like tails."

"Ooooooh, gross!" Princess scowled.

"Don't worry, Little Sunshine. They've been extinct for many years, but the Hyanthians don't know that. But maybe we can use that to our advantage."

As the smells of bacon, eggs, and biscuits soon permeated the mess hall, the two men sat with their coffees and planned the next move. The conversation was, as usual, way over my head. My curiosity, however was too powerful for me to be entirely excluded from the conversation.

"Grandfather?" I hoped I wasn't too annoying. "What happened to the trees on Thera?"

"Whew!" Dobber exclaimed and leaned back in his chair. "This oughtta be good. Do you really know?"

"Well of course. You didn't think you were being led by a dilettante. Did you?"

"'Course not."

"Well, then shut up and listen." My grandfather smiled at him. He seemed more at ease than I ever remembered. "It was about 80 or 90 years ago. As part of the interest payment on our loan to the Nichans, we were required to provide them with billions and billions of tree seedlings. They had depleted their forests and needed the trees. We thought we were getting a great deal because we had vast government-owned nurseries, and giving them the little trees was pretty cheap to us. Or so we thought.

"This went on for about 30 years; long enough for those seedlings to reach maturity. All during this 30 year period we were sometimes slowly, and sometimes quickly, eliminating our insect populations. There were certain species we wanted to kill off, and some we wanted to protect. They said it couldn't be done, but by the Gods, we did it. We killed all of them. It was a fatal mistake.

"Originally, the Nichans didn't really want a war with us. They only fired back when they discovered the planet was worthless, though its worthlessness was partly a result of their own actions. They wanted the whole planet. Loaning us money was their way of doing it. It's called a 'war of attrition'."

"I don't understand, Grandfather." My head was having trouble absorbing all this.

"A war of attrition, in this case it means, 'taking over, little by little, in secret, without the others knowing what you're doing." Cleo clarified for me.

"After the insects were eradicated and the seedlings from 30 years of production were removed from Thera, the Nichans launched a missile at us. It seemed to fizzle out and die in a cloud of smoke in the ocean. We thought it was a complete failure.

"It didn't hurt anyone. It didn't kill anything. We thought it was just a big flub. They wouldn't say why it was launched at all, just that it was a terrible miscalculation, and that it was supposed to be directed elsewhere. The missile supposedly had a major computer malfunction which caused it to crash into our ocean.

"After the ruckus died down in a few weeks, no one thought anymore about it. A few of us knew something was up the next year when the trees bore not a single seed. None the year after that or the year after that. By that time, my associates and I were pushing the panic button. Trouble was, no one would listen to us. The world went on like nothing was wrong. But things were horribly, horribly wrong.

"After six years, the government had to admit that we were looking at the imminent doom of all life on the surface. Maybe not the ocean, but everything on land was going to die. And that included the whole Theran race!

"Scientists the planet over were creating trees from stored DNA. Surely they could clone a few dozen species and soon all would be right again. In the meantime, we could buy oxygen from Nicha.

"Now the Nichans had us where they wanted us. All the toys, tools, electrical and plumbing supplies, all the equipment they had sold us in the past wouldn't be a drop in the ocean compared to selling us oxygen. Soon the whole planet would so indebted to them, they could just walk in and assume power . . . . thus the victory of this war of attrition."

"So," Dobber finally got a word in. "What happened to the cloned trees? Did it work?"

"Yes and no. The trees grew to maturity, or what seemed like maturity, without event. Just one problem."

"What was that?"

"They too, were sterile. Another thirty years went by waiting for them to mature, and not a single damned seed. Not one.

"There were scientists scrambling like mad to arrive at a solution, but nothing panned out. The trees that were left were all we would ever have except for the clones we were creating. Tornadoes, hurricanes, drought, disease, old age; the trees disappeared, sometimes a few at a time. Sometimes thousands at a time. We were watching our planet die and there wasn't a damned thing we could do about it.

"The Nichans would simply have landed and declared Thera theirs, except for one little problem."

"What was that?"

"The Oxecmis"

"Huh?" This was getting really hard for me to follow.

"The Oxecmis and the drug cartels and drug companies and the doctors had created a population the Nichans didn't want. The underground minerals of Thera were depleted. The ecology had been destroyed; the Nichans had seen to that. And now the former, industrious, vibrant population of Thera was a sorry lot of fat, lazy, unproductive drug-addicts.

"That's when Nicha decided it was best to cut their losses. Enter Borghe the idiot."

SPRINGFIELD, MO

T houghts of Kinley Thorsen, Anthropology Grad Student
My tiny office didn't provide enough privacy for what I planned to do. I dared not go home. There was no way I could hide this from Lois. That's when I decided to lie.

I started to call her, but then I already knew which direction the conversation would go. I decided to send her a text instead. I know, I know. Coward's way out. I confess, I was a coward. What I needed to do was more important than the appearance of my bravery, or the lack thereof. "goin to vis my bro in txark," the text read. "wont b home for cpl days. Mbe we cn tak thn. Luv U."

I gathered my equipment and the recording and headed east toward Poplar Bluff, hoping against hope that I couldn't be found. I hated to go by the ATM and get my picture taken, but better to leave an electronic trail in Springfield than in Poplar Bluff. I withdrew the maximum cash it would let me have, four hundred measly dollars, but it would surely be enough for my trip. I'd be back in forty-eight hours, and that would be more than enough money. I had no clue that this was the beginning of a journey from which there was no return.

I turned on to Highway 60 and let my thoughts concentrate on the recording . . . . not on me and my personal problems. I'd heard many times that there was nothing new under the sun, moon, and stars; that it had all been done before. And until the last few days, I had had absolutely no concept of the truth of that statement.

Could this be legit? Could we be repeating the exact same thing that had happened before? I'd read parts of Gibbon's "Rise and Fall of the Roman Empire", and could make comparisons to today's dire circumstances, but this? Was this the work of some modern day satirical jokester as Lois had claimed? Or was this the real deal?

I had to do my own research, and the only way to do it was to make a copy. I needed to find someplace where they were especially fond of cash and didn't ask too many questions.

Seventy-five miles east of Springfield, I found what I was looking for. The desk clerk was a seriously obese woman with a cigarette dangling from her mouth when I entered the office. She barely took her eyes off the TV, blasting the Jerry Springer Show, long enough to take my cash.

"Number seven," she said. "Right up front." She handed me the key.

"Uhmmmm . . . . could I have one around back? My ex . . . . she's stalking me," I lied. "Don't want her to see my car."

"Yeah, sure." She couldn't have cared less. "Number 22. And no ruckus. If she finds you here, get out. Don't need the law showin' up here. Some of our customers use this place for, uh, chemistry experiments . . . . if you know what I mean.'

Great! I thought. I've got the most revolutionary evidence in the history of the human race in my hands, and I've got to do my research surrounded by meth-heads and Jerry Springer addicts. No wonder the society was falling apart. I prayed they didn't blow up the place up before I got my ass out of there.

My car was completely hidden from the highway, and I was 200 miles from where I was supposed to be, so maybe I could get this done in peace. I got the equipment into the room, and though I was starving, I started copying the recording. This might be my only shot. If someone as un-influential as Lois could keep this suppressed, what would happen if the Feds got hold of it?

I didn't dare take the luxury of listening to this as I copied it, so the transfer to my laptop was at a very high speed. However, due to its extreme length, it still took half an hour, and another half-hour to copy it to a new zip drive.

Relieved that it was done, I stepped out the door to get some dinner. There were three more cars that had pulled in the rear lot since I had entered my room. *None were black SUV's,* I laughed to myself. I hadn't noticed it earlier when I first spotted the motel, but there was a truck stop just two hundred yards east, on the other side of the cow pasture that bordered the motel parking lot.

Because it was a pleasant September evening, I decided to hoof it up there and leave my car and my laptop at the motel. My copy and the original recording, however, would not leave my person. The highway was fairly busy, and the shoulder was not nearly wide enough for a comfortable walk. The parking lot of the truck stop wasn't even paved. It was gravel with large, water-filled depressions all over it, attracting millions of mosquitoes. They and a billion other insects circled the overhead lights, as summer wasn't quite finished. I thought I sensed a few bats flitting around the edges of the light-soaked parking lot, flying their awkward leathery flap, hunting mosquitoes.

Trucks came and went as I made my way to the door. I found an empty table without incident and ordered the Wednesday Special. The waitress was friendly, but too thin and missing a few teeth. I'd learned the hard way what that meant. Only fooling myself if I chose to believe otherwise.

I finished my meal, and had to admit, the food was good, and it settled my nerves as well as my need for sustenance. I tipped the waitress, knowing full well that it was going to be used to feed her habit.

As I exited the restaurant door, a huge explosion knocked me flat on my back, and glass showered down all around me. I was sure a fuel truck had exploded, but after I got back on my feet and looked around, the parking lot and all the trucks seemed to be intact.

A huge flame rose high into the night sky just off to the west. The motel, my laptop, my car, and God-only-knows what else were engulfed in flames. I could easily see across the pasture that my car was ablaze. I stood there, dumbfounded, not knowing what to do next. Fortunately, the decision was made for me. My car suddenly exploded, and debris rained down, all the way to the truck stop. I felt a sharp pain in my neck, but there didn't seem to be any wound. Two other cars in the motel lot then caught fire.

I found the nearest truck driver fueling his truck. Mustering all of my courage, I walked up and asked for a ride.

"Which way ya going?" He was a big man in overalls with a sunburned face. Unusual for a truck driver, I thought.

"East, going to see my girl. Lost my car in the fire . . . ." I pointed toward the motel.

"Need to wait for the cops and file a police report?"

"Nope, not worth insuring, "I lied again. That made four times today already; a new record for me.

"You a user?"

"Absolutely not!"

"Didn't think so. You don't have that 'look' about you."

"Can I get the ride?" I wanted to get out of there fast.

"Sure." He was quiet for a bit, then asked, "You know that place was almost entirely a working meth lab, don't you? I come through here all the time . . . never seen nothin' good come of there . . . . till now, that is."

We climbed in the cab, when much to my surprise, he admitted, "Me and some of my buddies leave gas cans around that joint all the time. Looks like if finally paid off. But I'm sorry you lost your car."

My personal possessions didn't seem significant at that point. In a few hours, however, I'd realize how much I needed that car.

Hmmmm. A little gas. A lot of meth. If I had waited another half an hour to get some dinner, I'd have been a casualty of the fire, along with my precious zip drives. But since I survived, I was a fugitive, without a friend, a home, or a car. And all I had was $340 to my name.

THE PRE-MAYANS

G randfather spent the rest of the day telling us about the stupid things that President Borghe had done that sealed Thera's fate. I couldn't believe any adult could be that stupid, let alone someone who had become President, but according to Grandfather, it was true.

After lunch the conversation began to lag, especially for me. Princess had lost interest a long time ago. I couldn't believe that our world leaders could be as bad as Grandfather said, but he was the smartest man I knew, so he must be right. They certainly didn't teach me any of these things in school.

"Caesar?" Cleo asked during the aforementioned lull in conversation. "What do we do now? We made it, but it seems as though no one else did. We're alive, but for what purpose?"

"I wish I knew the answer to that. I've been asking myself that same question for weeks now. The only answer I have, is that we must, if we intend to survive long term, assimilate ourselves into the native culture. They know how to survive, no matter how primitively, on this planet, in this environment. We must join them."

"I understand that. But what about the Quetzalcoatl incident? Was that wise to put them in fear of us?"

"In retrospect, I'm not so sure. I felt that a display of our strength and technological superiority would protect us and insure that they remained in fear. I don't know, now, that it was the proper thing to do. But it's done. I can' take it back." He hesitated

33

for a moment, then added, "If anyone has any suggestions, I'm happy to listen. This is a new experience for me as well as all of you."

There were several minutes of silence, finally interrupted by Princess having tea with her imaginary friends. It was only when I turned to tell her to be quiet that we realized the friends *weren't* imaginary.

A naked Princess, along with three other unclothed, very dark-skinned, but completely bald-headed little girls sat at Princess's tea table, drinking imaginary tea and eating imaginary scones. My sister was doing all the talking; the other three sitting in silence as though they understood what she said. They must have, but I certainly didn't understand a word she was saying.

"Princess!" I yelled. "What are you doing?!"

She replied with a reprimanding tone, but I didn't understand anything that came out of her mouth. I started to yell at her again, when my Grandfather put his hand on my shoulder and put his finger to his lips to shush me. "She's speaking Hyanthian!" he whispered excitedly.

"She's what??!!" Dobber couldn't fathom what Grandfather was saying.

"She's speaking to them in Hyanthian! I don't know how. No one ever teaches it anymore. Especially not to six-year-olds!"

"She's naked!" I hissed at Grandfather.

"I know, Solly. I know. Just be calm. We will probably all be naked before long." His comment caused no slight excitement and embarrassment in me. I always hated wearing clothes, but was always afraid to be seen naked.

"How did they get in here?" Dobber wondered aloud.

"I let them in," Princess said matter-of-factly, as though she'd been listening to our conversation all along. "They were standing outside and wanted to come in. So I let them. We're having a tea party." I was amazed at how childish and yet how mature she could be all at the same time.

"Princess," Grandfather said as calmly as possible, "don't you think you might want to put some clothes on?"

"No, Grandfather." She seemed absolutely sure of herself. "We're not on Thera anymore. If we're supposed to join these people, we must do as they do."

I couldn't speak for the rest of them, but I was dumbstruck. My little sister was giving my Grandfather orders!

The three adults looked at each other with questioning eyes, none of them knowing what do next. I stared at each of them, hoping for some guidance, but found none. Finally, Cleo broke the baffling silence by whispering, "She's right, you know."

Dobber and Grandfather reluctantly nodded, neither having a clue how to segue from agreement to action. Cleo got up and left the mess hall and retired to her room. Grandfather eventually ventured a question to Dobber, "How do I maintain the Quetzalcoatl routine? I can't wear that get-up all the time."

"Oh, forget the tail. "You'll have to wear the headdress, and we'll make some of kind of a robe you can wear to appear regal. The rest of us will have to be your servants."

"Well, there's a question you're going to ask, and I need to answer it before you ask it."

Dobber shook his head in confusion. "What does that mean?"

"You remember the conversation we had about my age a few days ago?"

"Of course. How could I forget that?"

Grandfather hesitated, as though he was trying to figure out how to tell Dobber in a way that wasn't too shocking, and tell it in a way that was still believable. "How do I begin?" He scratched his bald head, puzzling for a way to start.

After what seemed like ten minutes of silence, but was probably not more than two, he confessed. "I lied to Princess about the Wyverns. They're still in the population . . . . or at least they were until Thera was destroyed. They just don't look like Quetzalcoatl anymore. They had assimilated themselves into the Hyanthian population many centuries ago. You can't tell a Wyvern from a Hyanthian by physical appearance. They have the same type of bodies that we do. And we, in fact, are actually Hyanthian . . . . or what's left of them."

Dobber waved his hand in a circle, encouraging Grandfather to continue. The older man seemed to be searching again for the right words to finish his confession.

"These people," he waved his hand around the mess hall, indicating the natives, "are directly related to us. They *are* the Hyanthians. The ones who couldn't be implanted."

"Couldn't be *what?*" Dobber shook his head.

"Implanted. You, Cleo, and Solly have been implanted by the Wyverns. Princess has not. I've known it for a long time. I don't know how they missed her, but they did."

"What about you. I notice you left yourself out of that statement."

"I'm not. That's why I'm over 260 years old."

"Oh, c'mon, Caesar. You're jerkin' my chain!"

"Sorry . . . . but I'm not. I escaped as a young boy. By not being implanted, my mental prowess was unrestrained enough that I continually escaped round-ups to implant, kill, or deport the uncontrollable portion of the population.

"These people here were "un-implantable". I think the only reason they weren't slaughtered like cattle has to do with reincarnation."

"Reincarnation????" Dobber asked with a renewed incredulity, which Grandfather ignored.

"If they couldn't be implanted, it mattered not that they were murdered. They would return in a new body and *still* not be implantable. The Wyvern's eventually gave up and deported them all here . . . ."

He was about to say something else, when Princess approached and interrupted his train of thought. "I have a name for this place, Grandfather," she announced with authority. "As a tribute to Thera, I have rearranged the letters and will call it "Earth!" She was quite proud of herself, which only served to further irritate me, particularly because of her total lack of embarrassment at her own nudity in front of Grandfather.

"Thank you, Princess. That's good work." His praise only fueled my ire. "These people," he began again, "were the best of the best. They could not be made into slaves . . . . slaves to mortgages, credit cards, automobiles, fast food, drugs, ad nauseum. That's why they're here."

"O.K. I'm following you so far, except for one thing. What's this question I was going to ask?"

"Have you noticed that they have no body hair?"

"Yes. I also noticed how pronounced their sex organs are as well. The women as well as the men. Can't say it offends me . . . ."

"That's because the lack of the implant. A true Hyanthian has no body hair. They also have a very attractive scent . . . ."

"Oh my God!" Dobber exclaimed. "That's what I'm smelling! The three girls!! I thought someone brought in a bouquet of flowers!"

"Hyacinths, to be exact. The flower was named after us . . . ."

"Cleo and I have body hair." Dobber suddenly realized what Grandfather had said.

"That's because of the implant."

"Huh?"

Dobber was having as much trouble as I was at wrapping his brain around this conversation.

"I don't, Grandfather!" I proudly announced, rubbing my smooth arms.

"Not yet, son, not yet. But you will." I have to admit, my heart sank. I wanted the same acknowledgement and approval he had given my baby sister.

"When you receive the implant, it starts the growth of body hair. All Wyverns have body hair. Hyanthians only grow the body hair when they are implanted."

"I still don't get what the question was, Caesar."

"I just answered it for you . . . ." he replied to a still-dumbfounded Dobber. "I'm not *implanted*."

Dobber slowly absorbed what Grandfather was saying, though it was still lost entirely on me. The first mate began to shake his head in understanding, finally grasping the point of the conversation. It wasn't until three days later when we all shed our Wyvern-enforced Theran clothing that I understood what Grandfather was trying to explain.

THE PRE-MAYANS

Part II

To say the least, my Grandfather struggled with his ridiculous costume. Now that he'd started this game, he didn't know how to stop it. The locals were in awe, maybe even fear of him, as they bowed down before him the following morning as he stepped out on the deck of our ship.

They had disappeared the previous evening, returning to wherever it was they went. If we had known what magnificent architecture they were capable of, we might not have considered them so backward. Maybe they weren't backward at all, but they had no clothes, no vehicles, no electricity, no airships of any kind. To me they were backward. My Grandfather, however, had different ideas. Princess, too, but I didn't dare agree with *her*.

"Their ancestors," Grandfather began, as we sat around the mess hall after his morning greeting of our new friends, "were every bit as advanced as we think we are. They had all the modern conveniences that we have. The Wyverns knew that the only way to suppress them and their success on this planet was to *spoil* them."

"Spoil?" I didn't understand how spoiling somebody suppressed them. Maybe I didn't really understand what 'suppress' meant. "The kids that I knew who were spoiled had all the things I wanted that I couldn't have!" I nearly whined.

"Exactly," Grandfather stated absolutely. "The Wyverns spoiled the Hyanthian children."

39

"Why did they want to spoil their enemy?" It didn't make a lick of sense to me.

"By having everything given to the children, they had no desire to learn the things that their parents knew. I know this is hard for you to understand, Solan, because every child thinks that *things* will make him happy. Only when one grows up and grows older, does one realize that the things he owns soon *own him*."

I didn't get it. Maybe I never would. I only knew that my Grandfather was the wisest man I knew, and although he didn't shower me with gifts like Mom did after she felt guilty for going on one of her benders, he truly loved me, and Princess too, even if she was a thorn in *my* side. If he said it, it must be true. It was up to me to wrap my brain around it and understand why he said the things he did. Maybe I was really growing up.

Grandfather could tell I was struggling to understand, "O.K., Solan. Let me ask you a question."

"All right."

"Did the 'spoiled' kids that you knew like their parents?"

I thought about that for a moment before I answered. "Not really. Most of them talked about how stupid their parents were; how they didn't know anything, and how easy they were to manipulate." *Manipulate.* That might have been the biggest word I'd ever used. I was more than a little proud of myself. "They pretended to be nice in front of their parents, but after they got what they want, they acted like pricks."

I could see some chagrin in Grandfather's face at my use of that word, but he didn't comment.

"O.K. How about the kids who had jobs and helped their parents out with the bills?"

I really had to wrack my brain on that one. I couldn't think of any that actually worked or helped their parents. Finally one came to mind. His name was Uncas and he came from down south somewhere. I don't think his family even had a car or electricity. I mostly didn't talk to him because he was so poor, and though he was a nice kid, I didn't want to be seen talking to him. I didn't want to confess that to Grandfather, however.

"I-I-I knew one," I admitted sheepishly.

"And you didn't want to associate with him?" I told you my Grandfather was wise.

"Y-yes."

"It's O.K., Solan. You're not in trouble. That's the society in which you grew up. That's what was expected of you." He paused for a moment, then asked, "Doesn't make you feel very good about how you treated him, does it?"

"No." I didn't want to elaborate, and desperately hoped this conversation would take another turn.

"What about the ones who didn't have rich parents who didn't work?"

"They all got money from the government for not working." I justified my expectations of *support* from others.

"Where did the government get the money that they gave to the people for not working?"

I knew this was a test to see if I'd been paying attention to earlier conversations. All at once, it came to me. "Nicha?" I asked more than answered.

"Exactly." He stopped abruptly and waited for the significance of my half answer to sink in.

"Oh my God!" I yelled as I suddenly cognited on the awful truth of why we were here.

"You see, Grandson," he smiled as he tousled my hair. "Everyone needs to contribute. Nobody gets anything for free. Somebody had to make everything. For one person to work while another loafs on the other's work *always* eventually leads to failure. It's happened time and time again throughout history. And only when a group of people thinks they no longer have to contribute something good to the society, does the whole society begin to fail.

"I tell you these things because this responsibility that I have borne for so long will soon fall on your shoulders. And whether you succeed or fail, will depend on how much you understand these things I tell you."

I'd not get a chance to use this knowledge in this life, but like an audio tape that bleeds through to the next loop, his words haunted me for many millennia yet to come.

"These people here once had all the things that we just left behind. But the Wyverns started a planet-wide program to spoil the children into believing that they did not need to contribute. What the Wyverns hoped to accomplish by this can only be understood by understanding insanity, for when Nicha wiped out Thera, the Wyverns were wiped out too."

"That seems stupid, Grandfather. I thought adults were supposed to be smart."

"One would think so, Solan, but as one grows up, one begins to understand just how stupid adults can be."

"There's something I don't get," Dobber interjected. I didn't even remember he was still in the room, he'd been so quiet. "If these people were un-implantable, as you say, why weren't they able to rebuild a civilization here?"

"Oh, they have. You haven't seen it yet. They have quite a civilization. It just lacks the technological superiority that we have—er, I mean, *had*."

"But why does it lack that technology? If they're not implanted, can't they create the technologies we had on Thera?"

"The answer to that question is three-fold. First, it has to do with the spoiling of the children, as I was just saying, so that they refuse to learn the things that their parents knew. Second, the Wyverns wiped out all the adults when they shipped these Hyanthians here. No one over the age of twelve was left alive."

"But you mentioned reincarnation . . . . which I hold in serious doubt. Everybody knows you only live once!"

"Believe what you will, Dobber. But think back to memories of things you know didn't happen in this life. We all have those memories, and we hold them in some sort of mysterious reverence; which brings us to the third part of the answer.

"They couldn't be implanted. But there was one process which could be run on them. It's usually part of the implant, but in the case of these people, it was the only part that worked."

"Well, what is it?" I was growing impatient. I don't know why adults have to drag everything out so.

"Memory erasure."

He let that sink in for a minute as the three of us sat there in silence.

Just as he was about to elaborate, Princess and Cleo walked in the mess hall, and this time Cleo was as naked as Princess. Not only that, but her head was as bald as Grandfather's. I knew she was Dobber's girlfriend, but I was in love, hopelessly, forever, in love.

HIGHWAY 60 SOUTHERN MISSOURI

"**S**o where ya headed?" the truck driver asked me.

I seemed to have become a professional liar in the last 24 hours and it didn't sit well with my basic constitution. For lack of a better answer, I said, "Poplar Bluff."

"Any place in particular? I feel guilty about your car getting destroyed. I'll take you anywhere you want to go."

I had a cousin up near Farmington that Lois knew nothing about. This truck driver, past his prime, with his sunburned face and white forehead seemed trustworthy to me, especially with his extreme prejudice toward meth-heads, so I asked *him* a question instead of letting him do all the asking. "Where are *you* headed?"

"St. Charles. Then turning around and heading back to Dallas."

"You going up 67 or 55?"

"Sixty-seven."

"Well . . . ." my anonymity and disappearance from the system might be the only thing that saved me, and I wasn't sure I wanted to divulge that to him. Even if he was completely concerned with my well-being, did I want to involve him in my crime?

"Are you in some kind of trouble?" Curiosity finally got the best of him.

"Sort of. I took something that technically didn't belong to me. I was going to return it, but since the explosion and the loss of my car, I'm in over my head." I put aside my suspicion for a moment and confessed that I might be in big trouble.

"I'm sorry. I feel responsible for your situation . . . . at least part of it. Do you mind if I ask what you took?"

"Well . . . ." I hesitated again, not sure how much to say. "Let's put it this way. It's not something that a normal person would want. It is, however, something that certain people would not want distributed amongst the public."

"I hope you're not talkin' about dope, cause if it is, you're getting out at the next exit." His ire for the drug culture made me like him even more.

"No, no. Nothing like that. It's what they call 'intellectual property'. Technically, you could say that it belongs to Southwest Missouri State University. However, if the Feds ever got hold of it, the University's claim to it would evaporate in a nanosecond." I didn't want to tell him that Lois would probably be the one who turned me in, as that would only make me an even bigger liar in his estimation of me. "But in reality," I continued, "it belongs to all of the human race."

"It would probably be better for both of us, especially you, if you didn't know what I have. As they say in politics, 'plausible deniability'."

"Are they pursuing you now?" Now he felt jeopardized and even though it might have been my imagination, it seemed as if his sunburned face grew even redder above the glow of the dash lights. As much as I hated to involve him, if he hadn't blown my car up, he wouldn't be in this situation.

"No. As far as I know, no one even knows it's missing yet. And I provided a red herring to send any possible pursuit in the opposite direction. Even with goddamn surveillance cameras everywhere, it'll be some time before they realize which direction I headed."

"What about credit card transactions?"

"I'm smarter than that. I went by the ATM before I left home, so the only record they have of me is in my home town."

"Where's that?" This was beginning to turn into an interrogation, and I was getting miffed.

"Do you really want to know that?" I asked him. "Think about that for a minute. You're involved now, whether you want to be or not. I'm sorry that you are, but asking more questions only puts you at greater risk. Like I said, the less you know, the better off you'll be."

He didn't say anything for several minutes, and I soon began to see the lights of Poplar Bluff. "You can let me out at the next exit if you want." I finally broke the silence. "I'm not trying to get you or anyone else in trouble, so the sooner you get rid of me the better. I can find another ride, as long as you don't call all your buddies on the CB and get me jinxed."

He remained silent for a few more seconds then admitted, "I'm sorry, amigo. I realize I shouldn't have taken it upon myself to fire-bomb that meth shit-hole. I was just trying to do the right thing, since nobody else would do anything about it. I'll take you wherever you want to go, and I won't say a damn word. But even if there's no fucking surveillance cameras where you get off, they'e got satellite photos of damn near everything. Hell, even my neighbor got busted by a satellite photo of his pot plants.

"If they question me, I'll have to tell them where I let you out. Otherwise I'll go to jail for lying to the authorities. Just ask Martha Stewart about that!"

"Yeah, yeah, I know. Let me think for a minute. There's got to be someplace I can get out that won't be so obvious." We both sat quietly for a moment, when I added, "I really don't know how interested they are in me and what I have. There's really only one person who would blow the whistle on me . . . ."

"Speak fast, we're comin' up on a scale! Maybe you better crawl back in the sleeper!"

I crawled back through the opening to the sleeper and found a comfortable place that my driver must have spent many a night.

"There's storage under the mattress. Lift it up and crawl into the storage compartment." I did as he ordered just as we exited the highway into the scale area. I could only hear muffled sounds and didn't hear any conversation for some time as the truck inched its way to the scale. Finally I could hear him talking to someone outside the truck, but couldn't make out any words.

After what seemed like an eternity of hiding and hearing my heart pounding in my ears, the truck began to creep forward again and I heaved a sigh of relief. My joy, however, was short-lived, as my driver only went about 200 feet and wheezed the truck to a halt. I heard the sudden discharge of air as he set the parking break, and his slightest whisper, "They're pulling us over."

I nearly shit my pants.

EARTHBOUND HYANTHIANS

"Cleo!" Dobber shouted, not quite knowing what to say next.

"What?" she demanded

"Clothes! And what happened to your hair?"

"You don't get it yet, do you, Dobber?"

"Get what? This is just ridiculous!"

"Dobber," my Grandfather said as calmly as he could, "she's right. We have to assimilate ourselves into their society. They associate clothing and body hair as exclusively Wyvern. I believe I have made a tragic mistake by making them think I was Quetzalcoatl. I only instilled fear, and we don't have the power to maintain that fear. No matter how unpleasant it may seem at first, we must do as they do if we hope to survive. Princess may have saved us by inviting in the local girls and speaking to them in their native tongue. I'm sure their parents thought they were going to be sacrificed to me, and the fact that they were released unharmed may have brought us some margin of safety."

"Men," Cleo announced, "think of war and how to win it. Women, on the other hand, think of how to get along and maintain a pleasant society. If we do not join them, we will remain enemies. How long do you think Caesar can keep up that ridiculous charade before he is discovered? And if I understood him correctly, when he so cautiously explained that he was un-implanted, he has no body hair. They will recognize immediately that he is indeed, not

Wyvern, but in fact, one of them. How do you think that's going to go over?"

"We just have one problem," Grandfather stated. Princess will be safe. She will never grow body hair, as she is not implanted. The three of you on the other hand, will continue to grow it. Solan as well, will grow it in as little as a year. You'll be able to keep it removed for a while, but eventually we'll have no more razors, and the consequences could be severe, if they discover you actually grow hair anywhere on your body."

"I guess we'll worry about that when it comes," Cleo announced. We have razor blades, shaving cream, and electric razors. As long as we can maintain solar power, we can maintain the baldness. As for the distant future, I guess we'll worry about that when the time comes." She hesitated for a moment then gave a stern look in her lover's direction and said with a half question, "Dobber?!"

"Wait, wait a minute. I'm not ready for that just yet. Don't know that I ever will be. You interrupted Caesar just as he was about to tell us about the third reason why these people haven't developed any of our technologies."

"Memory erasure was what I was saying," Grandfather repeated his earlier comment as he stood and did something that shocked me beyond belief.

"Upon the death of the individual," he said as he removed his shirt, "the Wyverns maintain what they term the 'Transmutation Station'. That is the point at which most Hyanthians are implanted. It's where people have no bodies and exist as spiritual beings only. However, with these people," he paused for a moment and unbuckled his pants; they quickly dropped to the floor.

I was immediately shocked, but jealous at the same time. He wore no underwear, and his penis was huge. My little inch seemed like a speck compared to him. At the time, I didn't know adults had pubic hair, so his lack of such didn't mean anything to me, and his stomach muscles were amazing.

"These people," he continued as he stepped out of his trousers, "since they can't be implanted, only have their memories erased. Remember, Dobber, what I said earlier about memories you have that you know shouldn't be there? Some of them bleed through after the erasure, like a primitive magnetic tape that didn't completely erase."

I don't know that Dobber heard a word he said; he seemed to be in total shock at my Grandfather's disrobing. I was too, but now Dobber and I were the only clothed ones in the room.

Cleo quickly changed the subject of memory erasure. "Is this why Princess has to wear a wig all the time?" I didn't even know she wore a wig.

"All this time, I thought she had some disease that caused her to have no hair on her head. It's just the lack of implant, isn't it?" There seemed to be a tone in her voice of irritation and jealousy at the same time.

"Yes, Cleo. She is in her natural condition. The condition called 'alopecia' is actually the natural state of a Hyanthian. There is absolutely nothing wrong with her." Now I was jealous. Grandfather looked in my direction and nodded, "It's O.K. Solan."

Suddenly understanding what he was saying to me several days ago, I stepped out of my shorts and shirt, and stood there in my underwear, afraid to go the entire distance. Cleo touched my bare shoulder and I could feel my penis suddenly protrude above the band of my briefs. "It's perfectly all right, Solan. That will happen for a while, but you'll get used to it. I thought Princess would start laughing at me, and my face turned bright red, but instead she removed the wig I'd never noticed and hugged me from behind.

Dobber broke the calm by shouting, "You all have lost your Godddamned minds!" and walked briskly back to his quarters.

"He'll come around," Grandfather stated.

"I certainly hope so," Cleo answered with little confidence.

Dobber's ire made me feel self-conscious, so I grabbed my shirt and shorts and headed toward my room. Only when I was out of sight of the others did I finally remove my briefs. I prayed to the Gods that I could be the man my Grandfather was.

The rest of the morning was filled with a quiet tension, as we waited for Dobber to regain his composure. I wasn't sure he ever would, but I could hope. He was my only friend.

After about an hour, Cleo came by with a trash can and began gathering our clothing. I wanted to hide something in case I ever needed it, but she searched all my drawers and closets. I was left with nothing but shoes, but the view of her lovely body made me cover my groin with my hands. She pretended that she didn't notice.

"You think Dobber will do it?" I asked just as she was about to leave.

"I think so. It's just kind of shocking to him, that's all."

"Well, it's kind of shocking to me too." I felt slightly superior to him.

"As far as your grandfather is concerned, maybe the locals won't recognize him without his Quetzalcoatl get-up, and he can convince them that the Wyvern God departed and left us behind."

"I hope so. I'd hate for anything to happen to him. He's so wise and we need him." My voice was nearly trembling.

"Don't worry, Solan. We'll be O.K." She tried unsuccessfully to ease my mind. "I'm going to talk to Dobber now and see if he's cooled off a little."

"O.K." I whispered. As she made her way down the corridor to the room she shared with Dobber, I was entranced by her bare bottom as I peeked around my door. I hoped I would be able to learn how to keep my penis from becoming a flagpole around the girls. I didn't understand what was happening to me, and though it embarrassed me, I was falling in love with the sensation.

After she entered their room, I sneaked down the corridor and pressed my ear to their door. At first I couldn't hear, so I pressed it a little harder.

"Damnit, Cleo, put some clothes on while we have this discussion!" I heard that clear as a bell.

"I can't. Caesar has ordered me to dispose of all the clothing on the ship. I have fulfilled that order except for yours. I won't force you to strip, but I will remove everything that you're not wearing at present."

"Will you just stop!!? Have you all lost your minds?"

"No, actually I think we've found them."

"What about the kids?"

"As long as no one is molesting them, what about them?"

"Well, it just isn't' . . . ."

"Yes, I know. It isn't done on Thera. But we're not on Thera anymore. We're on Princess's 'planet Earth'. And here, it is the way it is. And according to Caesar, it's the way it was on Thera until the Wyverns took power and criminalized Hyanthian bodies."

"Well, I'm not shaving my pubic hair like you did."

"Don't, but don't expect them to tolerate you." She must have been referring to the natives. "And actually, once you get over the initial shock, I think you'll quite enjoy it. Here, let me have your hand."

I couldn't see what was happening, but I envisioned her placing Dobber's hand on her groin. Suddenly there was an indescribable sensation in my genitals and an explosion I didn't understand. I was overwhelmed with a sensation of great joy and simultaneous shame.

I turned and quickly ran back down the corridor to my room, not comprehending what had just happened. Before I got to my room, however, Cleo and Dobber stuck their heads out their door and noticed the mess I had made.

"See what happens?" Dobber admonished.

"You know good and well it happens all the time. We're just going to remove the shame. We don't feel shame when we eat, why should feel shame about sex? It'll be a little rough at first, but we'll all adjust . . . . and you will too."

I couldn't hear anything else that was said as I buried my head under my covers.

MAKING THE ADJUSTMENT

I didn't want to come out of my room, I was so embarrassed. Cleo begged me to come out, but I wouldn't. After about a half hour of begging, I heard a key turn in my door lock. Dobber stuck his head in and said, "Hey."

"Are you mad at me?" I asked.

"Of course not. Can I come in?"

"Sure," I said, though I wasn't sure. I stayed under the covers until he entered.

He'd finally removed his clothes like the rest of us. "Cleo has taken mine too," he said with a weak grin. It was then that I noticed, that unlike the rest of us, he had hair pretty much all over his body, and it was particularly thick around his groin, and he was nowhere near as big as Grandfather.

"We've got to adapt, they tell me," he said with no small level of discomfort.

"I-I don't know what happened back there, Dobber. I-I'm sorry. I didn't mean to do that."

"It's okay, son. It's just a normal bodily function. I know the first time it happens, it kind of freaks you out, but believe me, it's happened to everybody, and that includes me *and* your Grandfather.

"Are you serious? It's happened to Grandfather too?"

"Probably not in a really, really long time. It only happens on accident when you're young. As you get older you get more control and it doesn't happen by accident anymore."

With a sheepish grin, I admitted, "It was pretty good. Would it be okay if it happened again?"

He stammered a bit, then confessed, "I don't know how to answer that question, Solan." He waited for me to say something, and when I didn't, he changed the subject. "Come on down and get some lunch. Cleo's fixed your favorite pizza.

That was the first of many meals we would eat together in the nude. Princess' wig was gone for good, and her head was as smooth and Grandfather's and Cleo's. Cleo, however would require constant shaving to prevent her from being mistaken as a Wyvern by the natives. Dobber and I would have to do the same. At the time, none of us realized the hair problem would soon be solved . . . . along with a few others . . . . but not in a good way.

After lunch, Grandfather asked me to remain seated, while Dobber and Cleo went back to their room. In a moment they returned with shears, shaving cream and a razor. My beautiful blonde hair soon lay all over the floor. Cleo lathered up my skull and shaved me bald as Grandfather. I was sad to see it go, but yet I was glad to be like the others.

When they were finished with me, all eyes turned on Dobber. Compared to the rest of us he looked like a bear. "Not out here," was all he said with a resigned sigh.

When we saw him the next morning, he was smooth as the rest of us. Cleo must have spent hours on him.

After breakfast, Grandfather announced, "Today, we go out among the people. Although my seniority would ordinarily demand that I lead the party, because Princess had already made friends, I believe she should be the first one they see."

Although I had a lump in my throat the size of an orange, Princess just said, "I'm ready, Grandfather."

The heat and mosquitoes hit us without mercy. Our clothes would have been unbearable in this heat, but might have given us some protection from the mosquitoes. A remedy, however, was soon at hand.

Princess' three little friends approached her bearing some type of leaf and began to rub it all over her body. The mosquitoes soon departed, and it seemed as though the ones that left her abruptly added to the number of those attacking the rest of us. Within a matter of seconds, six women emerged from the thick jungle growth armed with similar leaves and began to rub all of us down with oil from the crushed leaves. The mosquitoes immediately left us alone, I suppose to find somebody or something else to bite.

An old man approached Grandfather and began speaking to him in that strange tongue that he and Princess had been using. First the old chieftain had an expression of fear and anxiety on his face, but it slowly metamorphosed into a smile and he was soon embracing my Grandfather in an exuberant hug. It seemed kind of funny to me at the time, but as it was the custom here, I soon grew accustomed to this strange exchange of friendship.

"What did he say, what did he say, Grandfather?" My excitement was spilling out of me.

"Easy, Solan, easy." That's when I noticed that several of the men seemed to be laughing at me. Except for one who stood off to the side with a frown of extreme displeasure.

"I told him that the Wyvern Lord, Quetzalcoatl had brought us here to our Hyanthian Brothers, and that he had left us to show them new things.

"The chieftain is very grateful and has invited us back to his village. I believe we all should go. I know this is a big first step, but we must become as they are if we hope to survive."

"I suppose you're right, Caesar, but what will we do when the hair starts to grow back? We can't take shaving gear with us," Dobber asked with no small measure of anxiety.

"You should be able to go a day or so without shaving. Then we'll come back here and you can shave again. Until we figure something else out . . . ."

"Yeah, like that's gonna happen. We were still shaving on Thera and how old was our civilization?"

"I get it, Dobber, but I don't know what else to do."

Off we went through the jungle. The trail went through the undergrowth for what seemed like 2 or 3 miles before it turned onto a wide road that almost seemed to be paved. Our new found friends stopped once we reached the road and offered us water and what I later learned was jerky. It wasn't bad and replenished our quickly vanishing energy.

We walked all the rest of the afternoon, and in late afternoon, a wicked storm blew up and a pelting rain began to hit us. I wanted to seek shelter, but the water was warm, and our companions kept walking as though nothing had changed, so walk, we did. One of the boys, who appeared to be about my age, taught me which leaves to look out for, as they held lots of water from the afternoon's rain. He took one, which seemed to have a good pint in its fold and held it to his mouth, and let the water run in. It ran all down his face as well, but he smiled a friendly smile and bid me do the same.

I, too, had water run all down my face and chest, but without clothes, I had nothing to get wet except my skin, and it was already wet. We both laughed together, and it appeared I had made a friend, though we understood not a word each other said. I could tell I was going to have to get back to the ship and learn Hyanthian . . . . quick!

If we had known our party of five would soon only be three, I'm sure we'd never have ventured out that morning. One would be an accident, the other outright murder, and it would be months before any of us made it back to the ship.

I would make my last entry into this diary on that visit.

NORTH OF POPLAR BLUFF

I lay there silently in my 'tomb', barely daring to draw a breath, for what must have been two hours. The droning truck engine drowned out any conversation that might have been taking place outside. My mind raced with all sorts of horrible outcomes, disgrace, prison, beatings by the police, but even more than fearing for myself, I was most distraught over what might befall Professor Kurtz.

He was a kind man, one of very few I'd known in my life. He always had a smile, was always eager to help, and though often out of place when surrounded by his in-laws, he excelled with his students and those he mentored. Lois was the exception to the rule.

I was still unwillingly single, but he had five children, three of whom were still in high school. I desperately needed to get a message to him. E-mail was out of the question. Too easily traced. Phone calls too. That left snail mail only. I needed to advise him that I alone was responsible for the theft, and he should tell the authorities that very thing. Would he do it? Only time would tell.

After the eternal hell of waiting in ignorance, I heard the truck door slam shut and the grinding of the transmission as someone searched for a gear. Trying to channel all my senses into hearing only, I barely discerned the faintest whisper, "Stay put till we get a few miles down the road."

I know it was less than five minutes, but my anticipation made it seem like another five hours, when I heard him say, louder this time, "You can come out now."

I eased my head out from under the plywood deck that supported his mattress to see we were moving rapidly down the highway, and my driver was at the wheel. My sigh of relief was audible even over the rumble of the engine and the tires.

"What happened?" I couldn't contain my need to know.

"Oh, it was just stupid. I had two tail lights out; the only two that hadn't been converted to LED."

"What took so long?"

"I had to call a truck stop down the road and have them deliver me some tail lights. DOT won't let you move until everything passes inspection. Took 'em an hour to get here and 10 minutes to change the bulbs."

"How long were we stopped?"

"About two hours."

"Seemed more like ten!" I whined as I climbed out of my temporary tomb and stretched my cramped muscles.

"I'm sure it did, I'm sure it did," he agreed, with more than a little empathy.

There was another extended silence as neither of us knew what to say next. Eventually, my concern over my situation got the best of me and I asked, "You got any stops before St. Charles?"

"Yeah, at the boss's place, just outside a little ghost town called Doe Run. Gotta make a delivery and pick-up there before I head to the city. Its, uh, kind of off the beaten path. Might be a good place to get out."

"Is there any way we could stop at a mailbox before we get there? I've got to warn somebody to be sure put all the blame on me."

I could tell by the reaction in his face that he hadn't expected that part about blaming myself. "You just earned my respect, amigo . . . ." I was certain he was going to ask my name, when I stopped him.

"Thanks, but if you're thinking about asking me who I am, let's just say it goes back to 'plausible deniability'." After a brief pause, I added, "and I'm not going to ask yours either."

"There's a Wal-Mart up the road about twenty miles. It's one of the few places I can get this rig off the road. They've almost always got a mailbox, but I'd better get out and mail it myself. They've got about fifteen surveillance cameras on the goddamn parking lot."

I hurriedly scribbled a note to Dr. Kurtz, confessing what I had done. In the note I asked him to put all the blame on me, deny any knowledge of what was on the file, and to burn the note as soon as he was done reading it, and to replace the original thumb drive I had included in the envelope. I hoped his naiveté didn't circumvent my wish for him to remain a non-participant in this crazy game.

Now that I had this file, what the hell was I gonna do with it?

AUTHOR CLARIFICATION

A s you may have noticed, this is written in the first person by two entirely different people. When Kinley asked to tell his story, I thought it best for him to tell it as he saw it, not as though I was omnisciently viewing his involvement. So the story has two authors, each telling his account of the developments. And as the story proceeds, if you find it at all a worthwhile read, you'll be glad I asked him to assist.

In the first part of this tale, I dictated in my personal recorder as a diary. After we left the ship the first time, I made it back to make further entries on the recording, though it was several months after our initial departure from the ship.

After receiving the recording from Kinley, some thousand centuries after I first made it, I transcribed it and added a few things that I shouldn't have known at the time, in order to make it more clearly understood to you, dear reader. As an eight-year old, my grasp on the events was less than comprehensible, and I didn't want to confuse any of you with the erroneous assumptions of an ignorant pre-pubescent.

The chapter entitled <u>Making the Adjustment</u> was written after my return to the ship, along with several more yet to come. After my (Solan's) death, though, all the subsequent chapters could only have been written with the recovery of my memory upon numerous implant-liftings.

For those of you who have read the previous book, you know that I had to have many cycles of de-implantation before I even came close to recovering these lost memories.

My thanks to Kinley, and to Professor Kurtz, whom I never met, for providing me with the basis to tell you this story. Without this kick-start, you might never have known how you got here; and without his help, the story would never have been completed.

You will come to understand why Kinley and Janey became my septic tank installers, and that this wasn't the first time we had been compatriots.

TRAGEDY STRIKES

[Leo/Solan]

We'd been walking for a several hours and dusk was approaching when it happened.

The wide road that had been hacked into the jungle, turned back into a narrow path with brush and trees all around. The nocturnal animals were beginning to come to life, and the sounds were putting a primal fear in all of us, including the natives.

I was walking in front my fellow space travelers when I heard my Grandfather scream. I'd never heard him do that before, but I knew his voice, and whatever it was, it was bad; really bad.

I turned and ran back toward him when I saw the reason for his shriek. A large snake had apparently dropped from a tree and wrapped around his neck. If we'd been lucky, it would have been a constrictor, and someone could have cut if off him quickly and saved him. We weren't that lucky.

He was flailing wildly, trying to pull the snake off him as Dobber and Cleo ran to help. The natives didn't move.

"NO! NO!" he shrieked. "Stay away! It's poisonous!" He managed, after a prolonged struggle, to get his hands around the base of the snake's head and pull it off his body. Only when he got it to the ground, did one of the natives run up with a knife and cut off the snake's head. I cringed as the body continued to writhe on the ground for several more minutes.

"I'm bit! I'm bit, he said." The excitement in his voice had quickly transformed into a resigned acceptance. "Dobber, you've got to cut me and try to suck the poison out of my neck."

"Caesar," Cleo interjected, "it's too close to your carotid artery."

"You've got to try. If you cut the carotid, I die. If you don't cut at all, I die. There's no choice to be made. You've got to cut." The gravity of the situation was not sinking into me yet. I stood there frozen in fear, eyes staring fixedly at the lifeless, yet still writhing snake.

Grandfather knelt to the ground as Dobber was handed a steel knife by one of the natives. The impact of the fact that it was *steel* was one more significance that did not penetrate my mind that day.

Cleo held my Grandfather's head while Dobber made the first cut. So far so good. He began sucking and spitting the poison and little blood out on the ground. Then he made the second cut.

What happened next took everyone in our party totally by surprise. Princess began screaming, tears were flowing from Cleo's eyes, and Dobber's face expressed a fear I'd never before seen. Even the natives were caught off-guard.

A solid red stream of blood shot from Grandfather's neck as water once shot from my water pistol back home. Only this didn't stop like my water gun at the end of its stroke. Dobber and Cleo tried desperately to plug the flow of blood, but to no avail. They were both soon covered in blood as my Grandfather dropped the rest of the way to the ground and slipped into unconsciousness. In just a few minutes he stopped breathing and a foul smell emitted from his body. "He's gone," Dobber whispered. "He'd lasted 260 years on Thera, and didn't make it a month on this planet."

Princess continued screaming until one of the native women rushed up to her and took her off a good distance until I could no longer see either of them. Cleo sobbed relentlessly as Dobber kneeled like a statue beside Grandfather's dead body. The two of them were covered head to toe in his blood.

I stared at his lifeless corpse for several minutes, completely losing track of where I was, who I was with, or even that I was alive. It all seemed like some bad dream or a movie, but this time it wasn't. I'd say that numbness was all I could feel, but if one is numb, does one *feel* at all?

Slowly I returned from whatever dream-state I had been in, and began to realize there were nude people all around me. Much to my relief, on every countenance, there seemed to be an expression of grief or at least some sympathy. On every countenance, but one, that is. Out of the corner of my eye, I noticed that same one who had frowned so hard at me earlier today was now grinning! He was happy because my Grandfather was dead and the rest of us were all so sad! I knew immediately I didn't like him.

The boy who had earlier showed me how to catch water in a leaf, approached me, tears in his eyes. He spread his arms toward me, and I stepped into his hug. I never knew a hug could feel so good. I hoped that Cleo would hug me like that, and then I immediately felt guilty for thinking such a thing while my Grandfather lie dead in a pool of his own blood.

There was a nearby pool of water, more than just the result of the afternoon rain, but none of us had any idea how deep it was or what lurked beneath the surface. Cleo and Dobber walked to it and knelt down, trying to get enough water to wash some of the blood from their faces and bodies.

I neglected to mention earlier that Dobber, in spite of his lack of clothing, had the presence of mind to wear his holster and laser. Cleo wore a heavy gold necklace and a gold chain around her naked waist. Dobber's weapon would soon save Cleo's life, but at great cost.

The two of them were dipping water with their hands and splashing it over their faces and bodies when I detected a short, rapid movement, followed by a scream from Cleo. Some strange animal, with a head nearly as long as it's body; a head filled with sharp teeth, jumped from the water and chomped down on Cleo's gold necklace, exerting all its effort into pulling her in the water. It was easy to see she wasn't going to win this battle.

Dobber yanked the laser from its holster and without a sound, slashed the animal behind the head, and the severed body fell back into the water. The head, still not realizing it was dead, snapped at her again, aiming for her face, but without the benefit of a body, it too fell back into the water, which quickly turned crimson as the beasts' heart pumped its life-fluid into the murky water.

My two companions sat quickly back on their haunches and began to catch their breath. Just as I thought the worst was over, I heard a 'whoosh' past my head as something struck Dobber from behind and he toppled forward into the water. Bubbles came from around his mouth and nose as Cleo tried to pull him up. Our native companions soon rushed to help, but the spear that had been hurled at him had penetrated his heart, and he, too was dead within seconds. The small pool of bloody water turned even bloodier.

When they were sure he was dead, the old chieftain pulled the spear from Dobber's corpse and viewed it closely. There was some conversation I couldn't understand, and soon all eyes turned to the man who had grinned at Grandfather's death. He said something to the chieftain and pointed in the direction of the bloody, dirty, naked Cleo. I could tell by her expression that the fight in her was gone. The shock of both our men being killed in less than fifteen minutes, and the evil expression in the face of Dobber's murderer left nothing in her but a resigned acceptance.

I looked in the faces of each of the native men, hoping for some sign of intervention, but it soon became apparent that none would be forthcoming. As the murderer approached, I realized that only I stood between him and Cleo, and I would surrender my life to protect her. And surrender it, I surely would have.

He stepped toward me with a knife that would have glistened in the moonlight, as it was now dark and the moon was overhead. But because of the tree cover, no moonlight shined on the sharpened shaft, though I knew it was there, just the same, and I knew he wouldn't hesitate to kill me as he had killed Dobber. And I began to wonder if he hadn't personally dropped the snake on Grandfather.

DOE RUN, MISSOURI

[Kinley]

We exited Highway 67 and headed west on Highway W. I'd never heard of this town before and as soon as we entered it, I knew why. It was nothing more than the dregs of a *former* town. Not only was it a depressed area, it depressed me as soon as we entered it.

Run down mobile homes and chicken pens under front porches were interspersed with an occasional decent dwelling. Apparently a few stalwart souls were determined to improve their little plot of real estate in spite of the squalor of their neighbors.

"In my daddy's day, it was alcohol," the driver said. "In mine, it was pot. Now the drug of destruction is meth. I hate to be so cruel, but I wish it killed its users a little quicker. They live too long and cause too much social decay."

"Ever thought about starting any fires here?" I regretted my question as soon as it left my lips.

"Yep," he said without hesitation, "every fucking time I drive through here."

"Then why are we here?"

"I pick up herbs from a local farmer and take them to a processing plant in St. Charles. The farmer owns this truck and I work for him." He cut off any further questions by picking up the radio and calling someone named Marie.

"Hi Honey," the sweet female voice came over the radio. His wife, maybe?

"Hi, Marie. Just calling to let you know that I'm about six miles out . . . . and I have a passenger." He was giving her a warning but I knew not why.

"Bring him on. I'll put on an extra plate," came back the reply.

"Constance home?" he asked over the radio.

"She's at the school. Be home in about an hour."

"Roger that. Give her a heads-up, will ya?"

There was some undertone to this conversation . . . . something I was not privy to, not that I could expect to be, but I didn't understand the need for the mystery. The radio conversation seemed to be over, and when he hung up the microphone, I wanted to ask but decided I was butting into something that wasn't any of my business. We made a couple more turns and headed out of the scurvy little town and were soon back out into the countryside. Being a couple hundred miles north of Springfield, some of the trees were starting to show a little of their autumnal colors. Three low mountains soon came into view, and the bucolic feeling of the area made me a little misty-eyed. I have to admit; I felt foolish and turned toward the side window so my companion couldn't see my face.

We soon turned off the paved road onto a long gravel driveway and a three-story Victorian house soon came into view, with huge trees standing sentinel. The house was accented by a gargantuan old barn, numerous wooden outbuildings, and a more modern-looking concrete structure. We parked beside the barn; he set the parking brake and let the truck idle for a moment before shutting it down. He grabbed his luggage, and it was then that I realized the only belongings I still had would fit in my pocket.

We climbed out of the truck and walked across the dusty gravel driveway toward the house. Ancient oaks and maples shaded much of the house, and a long row of spruce trees sheltered the house from the south. Strange, I thought, that they weren't on the north side, but after a few days with my hosts, I realized the huge spruces were in the right place; breaking a nearly constant southern wind.

Someone was walking toward us, and I could soon make it out it was a woman; his wife I guessed, but if his boss owned this farm and the truck . . . . something didn't make sense. As she approached, it made even less sense.

I can't say for certain what I expected; perhaps a slightly overweight woman in an apron and her gray hair pulled back in a bun? I couldn't have been more wrong. The woman walking toward us appeared to be in her mid-twenties, the very peak of life. He husband looked like he easily could have been her father, perhaps even her grandfather! She was wearing a pale green sundress, cut just above the knee. She was a stunning sight in the pleasant September afternoon, even before I noticed that the dress was open on each side from armpit to hem. A ladder-type connection was made between the front and back sections of cloth to hold them together. Her tanned skin, revealed by the dress, caused my heart to skip a beat and huge lump to form in my throat.

She ran toward the truck driver, who dropped his suitcase on the ground. She jumped up on him and wrapped her legs around him as my face flushed in embarrassment. After a prolonged kiss, she released her grip around his buttocks and dropped back to the ground. "Who's your friend?" she smiled and extended her hand in my direction.

"Uh . . . uh . . . James. James Carter," I lied . . . . once again.

"Like the President?" she asked.

"Uh, yes." I felt like such a dumbass, but I hadn't expected any of this, and with the combination of her beauty and friendliness, I was a speechless boob . . . . far from the beautiful boob that was partially visible through her revealing dress.

"Well come on in, James Carter. I'll set a place for you at the supper table." She knew I was lying, and I knew that she knew I was lying, but she was gracious enough to accept me for the liar I was becoming. I knew this had to stop, but I had no idea how to do it. My mother always told me that when you tell one lie, you have to tell another one to make the first one believable. I was somewhere around five or six in less than twenty-four hours, and it seemed like I was just getting started. I didn't like it and I was beginning to not like myself.

"Sam, honey, you wanna get a shower before supper?"

"Sure," he answered her back. Well, apparently somebody's name had just been revealed.

While Sam went to shower and change, I was left alone with this beautiful creature and was getting a little uncomfortable. I started to ask her where I might wash my hands when she suddenly exclaimed, "Where are my manners? Wouldn't you like to take a shower also?"

"Uh, uh, no. That's okay. I just need to wash my hands." I didn't tell her it had been over 48 hours since my last shower. But I guess I didn't need to . . . . it must have been obvious.

"No, no. I insist." I guess that meant I stunk. "Follow me. There's another shower and you can use it. And I'll find something for you to put on." It seemed awfully strange to me that this woman, especially one so attractive, would be so friendly to some casual stranger her husband had dragged home. Remembering the infamous slave ranch near Kerrville, Texas, I was beginning to think I was in danger. I guess you could say that the only thing in danger was my credulity.

JUST US THREE

─────── ◈ ───────

[Leo/Solan]

Without a doubt, he'd have impaled me on his spear. His ugly gesture toward *my* Cleopatra, no matter how dirty and bloody she was, inspired in me a courage I'd only imagined until now. I leapt between the two of them, and he raised his spear to steal my life as he'd stolen Dobber's. It wasn't until much later that I discovered what else he'd done.

I knew I was going to die right then and there, but I would willingly, without reservation, sacrifice my life for Cleo. And in the process, I'd sacrifice it for Princess as well.

With the spear raised beside his head, I clamped my eyes closed and tightened every muscle in my body, as if muscle tightening would make me tough enough to withstand his thrust. There was a sudden flash of movement, and I knew that I must be dead. And in a moment or two, I thought there must be no pain in death, for I felt nothing.

When I opened my eyes, my opponent was lying, writhing on the ground, screaming in pain. Nothing made sense. I'm the one who should have been writhing in pain. He seemed to be trying to get up as I stood there in front of Cleo dumbstruck, unable to move. Was I paralyzed? Was I dead? Still trying to defend her after my death? Why was *he* lying on the ground, screaming?

I felt something on my shoulder and, slowly arousing from my stupor, saw a bloody hand beside my head. I jerked violently away, and in doing so, crashed to the ground. As I struggled to my feet, I turned and realized the bloody hand belonged to Cleo. She had touched me gently, and I had reacted like I was being bitten.

Finally realizing I was alive, I noticed my attacker had a big knot forming on the side of his head and blood oozing from it. The old Chieftain stood over him with the blunt end of his tomahawk aimed toward the attacker, uttering words I couldn't understand, but the threat was plain as day.

The look in Cleo's eyes was hard for me to grasp at the time, but apparently she understood what the old man said. He gestured toward her again, and said something else incomprehensible to me. Her expression slowly transformed from fading fear, into sincere gratitude, followed by relief.

Three women soon emerged from the darkness, each carrying some kind of container. They swarmed around her and I soon realized the containers all held water. They began bathing Cleo, washing all the mud and blood from her skin. Much to my dismay, she soon began to weep, and she sobbed the entire time they bathed her. I thought they were hurting her and started to intercede when she raised her hand to ward me away. "Its okay, its okay, Solan. They're only washing me. I'll be okay."

What my immature brain couldn't understand was that her tears were those of relief combined with those of suddenly-realized grief. The tenderness with which the women cared for her was the catalyst for the tears. It would be days before enough of the shock wore off for me to be able to cry. And when I started, I didn't think I'd ever stop.

The old Chieftain, whose name I later learned meant 'Father Mountain', hadn't killed my attacker, but had wounded him seriously. Why the old man would attack one of his own in defense of me was inconceivable, but as I gradually learned the language, I would understand why he did. Father Mountain then drove him from our group, and the attacker, still clutching his skull with both hands, disappeared into the black forest, shouting something that I could only imagine were words avowing revenge. I was hoping I'd seen the last of him, but as it turns out, I'd only seen the beginning.

The old chief moved us along, as it was now well after dark. The big cats that roamed the jungle at night were now, though unbeknownst to me, a real threat to all of us. I wanted to take Grandfather's and Dobber's bodies with us to be buried, but Father Mountain was adamant: We weren't conveying any dead bodies anywhere. I didn't need to understand the words to understand that.

The old man knew his jungle, and though it would be some time before I discovered the truth, Grandfather and Dobber weren't done protecting us that night. Their bodies became nourishment for two big cats that night . . . . their bodies instead of ours. I was gradually learning that Planet Earth was merciless.

And the trouble hadn't even yet begun.

*   *   *

When I awoke to the rising sun the following morning, I couldn't believe my eyes. I expected teepees, wood huts, caves, or some other primitive type of dwelling. Instead, massive stone buildings lined a stone-paved street. I knew a little about slavery, and felt certain that was why I hadn't been killed . . . . I was saved to be enslaved.

I looked around the room to see where I was. I was on a comfortable mattress that looked like it was very well made; far from the primitive bed of leaves I had expected. Princess, Cleo, Father Mountain and two other people also slept in this same room with me. They were still all asleep.

I ducked my head out the opening without a door and looked up and down the street. A few people were out and about, but it was the quietest street I'd ever seen. Since the few people I'd seen were as naked as me, I decided to go for a walk. Back home I don't think I ever paid any attention to my environment. It was there and had always been there, so I didn't even look at it, or even think to look at it.

This was a different situation, however, and I did my best to notice everything! The buildings all seemed to be connected together, except for narrow alleyways that connected the streets. I cautiously made my way down one alley to find another street that looked much like the one I had just left. I wended my way down another alley and another one, and soon I was lost. I didn't remember how many alleys I'd walked through. More and more people were out on the street now, and I found myself staring at a huge pyramid. It seemed to me to be over 200 feet high. It had huge staircases on all four sides and a flat top. I stared up at it while walking toward it, not paying any attention to those around me, when I ran into a huge man with a fierce expression.

He made a demand that I couldn't answer because I couldn't understand the question. My refusal to reply must have angered him for he grabbed me by the arm and started dragging me down the street. My screams were met with uncaring stares from the others in the stone boulevard. As Dobber had said to my Grandfather, "no one was going to come to my rescue".

I kicked and screamed, even trying once to bite him, when he cuffed me hard on the head. He said something, and even though I didn't know the words, I knew the emotion. "Do it again, kid, and I'll knock your block off!"

My fear of being separated from Cleopatra was far more powerful than my fear of his threats, and I tried once again to bite him, and I'll say this for him. He was true to his not-understood words. He knocked me out cold.

When I came to, I was in a field of corn. Fifty other boys of varying ages were there with hoes, weeding the corn. The sun, judging by its position, had been up for less than an hour and I was already sweating profusely. The other boys were too, as I noticed they were muddy from the dust mixing with their sweat. The big man stuck a primitive hoe in my hand. It had a wooden handle and a steel head on it. His gesture was clear: Get to work!

Two weeks ago I was a pampered, spoiled kid on a civilized planet hundreds of light years away. Now I was a starving slave, all alone. Two of those I loved most in the universe were dead, and I was miles from my precious Cleopatra and my little sister.

Hunger would soon become my closest companion and my driving force . . . . that and my desire to return to Cleo.

DISCOVERY

[Hinley]

I must admit that the shower felt pretty good, and not only did it seem to wash the grime of my crimes from me, but revitalized my waning energy. I still wasn't sure that I wasn't being duped, coming to this out of the way place, brought by a guy who blew up my car, introduced me to his ravishing, partially clothed wife. Was this all a set-up? What did they plan for me? Was I to be the new ranch slave? Was Doe Run the new Kerrville? Were they going to turn me in? A thousand questions ran through my mind as I noticed my same old clothes, now washed and dried lay folded on the bed.

The driver, Sam, she called him, said he worked for the owner of this place. Marie treated him like a lover, not like most wives treat their husbands. Was he having an affair with the owner's wife? And if so, where was the owner? Who was Constance? And the crazy dress? At least it was driving *me* crazy.

When I entered the kitchen, the smell of fried chicken filled the air, and Sam was already sitting at the table. He'd shed the overalls and ball cap for white shorts and tank top. His head was completely bald; not only that, but the sunburned face and white forehead seemed to have blended into a handsome tan. I was sure it was him, but he seemed twenty years younger than he had before the shower! Surely this couldn't be? Marie was finishing something at the countertop as Sam motioned for me to sit. She placed a bowl of mashed potatoes and ears of sweet corn on the table and joined us.

"Dig in!" she said. "Don't be bashful and don't expect us to beg you to eat. There's plenty here. Constance won't be here," she looked in Sam's direction and added, "Homer's coming in tonight." I didn't know what that meant but it had some deep significance to the two of them. We ate in silence for a few moments when she asked, "So, James, where you from?"

I sat there stupidly wondering where James was, when I realized she was talking to me. Lies beget lies. "Oh, uh, Joplin."

"What do you do there?"

I started to search for another lie when Sam spoke up. "I called her and told her about you when we got pulled over at the weigh station. I think it's time we all started telling the truth." They both looked at me while my mind searched frantically for the next believable fabrication. "I'll go first," he added.

"Marie and I are the owners here. People often think we're having an affair, the way we act around each other. She is my wife. Constance is our daughter. I didn't want you to know my identity until we were sure who you are." They both stared at me for a moment as my mind raced up and down a series of dead-ends searching for the right thing to say. "Your turn." He added, breaking my reverie.

"Jimmy Carter? Is that the best you could come up with?" the breathtaking beauty asked. Her look of disdain cut me like a knife.

"I lied," hesitating, searching for another lie, but found a way to be truthful without giving myself away, "to protect your husband. And now to protect you. I've done something that could get me in a lot of trouble, and my lies were to protect you from being an accessory to my actions."

"We appreciate, but don't need your protection," she replied. Her husband remained silent.

"Oh, I think you do." I couldn't fathom why either one of them would want to be involved in a criminal activity, or at least one that certain individuals would consider criminal.

"Have you watched the recording?" Sam inquired.

"Recording?!" How the hell did HE know? "What recording?"

"The one in your pants pocket . . . . on the zip drive."

"Oh, shit."

THE CLOUDS

[Leo/Solan]

For three months I hoed corn every single day. From sun up till afternoon rain, and it rained every afternoon. I made six new acquaintances, two new friends and one new enemy. Day by day, I learned Hyanthian; first the nouns, and as the weeks turned into months, I even learned the verbs. I couldn't conjugate the verbs very well, but at least we could understand each other.

My first objective, after getting something to eat, was to find my way back to the city I had been kidnapped from. That's where my new friends helped out, for when I was taken to the cornfield, I had no idea from which direction I had come. The big man's last blow had knocked me out and when I awoke with a pounding headache, I was in the cornfield.

All of us boys slept on the ground. It was warm at night and miserably hot during the day. If it hadn't been for the leaves we rubbed on our skin, the mosquitoes would have eaten us alive.

On my second week in the cornfield, my real trouble began, and the trouble was my hair. It began to grow back. The boy who became my enemy began to mock me and make fun of the stubble on my head, since the rest of them were bald as Grandfather had been.

From here on out, I will translate.

"What's wrong with your head, peach fuzz?" the bully asked. His name was Tornuku.

I rubbed my hand over my head and cringed. Maybe these boys didn't know about Wyverns. I'd bet my skin (because that's all I had left) that the adults did. "I don't know," I lied.

"Look at the fuzz ball, boys!" He was probably six or seven years older than me and at least 50 pounds heavier. He also seemed to be the oldest of all of us. Only boys worked in the fields; there were men around in the evening and early morning, but none between sunrise and sunset. He strode intimidatingly toward me and grabbed me around the head, rubbing my stubbly skull with his knuckles. "There's something wrong with you, fuzz ball!" He declared to the rest of the group. My cover was blown. When he told the men that evening, I'd probably be executed.

"C'mon," I begged, "just let me get back to work."

He scrubbed my head hard with his knuckles and tossed me to the ground. "Get back to work, punk!" he ordered.

At least getting away from him gave me a chance to think, and hopefully find a plan of escape. Then at lunch, I saw something that changed everything.

The two friends I'd made were named Marsalu and Kateche. Tornuku ordered Marsalu to follow him over a low hill while we broke for lunch. "The rest of you punks stay here!" he demanded. "I have a special job for Marsalu. The rest of you idiots aren't qualified to do it. Don't come over the hill or I'll kick your little asses!" The look in Marsalu's eyes was pure dread.

I guess Tornuku was too stupid to realize that the surest way to get someone to do something was to order them not to. Shortly after the two of them disappeared over the rise, Kateche and I shared a silent glance and surreptitiously skirted the edge of the low rise. What we saw shocked and enraged both of us, and the hatred I held for the Evil One who had murdered Dobber boiled up inside me.

Marsalu was on his knees in front of Tornuku with a leather strap around his neck and appeared to be nearly choking. The bully held the other end of the strap and was forcing his penis into Marsalu's mouth. With no plan whatsoever, I ran screaming toward the two of them, without a weapon to hand. Tornuku's size was his advantage over my petite body, but I hit him with enough momentum to knock him to the ground just as his semen erupted from his penis. Kateche ran up behind me and as Tornuku began to regain his breath, my friend handed me a large rock. With no thought of the consequences, I repeatedly crashed it down upon his skull, crushing the life from his body. He twitched and groaned as blood oozed from his ears, eyes and mouth. Bubbles soon emitted from his nose as his blood began to flood his lungs.

Kateche helped get the strap off Marsalu's neck and used his sweat rag to wipe the semen from his mouth and face. "Please, please don't tell the others what he did!" Marsalu begged.

"I think that's the least of our problems," I announced. I had killed someone and now the Evil One was next on my list. Was I becoming a killer? But escaping had suddenly become vastly more important than my moral state.

"What do we do?" Kateche pleaded.

"We've got to hide till dark. After that, you've got to help me get back to the city. I have to find my women." Marsalu's shame wouldn't allow him to return to the cornfields, I *couldn't* return and Kateche was left with no choice but to side with his friends.

"I'm with you, Solly," he announced. "I have no choice. My parents are dead. I can't go back. The masters will know that we are friends and I will be killed. I didn't want to be a slave, but better a live slave than a dead free man."

"The masters count on that, Kateche. That's how they enslave us." I guess Grandfather's wisdom had sunk in after all. "After dark, can you find your way to the city?"

"I think so," he answered. "I was kidnapped in the dark, as well as knocked unconscious, but I watch them come and go. There are four roads out of here, but your women must be to the south."

"Then to the south, it is." I looked at Marsalu, to get his thoughts, but he just shook his head in agreement, shame still clouding his countenance.

We headed to the cover of the jungle just as the afternoon thunderstorm began, fortuitously obscuring our tracks as we sought to hide ourselves from possible pursuit. Within a few miles we found a small cave with a huge deadfall of timber and brush in front of it, and we hunkered down to wait until dark.

The first sign we had that anything was wrong was the length of the storm. They usually only lasted an hour or so, but this one went on until way after dark. The afternoon sun which broke out from the storm clouds every single day, refused to show its face on this day. I looked out once after several hours of darkness and could find not a single star.

On the morning of the following day, we knew something big had happened, but had no idea what was to come. Daylight gradually eroded the darkness of night, but for the first time, there was no sun. A heavy cloud cover obscured the sky. If the Evil One had stayed banned from the city, the clouds might have lasted for centuries, but the activities on which he was about to embark, forced the Watchers to take an entirely different turn.

And then there was the thundering voice coming from the sky.

THE CAPTURE

[Solan/Leo]

U tilizing all his best prey-stalking skills, the Evil One skulked into the home of Father Mountain. The sun was still five hours from rising, so he had plenty of time. He'd been raised in this very house; before the old man had betrayed his own kind and accepted these foreigners as his own.

He knew exactly where she lay and knew the old man would do anything to protect her. It didn't matter that she was old and her belly sagged like her tired breasts, or that that the lips of her pussy hung out like dry tobacco leaves from bearing so many children. Father was loyal to her to a fault. Stupid old fart! The Evil One knew that women were to be used. When they grew old and their bodies weren't supple any more, they were killed—just like the children that they bore. Stupid, sentimental fools! Piss on all of them!

*　*　*

Two months earlier, as she knew it would, Cleo's hair began to grow back out. With no way to shave it off again, she knew the hair could get her killed. The memories of the Wyverns were old but they ran deep in the collective consciousness.

The old woman noticed it first, and fortunately for Cleo, had a remedy that would save her life. *Falima*, Cleo learned, was her name. She was the wife and mother of Father Mountain's children;

all twelve of them. Only six had survived infancy, and one of the six was damaged. She begged Father not to kill the child, as he could display a look of innocence and could shed tears that feigned his insincere regret. In spite of what she knew to be true, she defended him at every turn, knowing deep within her, that her husband was right. The child should be put down like a mad dog, but Father's love for her had spared the boy's life. A sparing she would come to regret on this night.

Falima approached Cleo one morning after Father had left the apartment they now shared with my two girls. "You have hair!" she hissed. "We must get rid of it! If the elders find out they will kill you surely as the sun rises!"

Cleo was taken aback, though she knew she had to be rid of the hair. But how did the old woman know about hair removers?

"Sometimes, babies are born with hair . . . . maybe only one of a hundred. For many years, the elders would murder the baby on sight, and throw them into the fire, in hopes of preventing the Wyverns from coming back.

"My grandmother and my mother worked for five years trying to find something to take off the hair so that it would never grow back. I had two sisters killed by the elders because they were born with hair, so it was imperative that they find a solution. They mixed several concoctions of leaves and berries until they found one that worked. They rubbed them all on my hairy little head until one finally worked! They saved my life. It wasn't until I turned eleven that they realized that I had hair growing in other places. They then applied the salve on my legs and arms, my armpits and here," pointing to her hairless groin.

"I save *you* now!" she announced with pride, as she began to rub the white salve over Cleo's head. The hair melted away like ice on a hot summer day. "Raise your arms," Falima demanded. Cleo complied and the sweet smelling salve was applied to her armpits. "Down," the old lady said and applied it to both her arms.

"Now, wash!"

"Is it that fast? I thought it would take longer."

"Very fast. Go wash up and then we do your legs and your pubic hair."

Cleo did as commanded and was surprised to feel how smooth her arms, pits and her head felt. "No more hair?"

""Never grow again," the old lady answered. "Lay down," she ordered. Cleo could see this was life or death. Embarrassed or not, she would comply. "Raise legs straight up." Falima applied the salve all up and down her legs, feet, and buttocks. "Raise legs over head," she was ordered again. The old lady rubbed the salve around her anus and the lower part of her vulva. In spite of her efforts to fight it, she could feel her labia begin to swell and her clitoris to protrude as the old hands manipulated her. "Legs apart," was the demand and she complied again. Falima rubbed the salve from her labia all the way to her hips and her navel.

"O.K. Go wash. You are safe now!"

Cleo went to the basin and washed the rest of the ointment off her skin. Her epidermis had never felt so good in her life! "What about Solan?" she asked Falima.

"If we ever find him, I will do him while he's young. No hair will ever grow." Cleo let out a little sigh of relief.

*   *   *

When the Evil One came in that night, his mother and father were sound asleep; as were Cleo and Princess. His first victim would be his own mother.

She awoke to sensation of the blade against her throat. She let out a little sigh of relief, seeing the intruder was the son she had borne and so long protected. Her relief was short-lived however when his only words were, "Wake him up, bitch!"

Father stirred from the sound of the voice in the room. He struggled to see in the faint light provided by moon, stars and torches in the street. His heart sank when he realized it was the son he should have drowned 30 years ago.

"Wake up, you old fuck!" the Evil One shrieked at his father. "I want the women! Both of them!"

"Not the girl!" his mother cried.

"Yes, the little bitch, too. And don't try to stop me." He jerked Princess to her feet, and pointed his blade at Cleo, "Outside,

Pussy! And don't try to run or I'll gut the little one right here on top of the old crone!"

"Please, son, please don't do this," the old lady begged. His response was a slash that slit her throat spraying blood over the room and its occupants.

Father jumped up toward Falima and was met with the blade in his chest. He stumbled backward and fell to the hard floor as the liquid of life pumped out on the cool stone floor.

Princess was certain this was her last night on earth, and the last of the Therans would soon be gone.

Only her timing was wrong.

THE CHASE BEGINS

[Solan/Leo]

When sunrise arrived, it was merely a lessening of the darkness. For the first time during my short stay on this planet, the sun was completely obscured by a heavy overcast sky. The brilliant orange globe that usually brought the morning to life was nowhere to be seen, and for the first time, it seemed as though the morning was cool, unlike the steamy days I was growing accustomed to.

The usually chatty animals were quiet, and the pallor of death seemed to permeate the atmosphere. I don't know why I felt that, except that it seemed like an ancient forgotten fear seemed to have been subconsciously remembered. From their facial expressions, Marsalu and Kateche must have felt the same.

"It must be the end of days!" Marsalu whined.

"I know. I feel it too," Kateche added.

"What do you mean?" I asked, trying not to reveal my sense of foreboding, all the while hoping they might reveal their thoughts while I kept mine to myself.

"The Devils have returned! They returned because you killed Tornuku!" Marsalu was trying to explain, but my confusion only deepened. "When the Devils return, they steal the sun and all the light. The people go mad and begin to kill each other, and as the grey sky lingers, we retreat to the jungle and live like animals!"

I didn't say so, but thought I'd been living like an animal ever since I got here.

Without warning, a deafening clap of thunder made the three of us drop to the ground, shivering. Just as we began to gather our senses and stand up, a booming voice came from the clouds. One that we'd soon come to expect many times a day.

"STOP!" it shouted. "GO BACK!"

The three of us stood in dumbfounded silence, wondering what to do next. Before we'd even made a step, it bellowed again.

"NOT THAT WAY!"

"We haven't even moved!" I screamed in retaliation. I felt stupid once I realized I was yelling at clouds. But who else would I yell at?

"Don't yell at the Devils!" Kateche hissed at me.

"Oh, they're not Devils," I tried to comfort the two of them, but to no avail. They weren't going to believe me, a kid their own age. I knew the "Devils" were nothing more than space travelers, just as I was, but how was I going to explain that to my two friends? They'd just think I'd lost my mind. I'd watched my Grandfather use our loudspeaker system to intimidate the primitives; I knew how it was done. But that technology was so far from the understanding of my two friends that I'd have had more success explaining to them the annihilation of Thera.

"Yes they are!" Kateche and Marsalu hissed in unison, as though they didn't want to be heard, yet insisting that they silence any of my potential future outbursts.

"No they aren't. They're just travelers in the sky!" I hadn't yet learned that most people don't want to know the truth. Truth just interferes with their preconceived, but stable, notions. The lie, the mystery, the myth, passed down from ignoramus to ignoramus, no matter how destructive, is comfortable. Truth rocks the slave ship like a hurricane. To most people, being an ignorant slave provides the stability that they *know* knowledge and freedom can't.

The truth was that sending the jobs to Nicha, buying all our fuel from Qari and living off credit cards while the stock market spiraled to new heights on a foundation-less technology boom set the stage for the death of our planet. But Thera's inhabitants were comfortable living the lie. And if it wasn't for the wisdom of my Grandfather, who refused to believe the lie, I would have died with the rest of them. Tears welled up in my eyes, as I realized how much I missed him and wished he'd gotten to watch me grow; if I somehow managed to grow on this godforsaken place.

When I discovered the real reason he had to die, I exacted my additional pound of flesh. When I finally learned the truth about what happened to him, a strange sense of serenity pervaded my being. But I'm getting ahead of myself and the story.

*   *   *

It took us two days to get to the city. We entered under cover of darkness, the streets lit only by the oil lamps lining the stone boulevard. Marsalu and Kateche had been taken from the streets, much as I had been, and were terrified of being caught once again. Perhaps we'd been wiser to arrive in daylight, what there was of it the last few days, but we had no control over the length of the trip or the time of our arrival.

Marsalu wanted to wait until daylight, as it seemed that only boys wandering at night were kidnapped and made slave laborers. Daylight was much safer, he insisted. I, on the other hand, was too impatient to wait any longer to see Cleo and Princess. If I'd known that they had left with the Evil One only two hours earlier, I'm sure I'd have waited. The grisly interior of Father Mountain's dwelling made my gut retch till I thought my anus was lifting through my throat. Marsalu was hit with it also; he hurried out into the street and heaved the contents of his stomach. Kateche wouldn't enter when he smelled the death exuding from the door.

"I have to go find my family!" he complained.

"As I do mine," I responded coldly.

"I'm going, Solan. Please come. Don't go in there!" he pleaded.

"GO, Goddamnit!" I yelled at him. "Just go! I have to find my girls!" As he disappeared, his selfishness felt to me as though it was completely unfounded, though I later understood that he missed his family just as I missed mine. I turned to look for Marsalu, but he was gone as well. I would enter the bloody apartment alone.

The smell was indescribable. A Hyanthian, normally so sweet-smelling in life, exuded a fierce smell when murdered. A natural death, I would later learn, left no horrific odor, but one as wrong as this tortured the nose and brain. It made a coroner's job significantly easier identifying the cause of death, as the murder victim left behind a burning virulence as an indicator of his wrath at being murdered.

If I'd hung around Marsalu's assailant a few days earlier, I might have noticed it, but we left so quickly, any smell coming from his body was wafted away as I quickly escaped with my friends into the jungle; and perhaps he wasn't truly Hyanthian. I wanted to escape from this foulness as well, but I had to find my girls, in spite of the odor and the blood.

I diligently searched each room, each closet, each potential hiding place without success. The girls were gone. I didn't have to be told who had done this and why. If I'd had no reason for living till now, I'd just found it. And I wouldn't rest until I'd carved him up . . . . alive.

HIGH IN THE SKY

———— ⬡ ————

"**W**e have to find her and kill her," the slimy old Grey told his companions.

"But why?" the younger and least slimy Grey of them all, asked, "She's such a pretty thing. Couldn't we just kidnap her and make her a sex slave?"

"She's too dangerous. You know she hasn't been implanted."

"Why can't we implant her now?"

"Too late. She knows too much. Only the ignorant can be implanted. Ignorance feeds on ignorance. Knowledge feeds on knowledge. She understands way too much. The old fart educated those two kids too well. The boy probably *can* be. But the girl will have to be killed. Right before she picks up a new body, we can implant her then. We always ultimately win, but for now, she will have to be killed immediately."

"But we've lost track of her, sir. She and her teacher have been kidnapped and taken into the jungle. We've completely lost track of them."

"Change of plans," the slimiest one said without emotion. "Instead of five hundred years of cloud cover, we drop the nuke. The results are a little more dramatic, but the resultant apathy is extreme, in spite of its short duration.

"It's really kind of funny," he mused, "that you can destroy everything in sight and they manage to pull themselves up by the bootstraps and rebuild, but if you put the cloud cover over the planet, they dwindle into a motionless depression that takes thousands of years to overcome. The effect that their star has on this planet and these people is phenomenal." He had drifted so far from his original thought that he forgot why he was dropping the bomb. Suddenly remembering his logic, he added, "The bomb will surely kill her. After that, the cloud cover won't be necessary, and the budget will allow either the bomb or the clouds, but not both.

"I can explain it to the board that it was necessary, and though the cost is about the same, ultimately the cloud cover requires more maintenance, while the bomb is quick and effective. The board usually prefers the cloud cover and thousands of years of apathy over the quick and wide-spread destruction of the bomb. The bomb is messier, but the resultant cloud only lasts about 100 years. You know how the humanitarians complain back home . . . ."

* * *

Twentieth Century Scientists would explain it as an asteroid or a comet, because the truth was required by law to be hidden from the public, but what struck off the coast of the Yucatan was a nuclear bomb fired from those who were determined to keep my baby sister from realizing her potential. And though it wasn't the first time they'd done it, and they wouldn't completely thwart her rise to power, they would manage to delay it by tens of thousands of years.

In another 45,000 years, there would be an asteroid; one from the remains of the fifth planet in the solar system, the one the humans never bothered to name.

WELCOME TO DOE RUN

[Kinley]

"We know about the zip drive, 'Jimmy Carter'," Sam didn't mince words.

"We also know your name is Kinley Thorsen," his beautiful wife added.

I was dumbstruck! How the hell did they know? "Wha—? How do you know?" I had a sinking feeling in the pit of my stomach. What the fuck did I get myself in to? "I—uh, I—uh, think I need to go. Which way is the highway?" I had a desperate urge to run, but knew it was pointless. If they knew this much and had gone this far to get me here, they weren't going to let me go now.

"You're not in any danger here, Kinley," Sam tried to reassure me.

"What were you going to do with this once you got it?" Marie asked.

I hadn't thought that far ahead and she knew it. "I—uh, I—uh need to get it to someone who can tell the story."

"Who might that be?" she asked. She was beautiful, but intense. "Who would you take it to? The Media? You know they're in the pocket of the Emperor." Did she just say "emperor"?

"We are the people who need custody and control of what you found." *She* was certain, but I sure as hell wasn't.

"Why you? What's so special about the two of you?" They looked back and forth at each other for a few moments without answering. "And how the fuck did you know about me?" I was really becoming paranoid now.

"I don't think it would do any good to explain, do you, Marie?"

"No. He'll have to be shown, same as us."

I didn't know what the hell they were up to, but my heart was throbbing in my ears so loudly, nothing else they said penetrated the pounding in my skull.

"We need to go to the mine. I know some of Cleopatra's people are still there; they keep it functioning as a back-up in case anything happens down below Fredericktown." Marie said it, but I swear I never heard it. Even if I had, I wouldn't have understood a word of it. My mind was racing, trying to find some way to extricate myself from these people; people about which I knew nothing; people who knew *way* too much about me.

"Will you go to the mine with us?" Sam was polite enough to ask.

"If we get there and you don't feel the pull, you don't have to go." *The Pull?* "But if you don't go in, we get the zip drive. We'll buy you a bus ticket back to Springfield and you can go back to Lois." How the hell did they know her name?? "You can report your car stolen and collect the insurance money." We'll even pay your deductible.

"You can go back to your life and pretend none of this ever happened. But if you decide to cause any trouble . . . . remember, we found you once. We'll find you again."

"Okay, okay. I'll go. If I don't feel this 'pull' as you call it, you get the zip drive and I disappear from your lives. But I just have one question."

"What's that?" Sam asked.

"You haven't answered any of my other questions. Why would I think you'd answer this one?"

"Was that your question?" Man, this beauty could be sarcastic!

"No, smart ass. It wasn't."

"Why do *you* get the zip drive?"

"We know that what you found is legitimate. And we know how to get it disseminated, yet protected. And best of all, we know who dictated it." I think I vaguely remember passing out.

When I regained consciousness, we were at the entrance to the mine, my hosts were completely nude and to top it off, Marie was as bald-headed as Sam. I think I passed out again . . . . but not before I felt it.

PAIN

❖

[Solan/Leo]

"**Y**ou fucking bitches are gonna do what I tell you . . . . WHEN I tell you! You got that straight!?" The Evil One threw Princess to the ground and sat on her. With a leather strap he tied her hands behind her back and hobbled her ankles. She could still walk but not run . . . . like she'd done a few minutes earlier.

It was much easier for him to control Cleo by threatening Princess than it was to control Princess by threatening Cleo. It wasn't that Princess cared less about Cleo than Cleo did for her; it was because the youngster was more confident in her ability to outsmart their captor. Unfortunately, she underestimated his cruelty.

Now that he had her restrained, he could go back to what he was really after—Cleo. She was tied with her back to a tree, her heaving breasts protruding even more because her shoulders were pulled back tightly against the tree. Her ankles were also tied to the tree trunk. She'd kneed him once in the groin, and he retaliated by hitting her so hard she saw stars . . . . he wouldn't give her another opportunity to keep him from his prize.

He built a small fire and heated a pointed metal rod. Cleo had noticed when Grandfather had been snake-bitten that the Hyanthians had steel. They were definitely not a stone-age people, and now that very same steel was about to torture and imprison her.

The Evil One laid out four metal rings. They formed a complete circle, and like a key-ring, the circle was completed by a short lap of one circle over the other. They were split so that things could be hung on them. Cleo would soon find out that the thing hung on them would be her.

The cloud cover was three days old by this day, and though it wasn't cold, it was cooler than it had been since our arrival. Cleo's nipples stood erect, pointing toward the sky. To tighten them even more, her captor poured cool water over her breasts, which cascaded over her belly and between her spread legs.

After the metal rod had cooled a little, the Evil One picked it up and approached her. He stuck it up under her nose, and with a sneer, made his intentions clear. "I own you now. I own your tits. I own your pussy, and I own your asshole. You are my property!" With no further warning, he grasped her left breast with his left hand, squeezing the nipple and areola, then plunged the pointed rod through her nipple. She grimaced in pain but let out no sound. Blood began to trickle down her belly as he grasped the right one and did the same.

He began licking the blood from her belly until he had cleaned it of the red fluid, and deftly, yet excruciatingly, inserted the rings through her nipples.

He once again went for the metal rod. She cringed, knowing what would come next. Grasping each of her hairless labia, he pierced each one and began to lick the oozing blood from her vulva. In spite of the pain and revulsion for him, she felt her body react, almost as if it were completely independent of her mind. Her labia began to swell, her clitoris grew firm and she suddenly felt a wetness between her legs she knew wasn't blood.

"Good," she thought. Let him believe I like it. Maybe he'll let down his defenses. "You can do anything you like to me, and I won't fight back on one condition."

"Say it!" her captor demanded. "Maybe I'll honor it. Maybe I won't."

"Don't hurt the girl," Cleo voiced.

"Bah. I'm not interested in little girls. I want a woman! But if she doesn't behave, maybe I'll break her leg."

"I'll talk to her. Do anything you want to me, just don't hurt her. I'll get her to behave."

"Good luck," he muttered sarcastically. "But if she tries to run away again, I'll . . . ." He didn't finish his sentence, as he went back to his collection of trinkets and dug out pieces of chain. His civilization was even more advanced than she thought.

He attached the chain to each of her nipple rings, then connected another to her labia rings, then connected the two chains together with another than ran vertically the length of her belly. He then ran his leather strap through the vertical chain and tied it around his wrist. The only way to escape was to rip the rings from her body. Then he reached around behind the tree and untied her ankles and wrists. She could move her arms and she could walk, but now she was a more a prisoner than ever.

The captor pulled on his strap, sending shock waves of pain throughout Cleo's body; pain accompanied by a strange sense of pleasure. "Pain and pleasure," Cleo thought to herself, "That's what sex is all about in the first place. Pleasure mingled with pain." He jerked again and this time, it was all pain. The pleasure had evaporated.

Princess tried to run toward them, but the hobbles kept her from doing anything more than shuffle in their direction. The Evil One laughed as the little girl tried to attack him. He'd put a stop to this! Without warning he kicked her to the ground and raised his machete.

"NO!" Cleo screamed with every ounce of voice she could muster. "NO!"

He paid no heed as the blade came down and struck Princess on the ankle just above her foot, severing the tendon that allowed her to raise and lower her foot. There was little blood, but Cleo could see that the damage was done. Princess wouldn't be able to walk, let alone run . . . . ever again. The little foot flopped helplessly as she tried to stand and attack the Evil One one more time.

"Oh, you son of a bitch!" Cleo screamed at the top of her lungs as Princess lay writhing in agony. He slapped her to the ground and ripped the rings from her nipples. Pain shot through her breasts as she covered them with her hands, hoping to stifle the pain.

"She'll be less trouble now," he said to no one. He then turned to the weeping and bleeding Cleo and ordered, "Do your duty, bitch, or I'll cut *your* ankles too." He pointed to his penis, which had become erect at the sight of the girls' pain. If that's what aroused him, Cleo knew what to do, and complied with his command. He grabbed her by her necklace and tightened it around her throat as he pulled her face to his groin. On all fours, she rested on her left hand and grasped his penis in her right and placed it in her mouth. He quickly jammed it in till it hit the back of her throat.

Knowing what must be done, she pretended to caress him and attend to his biological, yet abusive urge. Once she had his confidence, she looked up toward his face and saw that his eyes were closed. Knowing that this was her one opportunity, she took it and bit down with every gram of adrenaline she could muster. It didn't sever completely at once, but blood soon filled her mouth as his erection quickly collapsed. He jerked back away from her and using both hands to cover his mortally wounded member, dropped the machete.

Princess took advantage of her position and though it weighed nearly as much as she did, grasped the machete and struck the back of their captor's right leg, severing the calf muscle.

As he collapsed to the ground on his backside, Princess looked him hard in the eyes and said, "How do you like that, ASSHOLE?"

Cleo grabbed the knife from his belt and quickly cut the leather thong tied to her chains, and stepped back away from him so he couldn't reach her ankles. Thinking only of escaping, she hadn't at all counted on Princess' next move. The six-year old raised the machete above her captor's head, intending to cut his throat, but missed, and the blade landed parallel to his open mouth, cutting his cheek clear to the back of his jawbone.

They should have killed him then and there, but all Cleo could think about was escaping into the darkness of the jungle. She hoisted Princess on her back and grasped the chains that were still attached to her labia, and handed them to Princess. They'd remove them when they were far from the Evil One, but until then, Princess had to hang on the chains to keep them from inflicting any more damage to the injured Cleo.

Worried about the injury to her charge's ankle, Cleo held little concern for her own plight. Had she realized Princess' incredible ability to heal, she might have spent a little more of her energy caring for herself.

THE PULL

[Hinley]

I felt it; much as Billy Gordon must have felt it, though I wouldn't meet him for a few more weeks. Once I was right above the mine entrance, The Pull was as strong as a magnet on a paper clip. Somehow, I got the sensation it had been pulling me all the way from Springfield, and that none of this was an accident.

You know that sense you have that you somehow don't fit in? That sense of always longing for something that you fear will never be found? The soul mate you spend your entire life searching for but never find? A hunger that burns your soul, but you can't describe it because no words exist for it? You settle for a job. You settle for a spouse. You settle for hundreds of things that seem so far from your true aspirations. You settle because you must. If not, you become an endless wanderer. It seems romantic and adventurous until you're about 25, and after that, if you're still wandering, you're wandering to wander . . . . not to get anywhere or accomplish anything. The destination ceases to be the goal. You're only journeying for the journey.

All those sensations, all those longings, felt as though, for the first time in my life, that they were on the verge of being fulfilled. And all I had to do was accompany two naked people into an abandoned mineshaft in a little Podunk town named Doe Run. Now that I verbalized it, I sounded like a raving lunatic. Well, being sane and normal hadn't gotten me anywhere. If normal was an average of all the range of humanity, brown must be the average of all the range of colors. Brown—the color of shit and dirt and death. All the beautiful colors of stone, all the colors of flowers, sky, birds, animals—averaged out, it became all brown. Normal. Just like me . . . . the color of shit, dirt, and death.

I might be crazy as a bed bug (don't know where that phrase came from) but I was going to follow these two naked bald people down into a hole in the ground. Hell, even if I died down there, if the story got disseminated, wouldn't it be worth it? Would death be so much worse than the life I'd been living? I mean, really, would it?

And if the story got in the right hands? Maybe, just maybe someone might be able to save this planet from the same fate as Thera? Little did I know at the time, that the plan was already well underway to rescue the human race from its idiot self, and I had landed smack dab in the middle of the most determined, hell-bent bunch of people I would ever have the privilege of meeting.

So down we went.

*   *   *

I don't know what I expected, or even if I expected anything at all. A dark hole in the ground? Dripping water? Stalactites and stalagmites? What I didn't expect was the hum.

It was the first thing I became aware of that didn't fit into any preconceived notions I might have had. A low hum. Not deafening, not even loud; but noticeable.

The second thing I became aware of was not really capable of being called 'light'. It was more like an absence of darkness. It seemed to have no source . . . just as the sky does on an overcast day when the sun isn't visible, and light diffuses through the clouds. But I could actually see clearly. Not great distances, mind you, but I could make out the pleasing naked backside of my female companion. Sam wasn't ugly by any means, but I prefer girls . . . .

"Why do you two have to be naked?" my curiosity finally got the best of me and I regretfully blurted out the question.

"Don't HAVE to, WANT to," they replied in unison, but didn't elaborate further.

"Well, can I ask why you WANT to?"

"Sure." I should have expected the lack of elaboration to Sam's reply, as he exactly answered the question I asked. "You can ask."

"Well, why, then?" I was growing impatient, feeling awfully ignorant of a situation about which they seemed totally certain.

"Were you born with clothes on?" Marie asked.

"Stupid question. Of course not."

"Why do you wear clothes?"

"Because we're supposed to, it keeps us from being animals. It keeps us warm. Besides, you get arrested for walking around like that where I come from!"

"Ah. Supposed to." Marie was more than a little smug. "By whose orders?"

"I don't know, God? Jesus?"

"Okay, so what you're saying is that you are supposed to do something because someone . . . . you're not really sure who . . . . said you're supposed to do it."

"I guess. I never questioned it."

"Never questioned it? Hmmm. If someone told you that you were supposed to stand on your head at the bottom of a cesspool, you would do it then?"

"Of course not . . . that's not the same thing."

"I agree. It's not the same thing. It is, however, a thing called 'now-I'm-supposed-to'. C'mon, Kinley. You're a smart guy. You didn't take all these risks because you are stuck in a 'now-I'm-supposed-to'."

I had to ponder that for a minute, and the two of them must have picked up on my pondering, as they both remained silent. How many times during the day are we doing 'now-I'm-supposed-to' without any thought or reason why? An automatic response. "It's how we get along in this society!" I finally protested.

"And how's that workin' out for us these days?" Sarcasm dripped from Sam's words. I didn't reply because we both knew the answer.

"At one time, the human form was a work of beauty," Marie broke the silence.

"And in the case of you two, it is!" I paused as my self-consciousness struck me like a fist. "But not me. I could never take my clothes off in front of other people. I don't have the body for it. Even if I did, I couldn't do it."

Neither of them said a word, but the extended stare they gave each other told me that they knew something else that I didn't. "I'm just gonna shut up now." I added with some embarrassment.

"That might be a good thing," Marie actually turned around and smiled at me. Even without hair, she was strikingly beautiful. Her physique was perfect, like something Michelangelo would have created.

The hum grew louder, the light with no source became brighter, and the Pull increased with every step. In spite of all my verbal protests, and 'now-I'm-supposed-to's', the Pull grew stronger and stronger. Resistance became futile.

If, two weeks ago, I'd been told that before this day was done that I'd be hairless and nude in the bottom of an abandoned mine, I'd have told you you'd lost your fucking mind.

I'd have been wrong.

LIKE SHYLOCK

[Solan/Leo]

I had no reason to know which way to run once I'd left the city. No one was going to help me; no adults, no friends, no one . . . . I was completely on my own and it was up to me to save Cleo and Princess. I don't know why I ran the direction I did. It just seemed like the right way to go. My sister was helping me and I wasn't even aware of it.

I must have made fifteen miles the first day, and it was hard going. The temperature and humidity were unbearable, and I had to stop three times to rub the mosquito repellant plant on my skin. By nightfall, the creatures began to stir again after resting during the heat of the day, and I knew that not only I, but maybe the girls as well, were in danger of being *something's* evening meal. And with Cleo's wounds, the smell of blood would make them that much more attractive to the nocturnal carnivores. It was a thought I didn't relish, though at the time I was only guessing; I knew nothing of her wounds.

I found a rock overhang, which though unneeded, gave me some sense of security, and at the very least provided protection from one direction. That only left me three to watch. And though I dared not sleep, my exhaustion finally overtook me and I dozed off.

I don't know what awakened me, but this formerly over-protected city kid was tuning his senses and becoming a child of the jungle. If I hadn't awakened, I'd never have lived to rescue my girls, pointless as it turned out to be. But I'd be damned to the fifteenth level of Hell before I'd let that evil bastard make off with Cleo and Princess as long as a breath remained inside me.

All I had to protect me was my club and a knife I had taken from Father Mountain's apartment. Though I might be able to inflict a fatal wound with a knife on a cat as big as a small cow, he'd surely rip me to shreds in the process. My club was my best bet and I quickly raised it over my head in a threatening pose.

The cat, which was blacker than night itself, and fangs in excess of six inches long, sized me up like a butcher might eyeball a prize-winning steer. I could see him estimating which parts of me would taste best. He paced back and forth, as if to locate a proper spot from which to pounce.

To and fro, back and forth, he paced; his impatience with the situation as annoying as mine. Finally analyzing the best spot, and with me backed against the rock wall, the huge feline took his position. And I took mine.

When he leapt, I was ready and came down hard on his skull, the club snapping in the process. Maybe I hadn't been fortunate enough to kill him, but I'd damn sure slowed him down. It was then I noticed the blood on my arm. Blood or no blood, I had to kill him now. I reached in my belt for the knife and made a quick stab to his chest. I wanted to cut his throat, but knew it was too dangerous to be in that position in range of both his fangs and his claws. Blood spurted from his chest, but before his last breath past he made one more swipe across my backside, tearing the flesh from my back and buttocks.

He might be dead, but I could still bleed to death before I was able to find the girls. I found some leaves and a small vine to bandage the flowing wound in my arm, but my back was a different story. I had no way to reach it, let alone bandage it. I could only hope the blood would clot before I lost too much and passed out. My arms and legs all seemed to work, so I didn't think the muscle damage was too severe, and since sleep was now hopelessly out of the question, I trudged on down the narrow trail that seemed to tug me toward the girls. Like a magnetic beacon, something was pulling toward the last two Therans in the Universe.

The beacon was working, I knew not how or why, but my math was off. I wouldn't know for many, many years, but there were more than two. But they wouldn't make it to Earth for another 45,000 years.

As night slowly transitioned into a milky daylight, I found the two of them huddled together as if to protect themselves from a hailstorm, though I'd seen no hail in the jungle. As I soon found them I realized the hailstorm was more figurative than literal.

"You made it!" Princess jumped up and ran to hug me, but fell flat on her face. It was then I realized that her foot didn't work.

"I'll be all right in a couple days, Solan," she announced proudly as she pulled herself erect.

Cleo looked worse than I ever could have imagined. Covered in blood and mud, her pallor was that of the constantly grey sky. I was afraid I'd arrived too late.

"Help me get the chains off her!" Princess pleaded. It was only then that I realized what he'd done to her. Her breasts and her vulva looked swollen and painful. Her nipples were ripped and deformed. "Give her a stick to put in her mouth and hold her tight, Princess," I ordered. Cleo just nodded her head and put the stick between her teeth.

I worked the chains off the rings as she struggled to remain motionless. Once I had the chains removed, I, as gently as I possibly could, slowly worked the rings loose from her flesh. I knew enough about infection that I knew she was in grave danger.

With her waning strength, she described two plants that I should look for, to crush and mix with water to make a poultice. I could only assume she had learned of them from Falima.

I hurried off to search after leaving Princess with a little water to wash some of the grime from Cleo's battered body. I knew a bath would make her feel much better, but how was I to get her that, way out here? Before the clouds came, it rained every afternoon, but since the continual cloud cover, the rain had stopped. I had to get her to a flowing body of clean water or she wasn't going to make it.

I found the leaves she described, which she had, indeed, learned about from Falima during her short stay with our now-deceased hosts. I found a depression in a rock and crushed them up with a little water. After I rubbed the poultice on the affected body parts, Cleo whispered to me. "Thank you. Now put the rest of it on my tongue."

I did as she ordered and gave her a swallow of water from my container. She lied down and whispered again, "Thank you." Tears fell freely from my eyes. My love for her was a burning, overwhelming emotion that I'd never felt before. Now I had to find the monster that did this.

"He's not dead," Princess said before I asked. "I hurt him bad, but he's not dead." She pointed to the north, "he's that way."

"Take care of Cleo," I ordered, unnecessarily. "I'm leaving my water with you. I'll find something else to drink. She's going to need lots of water, and you may need to cool her head if she starts to get a fever." Princess nodded as if it say, "I get it," but she didn't speak.

"I'll be back as soon as I can, but I'm not resting till he's dead."

"Come back in one piece, please, brother. I can't lose you too." In spite of her usual bravery, she began to sob. I gave her a tight hug and did my best to reassure her. "If I don't kill him, he'll just be back again."

"I know, I know, Solan, but he's a very, very bad man." She pointed to her ankle and to Cleo.

"I get it, Sis. By nightfall, I'll guarantee you he'll be dead." It was a big boast for an eight-year old, but I'd aged fifteen years in the last two months, and already killed my first man. And like making a million dollars, the first one is the hardest. With a wave to my sister, I disappeared into the jungle.

*   *   *

I'd scarcely gone a half a mile when I found him. He'd picked up a stick to aid his walking, and he, like Cleo was smeared in blood. He had a ridiculous looking smile on his face that I couldn't quite make out when I first glimpsed him on the trail. It wasn't until I got a little closer that I realized his mouth seemed to be stuck open. He made threatening sounds toward me, but his lower jaw wouldn't close, I learned later that his injury was from Princess' blow, because the muscle and tendon were cut when the machete crashed into his open mouth. He was a hideous sight to behold.

His leg wouldn't work properly and then I saw that the calf muscle in his right leg was laid open, also by Princess, I guessed. I had to smile, I was so proud of her!

All I had was my knife, and I was going to extract my pound of flesh, hopefully while the sick son of a bitch was still alive. He started to speak, but the words all seemed to be gibberish because he couldn't close his mouth. Then he made a slithering motion with his arm that mimicked a snake. Finally I made out the word, 'grandfather'. I looked stupidly at him for a moment while he tried to tell me something without words, only body motion. He was doing it to spike my rage and make me do something stupid. It worked.

I charged him with my knife and he knocked me to the ground with his stick before I got within five feet of him. He was about to cut down on me again, when I regained enough of my senses to roll out of the way. (Princess had taken the machete and knife; his walking stick was his only weapon.) As I made my roll, I slashed at his left ankle with my knife and toppled him to the ground. Now both his legs were cut and he'd die right where he was if I could have just left him alone.

Revenge, best served cold, was going to be a hot dish today. He swung wildly at me hitting me with the stick and knocking me down, and I fell on top of his legs. It was then that I noticed his badly mutilated penis was hanging on only by a small thread of skin. I took advantage of my position and stabbed him in the belly as he cut down on me again with the stick, stunning me into inaction for a second. I knew the next few blows would render me unconscious, when I remembered what Grandfather taught me. I began stabbing him in the leg, looking for that femoral artery that would quickly bleed him out. After the fifth stab, and the third blow to the back of my head, I found it. Blood pumped violently out of the wound and showered me. I stabbed toward the other leg, hoping to hit the other one as well when he hit me once more and I went out cold.

My last thought was the hope that he would lose consciousness before he beat me to death.

LOSING MY SHIRT

[Along with everything else]
[Kinley]

"If you'll take the punch, I'll do the deep freeze," Marie said to Sam while my brain tried to wrap around the implications of her statement.

"Deal," he answered. "I know you can take it, but I still can't stand to see anybody hit you." I shook my head trying to rattle something loose enough to understand what the hell they were talking about.

"Why does *anybody* have to get punched?" I complained. Things were getting weirder and weirder. Were these two really aliens, or just plain fucking nuts?

"To prove something to you," Sam answered. "You'll never believe it unless we show you."

"Maybe I will. You don't have to get hurt just to prove something to me."

"It won't hurt . . . . me, that is. He'd probably break your jaw and your nose!"

"Who's going to hit you? And why?"

"Like I said, there is no way that you are going to accept and believe what is about to happen. The only way is to show you. It's a 'Missouri' thing. You know, the 'show-me' issue."

"Well, you still didn't answer, 'who's going to hit you'?"

"His name's Kateche but the name won't mean anything to you. He's a friend and somebody who knew Solan."

"Solan?"

"You know. The kid who made the recording." I was still trying to wrap my head around all this, and didn't have a clue what he was talking about. I just stood looking stupid *and* stupidly, once again.

"The recording YOU copied that's on the zip drive that YOU risked YOUR life for!" Marie was nearly yelling at me. "God, Sam, we gotta get this kid's implant removed, so we can get him into present time!"

"O.K., O.K. I get it. But how the hell can he be the friend of a guy who died tens of thousands of years ago . . . . assuming that the recording is even legitimate!"

"Oh, don't worry about that. It's legitimate all right. No doubt about that!"

"How can you be so sure? I mean, I think it's real, but it's still such an inconceivable stretch to accept it completely at face value!" It suddenly dawned on me I was playing devil's advocate to my own belief, so I stopped talking. My bald, naked hosts just smiled at each other and kept on walking.

"O.K. O.K.," I acquiesced, knowing I was not going to win an argument with myself, especially when my companions had already chosen their side. "Tell me, please. How do you know it's the real thing?"

I'm sure they answered in unison, but the vision I next encountered, deafened my ears to their reply. If I'd actually heard what they said, the next few minutes might have made a little more sense.

Instead of a dark, dank, abandoned mine, I was in a well-lit room, huge, almost museum-like, but much more informal, with comfortable furniture. There were magnificent paintings on the wall, and exquisite sculptures dotting the floor. And all persons depicted in the *objets de art* were as nude as my two companions.

I gradually became aware that the room held several more people. People living underground? They greeted Marie and Sam as though they were old friends. Women hugged men, women hugged women, men hugged women and men hugged men. And every single one of them was naked as the day they were born.

Slowly my discomfort began to reverse. At first, I was anxious because I was in the company of naked people. And then the reversal; my discomfort was a result of being the one out of place . . . . the only one clothed . . . . and the only one with hair.

Oh my God! It hit me like Sam's semi-truck. The recording was legitimate! And I was surrounded by them.

I stood there like an idiot for a few minutes while they all seemed to be catching up on the latest gossip. Sam finally broke off his conversation with the well-endowed man to whom he'd been speaking, and introduced me to Kateche.

"You need to punch me," Sam informed the big bald man. "He's going to need to see for himself. Then Marie will do the deep freeze with him beside her, so he has no doubt that this is all for real."

"You want me to hit you now?" the big man asked Sam.

"Sure. Then you can hit Kinley and see if he can take it." I didn't see him grin at Kateche, and my body involuntarily clenched.

There was no way he could have faked that. If I had taken a blow to the face like that, my nose would be shoved into my brain and my jaw would have separated at the hinge. Sam just acted like someone had given him a pinch. He backed up a little, but seemed to have no damage to his face, and no blood came from his nose.

"How? How did you take that blow with no damage? And how is Kateche's hand not shattered?" I was incredulous. They both should have needed surgery after that.

"No implant."

"What implant?" I shook my head. Again, the conversation seemed to make absolutely no sense to me.

"The implant that every single person receives before being sent to Earth."

"Then why don't *you* have it?"

"He did," the big stranger said. "We removed it for him . . . . and Marie too." I had no idea what to say, so I stood there mutely. Kateche then ordered, "C'mon, let's go to the deep freeze."

While we were talking, Marie had walked off with the other strange nudists and was already inside the deep freeze when I got there. Kateche held the door open for me and I entered the room.

Its walls were glass on three sides and we could plainly see the people outside the room, as they could us. I didn't think anything about that until Marie's next statement.

"Take off your clothes, Kinley." It wasn't a request. It was an order.

"I-I-I'm not wearing any underwear," I sheepishly admitted.

"That's a good sign," she said, her first indicator of approval since I'd met her. "But then again, I didn't give you any to put on, now did I?" she smiled.

"I've never been naked in front of other people before." I think, in retrospect, I was whining.

"Not even in your own home?"

"Just with girlfriends, and then only briefly."

"OK, I understand your trepidation. Now take them off." If she understood, she sure didn't care. I reluctantly complied with her command and started with my shoes and socks, pulled my shirt over my head and dropped the shorts she'd given me. I felt oddly out of place, partially from being nude, but mostly because I was the only one with hair. The rest of them were completely smooth. I stepped out of the shorts and she held out her hand, as though I was to give them to her. I reluctantly handed them over; she turned and dropped them down a chute marked "Incinerator", and my heart sank.

I barely had time to contemplate the fact that I was now going to have to walk out of this mine totally naked when the temperature suddenly began to plummet. Eighty, seventy, sixty, forty, twenty. I began shivering and shaking so hard I thought my teeth might crack. I looked at Marie and she was as comfortable as if she'd been laying on the beach on a warm summer day. I was certain I'd be dead in another five minutes.

"Had enough?" she asked.

"Y-y-y-yes!" I chattered. "Please let me out or warm the room!"

She nodded to someone outside the room, and suddenly warm air began flowing from the vents and the temperature climbed to a balmy eighty degrees. My shivering gradually stopped, but my manhood looked like it had completely tucked itself inside my belly. The cold had virtually neutered me. What little that hadn't inverted itself was hidden in my pubic hair.

The door opened and I was led to another room which had something that looked similar to an examination table in a doctor's office. Marie told me to lay face-down on it, and the warmth of it felt so good that I didn't resist. Three more naked, bald women entered the room. Once came near my head, apparently to comfort me and keep me lying still while the other two lost no time in lubricating my anus and inserting a tube. Thinking I was done, I relaxed. Then, without warning, they returned with more lube and worked a much-larger, round-headed device that felt like a vibrator, into my rectum. I felt like I was being ripped apart!

"Am I being probed?" I managed to mutter with my face stuffed in a pillow. I'd heard so many rumors about aliens probing human rectums. My only reply was the giggles of Marie and the other three. None of them said a word.

Soon, I felt warm water entering my bowels followed by a sucking sound as though a small vacuum had been turned on. "How many times have you eaten fast food?" Marie asked sarcastically.

"I don't know . . . . thousands maybe?" I had to admit, I was feeling better with each passing second as I discovered that my intestines were being washed.

"Well, that's why your gut must be cleaned out. Nobody's interested in looking up your ass. We're saving your life and preparing you for the next treatment."

"Can it get any weirder than this?" I pleaded, my face buried in the pillow.

"Well, your hair goes and then we start on the implant."

"My hair?"

"Don't ask so many questions. Once the implant starts being removed, this will all make perfect sense." I hoped she was right. From my viewpoint of early this morning, none of this made any sense. But as the process progressed, the previous step became perfectly clear from the new perspective I gained after doing that step. And as I began each one, it seemed as ridiculous as the previous one had upon starting it. But once it was complete, I was amazed at how much my perspective had changed.

Finally one de-implantation process was complete, and everything seemed crystal clear, as though I'd known it and been able to understand all my life, when in fact, I'd been a whining, indecisive twit for all my existence. No wonder Lois had been able to manipulate me so easily.

Sam approached me now that I was "one of them" and the uncomfortable sensation of being around naked people was (mostly) gone. I was more at ease than ever before, and my chronic embarrassment when naked had vanished. I felt (almost) completely at ease.

"You're going to need a new identity and a job," he announced, calming the anxiety I had carried with me since leaving Springfield. "Hello, *Roy*. I've got just the job for you."

And though I was going from a cushy University position to a septic system contractor, I was, briefly, the happiest I'd ever been . . . . even if I had had to take the name of a singing cowboy.

LAST OF THE THERANS

[Solan/Leo]

I awoke to a sky on fire. The ground was shaking as though it would be rent asunder. I dreamt I was on a carnival ride back home on Thera, wanting it to stop, yet wanting it to continue.

My head pounded as though I'd been beaten half to death . . . . and then I slowly wrapped my awareness around the fact that I HAD been beaten half to death. When I could focus, a mangled, bloody penis was the first thing I could discern; of course it was hard not to . . . . it was right in my face.

I gradually came to realize where I was, but when I tried to move, my back and my neck and my head screamed with pain. When I pushed against the cold, motionless legs I was lying across, they did not respond. It was then I noticed the blood. All over my arms, all over the lifeless legs I lay upon, blood covered everything in my immediate view. And then there was the puddle of it pooled between his legs; legs that felt cold and had lost all resilience.

"THANK YOU, GODS! AT LEAST SOMETHING WENT RIGHT TODAY!" I screamed toward the sky at the top of my lungs. But in just a few minutes, I wasn't so sure that I was the fortunate one. Maybe the dead guy was.

As soon as I had pushed myself upright, a blast of hot air hit me and knocked me to the ground. It was followed by a second wave that distorted my vision and olfactory senses as the jungle became a cloud of smoke and then abruptly erupted into flames.

My skin felt as though it was on fire and I began to run, but there was no way to outdistance the overwhelming blast of heat. Fortunately the girls were a little farther away and I ran in their direction, but the heat seared my lungs and each breath became a scream of pain. With each step my body shrieked from the beating I'd taken, and I fell down into the ash-colored mud at least twice.

When I finally got to them, Cleo was a little cleaner than when I left her, but a few moments after my arrival the ash began to rain down upon us, and she soon looked as pallid as when I left them to extract my pound of flesh.

"Solan," she hissed, tears welling in her eyes, "you must get back to the ship and make a recording so that if anyone finds us, they know what happened."

A fine white powder continued drifting out of the sky and as it hit our skin, it burned. "You and Princess must come with me!" I shrieked.

"No, Solan," Cleo answered with authority. We stay. You must go alone."

"But you'll die here!"

"We'll die there too. And so will you. You must make the recording. None of us, I repeat to you, none of us are going to survive this. We'll be dead in twenty four hours out here. In the ship, you might last a week, so you must get busy and make the recording before you're too sick to talk."

"It can't be that bad!" I screamed at her. Was it all for naught? Had we escaped the death of Thera only to be annihilated on this godforsaken planet?

"GO, SOLAN! NOW! If you don't, I'm going to kill Princess and then kill myself. That way you won't have any reason to try and rescue us. NOW DO IT, DAMNIT!"

She'd never talked to me like that before, and as much as I wanted to deny it, I knew she must be right, or she'd never have threatened Princess. "This is radiation, Solan. Every living thing above the surface of the ocean is going to die, and that includes all three of us! Please! I beg you! Go!" I didn't know what 'radiation' was, but I finally understood her urgency. In a few days, if I didn't understand *what* it was, I sure as hell understood the effects of it.

My sobs only added to the difficulty I had breathing, but I took off running anyway. At this point I wasn't even sure I was running in the right direction, so I just ran. I stopped once to look back and could barely see the two girls, when to my horror, I saw Princess turn her throat toward Cleopatra, to offer her jugular for severing. Blood spurted from my little sister's neck as Cleo turned the knife toward her own throat and stabbed. I wheezed as I watched her fall to the ground and I started to turn back.

Her last breath was used to wave me onward. There was no one for me to save now. I ran as best I could, though each breath felt like a knife in my lungs. Finally the ship came into view and I used the last of my wind to climb up inside it.

Once inside, my breath recovered somewhat, and I found some clean water to drink. I located the recorder inside my grandfather's desk, and began to speak. I felt much better now that I was inside and felt sure I could survive this "radiation", whatever that was, yet, now that I was totally alone, I wondered why I'd even *want* to survive. I rattled off this story, ridiculous as it may seem, and then lay my exhausted little body down to rest.

For the next five nights, sleep only came in fits, as each time I closed my eyes I saw Cleo murder Princess and then kill herself. I cried most of each night, certain that I could have gotten them back to the ship and saved them. Why, oh why did she do that?

My answer came when I awoke the sixth morning. She knew what she was doing. My body is covered in red welts. My teeth seem to be coming loose, and one of my eyes won't focus . . . . but wait . . . .

Sorry. I just vomited blood. Had to step away from the recorder. Wait. I gotta puke again . . . .

Blood is coming out of my nose and ears. I can't see anything but a red haze out of my eyes. I think blood is seeping from my anus and my penis, but my eyes are so bad I can't tell.

Everything seems to be going numb and dark . . . .

INCONCEIVABLE

[Kinley/Roy]

"That's it? That's all there is to it?" I asked incredulously.

Now that I was naked, hairless, and at least partially de-implanted, Sam and Marie had taken me back to their house and let me hear the recording I had risked my life to copy. When it ended abruptly, I was left with a terrible sense of despair as though all had been lost. Of course I knew it wasn't, for I was standing here with this apparently alien couple today. But like a movie with a tragic ending, you can't help but cry even though you know they are just actors. I guess we all have long-forgotten memories of past tragedies that get poked when we see tragedy once again.

"They all died? Just like that? End of story?"

"Yes, they did," Sam answered. "But did you miss the larger point of the story?"

"You mean about the annihilation of the planet? No, that wasn't lost on me."

"Then you noticed all the subtle little correlations?"

"Of course, only an idiot wouldn't have noticed." I was a little put off by the insinuation that I might be that naïve.

"Well, sorry to say," Marie opined, "there are lots of idiots on this planet. They wouldn't notice those not-so-subtle nuances. That's part of the implant . . . . stupidity."

"Sure, Earth is headed for the same end result, though only on a continental scale, not an interplanetary one."

"That's why we're here." Sam informed delicately.

"Why *who's* here?"

"Us. And a handful of others. However, we need one more person to complete the entourage."

"Who's that?" I hated it when they were so damn cryptic.

"Solan," they answered simultaneously.

"Oh, you gotta be kidding me!! If there's any truth to that recording at all, he died tens of thousands of years ago! Are you people nuts?"

"I guess he's going to need another session, Sam." Marie looked at her husband with a raised eyebrow. He nodded in agreement.

"Did you not recall things from your last de-implantation session that could not be explained in a 'single-lifetime' state of existence?"

"I suppose, but I thought I must be making that shit up."

"Oh, no. Those recollections were real. Every single one of them."

"Okay, but didn't you just change the subject?"

"No . . . . You see, Solan is very much alive. He no longer goes by that name, and hasn't for many thousands of years. I don't know much of anything about him prior to the recording he made, but from what I can gather, he was a fearless warrior. Not a conqueror like Cortez or Pizzaro. Not an enslaver like Julius Caesar. But a mortal man who fought for the good of sentient and non-sentient beings everywhere. He fought injustice, stupidity, cruelty and any other form of suppression he encountered."

"What is he, some kind of fucking superhero?"

"But something happened to him at Thermopylae," Sam went on, completely ignoring my derogatory question. "In his next lives he became passive and weak, too willing to go along to get along. And in the subsequent lifetimes he has lived, each one has found him weaker and less able than before.

"And now we find him enslaved in a marriage to a shrew who denigrates him at every turn, pretending to be the faithful wife, while she sleeps with her co-workers. We wait for him to find that remaining ounce of self-respect to free himself of her and find his way back to us."

"Where do I fit in this yarn you spin?" not so sure my leg still wasn't being stretched to Greenland.

"We need you to help pull him out of his rut—nay, it's more like a rut in the bottom of a ditch in the lowest point of the canyon."

"So what can I do?"

"Let's go to Fredericktown," Sam said, like he was going to the hardware store and nothing more.

I had not a clue what he meant.

BACK IN SPRINGFIELD

T here was a knock on Professor Kurtz's door. He looked over the top of his glasses, and much to his chagrin, saw a young woman standing outside his office.

"Can I come in, Professor?" she asked, feigning sincerity.

"Sure. What's up?" He wasn't fond of letting unknown females into his office, but she looked so distraught, he couldn't refuse her.

"I, uh, I need to talk to you about Kinley."

"What about him?" The professor was well past the age of retirement, but still had passion for his career. Of course, being in proximity to thousands of beautiful female college students also had its reward, but only for the view. His fidelity to his wife and family was complete. Each year, though, he had a harder and harder time remembering students' names. After a few seconds he remembered Kinley, but had no idea the identity of this woman standing in front of him.

"He's been gone for days, and I believe his disappearance is related to something the two of you were working on."

"Disappearance?" It seemed to be the only word that held his focus. "Are you sure?"

"He left me a text message saying that he was going to Texarkana to visit his brother, but when he didn't return within a few days, I called down there. His brother said he hadn't heard from him."

The professor looked over his glasses again, as oldsters do when they sense that the truth is being manipulated. "Everything all right between the two of you?"

Lois looked out the window behind him, avoiding his gaze as well as his disdain. "No. Uh, not really. We quarreled and that's why he left. But now I'm really worried about him. He's been gone for five days and the one person who should have seen him had no idea he was even heading in that direction."

"Why are you coming to me and not the police?" A sinking feeling began to overtake him as he remembered this morning's mail and a package he hadn't yet looked at. The damn thing was right in front of her lying on his desk. He fought down a sudden urge to look at it, knowing his gaze would direct her attention to it. Yet he didn't know why he felt he shouldn't look at it and alert her to its existence.

"You and he were working on something you found in a dig in Belize."

"Yes, yes. I remember. That was a very long time ago. But what's that got to do with his disappearance."

"I believe he stole it, Professor. I don't know why. I told him it was just a stupid hoax, but he was convinced the recording was real."

The old man was suddenly grateful that he had avoided looking at the package on his desk, now that he knew which side of the fence she was on.

"I'm trying to keep you out of trouble, Professor, if the two of you are involved in the theft of University property . . . ." Her abrupt change of demeanor nearly caught him off guard, but he was an old hand at dealing with students, especially young women who hoped to seduce, then blackmail the male members of the faculty.

"I don't think you need to worry about me, young lady. I've done nothing wrong. Is there something you wanted from me? . . . . uh, I don't believe I got your name."

"Lois. Lois Lofgrin. I'm . . . . or was, Kinley' girlfriend. I don't know what I am right now." She tried to muster some crocodile tears, but failed as she realized her acting skills needed honing.

"Well, Miss Lofgrin, I think you should go to the police. If Kinley has been unaccounted-for for five days, it's high time someone started looking for him."

If he had opened the package when it came in, he might have been less adamant about the police, but it was too late now.

"I just wanted to give you the benefit of the doubt, Professor, before I went, I mean. You know, if you and he were involved in anything illegal . . . ."

Benefit of the doubt, my ass, he thought silently to himself. She was up to something. "You should go to the police now! And if they don't pay me a visit in twenty-four hours, I'll call them myself! Now, if you don't mind, I have work to do . . . ."

It wasn't until she stood up that he realized just how short her skirt was. He had been staring down at his papers when she entered, and hadn't noticed. This was beginning to feel more and more like a set-up. What was she up to and who was she working with? He couldn't help but stare at her as she walked out his door, but he knew perfectly well that she was up to something. College women don't titillate professors because they find them physically attractive. He was certainly too old fall for that antiquated ruse.

He waited a few moments and then went to the door to see if she was out of sight. He desperately needed to open that package and if it contained what he thought it did, he needed to get it back to the archives immediately. He eased around the door jamb, only to see her standing in the hallway, talking to an older man in a suit. This was looking worse and worse. He'd be under surveillance now. Just as he was about to duck back into his office, the two of them looked directly at him, and somehow, he couldn't quite make out how, her skirt got lifted up to reveal that she obviously wasn't wearing panties. Had she done it on purpose? And though the professor glanced away, she never once took her eyes off him.

He stepped back through his door, locking it before he hurried back to his chair. He heaved a heavy sigh as he plopped down in it and contemplated his next move. The pounding in his ears was preventing him from thinking clearly. He drew all the blinds in his office and paced in the darkness. They'd be watching his every move, and with surveillance cameras everywhere these days, he had to be as inconspicuous as possible.

Coffee always helped him clear his head, so he put on a pot. As the smell of the dark liquid began to fill the room, his saw his goal with clarity. He'd destroy it. He hated to do it, but he wasn't going to end his career in scandal. His wife needed his insurance, and if he was convicted of a crime, especially one against the university, he'd lose everything.

He opened the envelope, read Kinley's letter and shredded it and the envelope immediately, and stuffed the zip-drive in his pocket. He called the janitor to remove the trash, and headed for the restroom. On second thought, he realized he couldn't let the janitor carry the shredded remnants of Kinley's letter out the door. They'd have no trouble putting the shreds back together down at the crime lab. He grabbed up a handful of the shreds and dropped them and the thumb drive in the bowl and flushed, but the thumb drive wouldn't go down. He flushed again. Still it stayed in the bottom of the bowl, though the shreds disappeared down the drain. Again . . . . again, and still it wouldn't go down. He began to panic. He hurried out to the sink and filled his hand with liquid soap. This was going to be horrible, but he had no choice. He felt certain they'd be back with a search warrant in less than an hour. He pulled the drive out of the toilet bowl and wiped it down, then covered it in the liquid soap. He dropped his trousers and inserted the zip drive in his only hiding place. The pain was awful, but when he heard, "Professor Kurtz?!" he hurriedly finished the job.

"Professor Kurtz? We have a warrant to search your office and your person," the authoritative voice announced. At first he hoped he could hold it during the search . . . . and then he hoped he could get it out. He knew he'd have to do it himself. They'd be watching him now, so if he couldn't remove it, he damn sure couldn't go see a doctor.

After what seemed like an eternity, they left empty-handed, and he hurried to his bathroom to remove the device. He was a little worse for the wear, but after a half hour of straining, he got it out, but not without a little 'biological evidence'. Fortunately, this time the 'evidence' provided enough mass to take the zip-drive with it.

He heaved a sigh of relief as he realized the evidence, no matter how critical it might have been, was gone and he could retire with pride. It didn't take much consideration to decide that now was the time to retire. Being blackmailed by a panty-less sociopath outweighed his passion for his career. He would depart with his head held high, and she could find some other poor sap to blackmail.

MADISON COUNTY

[Kinley / Roy]

Madison County, Missouri, is one of the most conservative places on earth. Small farms owned by poor people and large farms owned by city dwellers. That's the way the world works these days. Miles and miles of forest dotted by a few open fields, ramshackle buildings and meth labs. Formerly populated by hard-working, industrious farmers, much of the population has evolved into a chemically-addicted, welfare-supported class of ne'er-do-wells.

Now before I get blasted by you remaining hard-working citizens, I'm not talking about you. You are the people who made this state and country what it once was. But now you're in the minority, and you struggle daily to keep your head afloat while the "entitled" on both ends of the economic spectrum bleed you to death.

When Sam and Marie first took me to meet Veronica and Charles, I had no clue what to expect. Certainly not what I found. Sam and I had passed through this county on our way north of Poplar Bluff, and except for some beautiful scenery, I gave it not another thought. Today, however, would be different.

I awoke that morning thinking what a crazy dream I had had. I looked around the room and reality began to sink back in. I hated to do it, and hesitated for several minutes, not wanting to know the truth. Finally I broke down and did it . . . . I touched my head. It was slick as an egg. Nope—not a dream! I threw the covers

131

off me and realized I had slept nude. That was something I had never done in my life. Lois had often harassed me about putting on underwear and pajamas after having sex. Not only was I naked, I was hairless as a new-born babe.

I looked around the room to find my clothes, when it suddenly dawned on me that I had none. Marie had disposed of my clothes when I arrived, and she had sent mine to the incinerator when we were down in the mine. I had come home without a stitch on! Then it all started to come back to me . . . .

I looked around the room to see if I could find something, but this was obviously their daughter's room I was sleeping in and there weren't any clothes for a man. The only thing I could find that remotely fit was a pink sundress, and I knew I'd look more ridiculous wearing that than my birthday suit, so I took a blanket off the bed and wrapped it around myself to go to the bathroom before heading toward the kitchen.

When I arrived in the kitchen, my hosts were sitting at the table drinking coffee wearing nothing more than what they were born with. I sat down at the table, trying to manage the excess fabric of the blanket as Marie asked, "Coffee?"

"Sure," I answered, half expecting her to get it for me.

"I'll get it for you." The voice was definitely female, but it wasn't Marie who had spoken. Was there someone else in the room?

Unlike Sam, Marie and I, she had a beautiful head of dark brown hair, but she was definitely naked. She was a vision of classical beauty, walking toward me with a coffee cup. "Hi, you must be Kinley, or should I say 'Roy'? I'm Constance. Sam and Marie are my parents. I believe you've been sleeping in my bed?" I suddenly felt like Baby Bare meeting Brownilocks.

I was embarrassed beyond belief, but she was apparently more comfortable being totally naked than I was fully clothed. I began to question my own hang-ups.

Marie just looked at me and said, "You'll get used to it."

"It's easier to take than it was yesterday," I admitted.

"That's because you've had the implant reduced," Sam explained.

"I understand you're going to Madison County today," Constance said with a grin, changing the subject.

"That's what I'm told," I said somewhat forlornly.

"Great! It'll be wonderful to have you on board!"

I wondered just exactly what I was boarding, but kept my thought to myself.

"I'll fix you some breakfast," the dark-haired beauty stated. "And then we'll head south."

"All of us?" I asked, hoping this striking Goddess was going with us.

"All of us," Marie stated matter-of-factly, not the least bit fooled by my 'innocent' question. "And FYI, Kinley, she's spoken for . . . . and lose the stupid blanket, will you?"

I think I blushed as I stood and took the blanket back to my bedroom and made the bed. I expected to blush even more as I returned in my natural state to the kitchen, but for some strange reason, it didn't happen at all. Apparently my lack of clothing was bothering me less than my ridiculous attempts at modesty.

We had a great breakfast of sausage, eggs, and pancakes. I offered to clean up as Constance and Marie packed coolers; the ladies and allowed to me earn a small part of my keep. Sam went outside to tend to some livestock and then brought a van up near the house. Marie and her lovely daughter carried the cooler in tandem out to the van and proceeded to put towels down on the seats, then sat down and beckoned me toward them.

"Clothes?" I asked.

"Not necessary where we're going," Marie advised.

"What if we get pulled over by a cop?"

"Really nothing to worry about, 'Roy'," Constance added. "If there's a problem, Dad'll take care of it."

I just shrugged my shoulders. I had no clothing left in this world anyway. If they weren't going to offer me something to put on, I'd have to go *au naturel*, just as they were.

We headed east on Highway 221 and turned south on 67, while they chatted about the farm and the school Constance created for the farm workers, without the slightest attention on their lack of attire; a condition to which I was slowly becoming accustomed.

And then it happened. A state trooper pulled up beside us and motioned Sam to pull over. I got a lump in my throat the size of a bowling ball. Was this really worth the risk of going to jail?

Sam pulled over and waited for the cop to walk up to the window. While I frantically pulled my towel over my lap, the girls and Sam made no effort at all to conceal themselves. I looked down at myself again, and I was wearing an Italian wool suit. It even itched.

Sam rolled down his window and I heard the officer say, "License and registration, please."

Sam had already pulled the driver's license from his wallet, which was lying on the engine cover; retrieved the registration from the storage compartment, and handed them to the officer.

"Going kind of fast weren't you, Sir?" the officer asked as though he hadn't noticed anything out of the ordinary.

"Not that I am aware of, officer. Thought I was actually a little under the speed limit." Sam looked directly at the officer who was somewhat masked by his sunglasses.

"Well, sir, I believe you are right;" the officer admitted in a sudden shift of demeanor. "I must have pulled over the wrong vehicle. My mistake. Please accept my apologies."

"No problem, officer. Could have happened to anyone. Have a good day, sir," Sam aided the officer in his apology.

I didn't say a word until we were back out on the highway. "I don't get it. How did he not notice we're naked . . . . especially you ladies?"

"If asked, he'll say we were all wearing light blue uniforms, except you in that ridiculous Italian suit, Roy, and that he just gave me a warning for barely exceeding the speed limit."

I looked around at my companions for some type of an explanation, as the one Sam had just given me didn't make a lick of sense. And how in the Hell did I get an Italian wool suit?

It was Constance who finally broke the silence. "Dad has a special ability . . . ."

I thought she was going to say something else but she didn't finish.

"Can you all stop being so goddamned mysterious and tell me what's going on and what you have to do with the recording I found? I've done every damn thing you asked me to do. Hell, I'm sitting here naked and hairless riding in a van to somewhere in Madison County. My memory is improved, but I'm still in the dark. Will you PLEASE fill me in? I'm sick of being odd man out!"

The three of them looked at each other as if to make a silent consultation. Sam nodded slightly as if to agree to an unspoken question. Apparently with his approval, Marie began to speak.

"We wanted to wait to get to Fredericktown so you could meet some of the people you will need to acquaint yourself with as you learn about us. But I suppose we can begin to tell the story . . . . especially since we're on our way . . . .

"We are trying to save this country and this planet from the fate that Thera suffered those many millennia ago. You will come to fully understand that the recording you found was entirely legitimate. We were friends of Caesar and his small entourage. However, we were late in our departure and when Thera was annihilated; the explosion blew us off our course. The people that Caesar was trying to reach on the radio was *US*."

"Oh, now you're just pulling my leg."

"Okay, Roy, can you accept the possibility of past lives?"

"Barely."

"Well, then use your '*barely*' and let it grow and mature. Every single one of us has lived multitudes of past lives. Though you're not fully cognizant of your own, doesn't mean that they don't exist. As you have further implants lifted, they will begin to come back to you . . . ."

"Wait a minute; won't that just clutter my mind with excessive memories? Most people want to forget—not remember!"

"Much to their own suffering," Marie answered. "The path to enlightenment comes through understanding and knowing all, not forgetting the past."

"That makes sense from an academic point of view, but what about from a personal trauma issue. Wouldn't we be better off not remembering past pain?"

"Remembering pain is not the same as re-living pain. Remembering pain teaches lessons; re-experiencing pain only weakens a person. And to answer your question, you are capable of remembering and knowing a thousand times more than you've been told you can. You are only limited by the restraints you put on yourself.'

"Are you saying I'm not restrained by the authority?"

"You may be . . . . in your current state. But I ask you, was Sam restrained by the authority that just pulled us over?"

"Apparently not, but I don't have his abilities!" I actually think I whined a little with that statement. I was beginning to not like that side of myself . . . . the whiner.

"Okay, I'll agree to that, but we're drifting away from your question. Whether you can accept it fully or not, at this time, the only way that this will make any sense to you is to alter your pre-supposed notions; to accept the possibility that we have all lived many times . . . . And Sam, Constance and I are all former Therans. And before the day is out you'll meet a few more yourself.

"Assuming you can accept that, I'll continue . . . . We were blown off course and were forced to land on another planet *within this solar system*. We, like Caesar and Company, had limited fuel, and once we landed we had no choice but to stay. Unlike Earth, the planet on which we landed was far more technologically advanced, so we had to be extremely careful where we landed to avoid detection. The next problem we encountered was documentation.

"In these so-called 'technologically-advanced' societies, everyone must have identification. The first people we encountered were a group of college students out hiking in the mountains. They had seen us descend and actually found us . . . . we didn't find them. They gave us their spare clothes, as the clothing we wore on Thera was so radically different, we'd have been noticed immediately.

"Constance was versed in many languages, and although she couldn't speak theirs word for word, we were able to communicate with them well enough to be understood. Being a group that was "on-the-fringe" of their society, they were able to get us identification and jobs in their more-or-less underground group.

"We met a master-forger, and he created new identities for us, complete with retinal-scan, fingerprint and DNA accessibility, as their planet was far in advance of this one even now."

"Well, what happened to you once you got established?"

"Just like everyone else, we lived out the rest of our lives like ordinary citizens . . . . until we were found by the Wyverns. Forty five thousand years ago they dropped a planet buster on us . . . ."

"Forty five thousand years ago?"

"Yes. But more about that later . . . . The planet was shattered to the core, and the explosion blew off the atmosphere of Mars, and sent a shower of meteors to Earth, killing off nearly all life above the oceans' surface. If it hadn't been half way around its orbit, it too would have had the atmosphere blown off it. Unfortunately for Venus, it was in its closest orbital position to Apollo when it took the hit . . . ."

"Wait, wait, wait . . . . Apollo?"

"The fifth planet from the sun. It's an asteroid belt now."

"Are you shittin' me?" She glossed over that era of history in a flash that was way too nonchalant for me.

"No, now will you let me finish?"

"OK, OK. Please go on."

"All life on Venus went up in flames, and converted all the carbon tied up in life forms into carbon dioxide. The resultant Greenhouse Effect raised the planet's temperature to such extremes that nothing but microbes have been able to withstand the temperature. Venus, the true Garden of Eden in this solar system was destroyed, perhaps forever. The only habitable planet left in the system was Earth."

I felt like the president of the 'Flat-Earth Society' at a fundraiser for Columbus. "That's impossible!" I shouted, way too loudly for the inside of the van.

"Then there's someone else you should meet." Marie answered with equanimity.

GRASSHOPPER

[Leo/Solan]

I awoke (though "awoke" seems an inadequate word for the experience) to a conversation. A conversation that began unintelligibly, but slowly began to make sense. I can't say I "heard" it . . . . hearing implies one has ears, and a brain. I had neither. I perceived it . . . . perceived it fully with absolutely no sense of a body whatsoever, and yet I was helpless to do anything but wait . . . . wait for whatever they handed to me.

"I can't believe this son-of-a-bitch is back again! I keep increasing the shock and he keeps showing up as a sentient being in a humanoid body!"

"Dumb him wa-a-a-y down this time. Don't give him two legs, or four legs, give him six. A few thousand lifetimes ending up as birdshit will surely slowly him down!"

"I don't know if I'm authorized to use that much energy," the other replied. "I got written up the last time I sent him back, and that was just with two legs. This mother-fucker is a tough nut to crack!"

"Well, put this jerk on the pole till we get authorization. Ten thousand Theran lifetimes stuck to the pole oughtta make him a little more tractable. And it hardly requires any energy. Just the maintenance flow, which is only a fraction of a percent it will take to send him back as an insect."

There's little for me to say about what happened next. If you can imagine someone describing the same bowl of Malt-O-Meal

139

he had for breakfast, over a period of about 200,000 years, always describing today's bowl . . . . never a single variance, a condiment, or even an electrocution, that's what it was like. If you can imagine a day in which you were completely bored, couldn't find a single thing to do, and multiply it by hundreds of thousands of times, that's the best explanation I can give you for being stuck to the pole. I almost think I'd rather have received blows and shocks . . . . at least there would have been some way to mark the passage of time, and my days and years and decades and centuries would not all have become an absolute nothingness. There's no point in any further attempt to describe that situation. You'd probably throw this book down in disgust, so let's move on.

*   *   *

The next thing I can remember is being in a huge forest. I'd never seen trees that looked like this, slender trunks topped by strange looking leaves. And the plant population was thick as hair on a Golden Retriever. I seemed to be on my belly, and I was appalled to sense how long I was from head to ass. Not head to toe, but head to ass. I could scarcely move my head from side to side, couldn't see my body and I couldn't seem to stand up on my back legs . . . . wait a minute . . . . "back" legs? What the hell was going on here?

About that time I noticed the huge locust staring at me. My God, he was as big as I!! I turned my right eye and there was another . . . . and another . . . . and another!!! Funny, I couldn't turn my head, but I could turn my eyes, and my peripheral vision was fantastic! These giants made no move to harm me; they just seemed ravenous in their appetites to eat these over-populated trees. I soon felt a gnawing hunger inside my belly, and the trees began to look very appetizing. Never having eaten a tree, I must admit, I was more than slightly taken aback, but once I dug my taste buds into their juicy nectar, I couldn't get enough.

Within a few minutes (I suppose it was minutes, though my sense of time was completely deranged) the other locusts and I had eaten every tree in sight . . . . and still I wasn't satisfied. Eat! Eat! Eat! Something screamed in my tiny brain and I leapt.

INCONCEIVABLE!!! I just jumped twenty times my length. No Theran can do that! What the hell was happening? As I tried to make sense of that, something spooked me and I did it again! Twenty times the length of my body! Absolutely amazing! Being stuck to the pole hadn't made me less powerful, it had made me more powerful! (Or so I thought for a few brief moments . . . . Man did that turn out to be wrong!)

Upon landing after my second jump, I felt something land on my back, and it immediately tried to violate me sexually. What in the thirty-seven levels of the Hells is going on? I rotate my left eye back and up to see another locust clinging tightly to my body. Within seconds I felt him ejaculate into me a mere second before he leaps away. Well, either I'm a homosexual (or he is), or I'm female . . . . but I still can't figure out WHAT I am. I simply cannot see my body no matter how much I contort myself.

I soon realize that every tree is now gone, and I'm looking at billions? Trillion? Quadrillions? Of giant locusts leaping away from me.

I guess being stuck to the pole for those innumerable millennia have made me a little slow on the uptake. As I try to wrap my discombobulated mind around what has just happened, a huge shadow approaches me from behind. Without a sound, it pinches me tightly on my neck, and the poor rotation I had of my head has become "no" rotation of my head. And now I'm getting a terrific aerial view of the denuded landscape, but I'm not jumping. I'm flying!! The thrill of being airborne almost masks the pain in my neck, but after a few seconds, it comes pounding back, and now I can't feel any of my body except my head.

I soon see a lone giant, a tree bigger than any I could have imagined, even in my wildest deranged dreams. I'm flying helplessly toward it, and as I approach, I see huge, cavernous mouths stretched to their maximum and I'm heading right toward them.

Their screeching is nearly making my ears bleed, and how I long for the mobility of my hands to cover my ears, but they are limp and useless it appears . . . . though I suddenly seem to have no recollection of even seeing my hands.

Within seconds my head is ripped from my body and for the first time I can see it. I can finally see my body. It's not Theran,

Hyanthian, Human or any other bipedal-type sentient being. Six fucking legs!! But it's soon torn asunder and shoved down the gaping mouths as I numbly watch from the detached viewpoint of my detached head. The hugest mouth of all approaches me as I lie there totally helpless and it snatches me up and swallows me.

As I drifted off into unconsciousness, I remembered one of the last things I heard before being stuck to the pole. "A few thousand lifetimes ending up as birdshit oughtta slow him down!"

I wondered . . . . As the lights went out . . . . "How many is a 'few'?"

Fortunately, for me (and you), the lifetime of a grasshopper/locust is pretty short . . . . if it was as long as yours, you wouldn't be able to read this for another hundred thousand years! And I wonder, is there any market for a book entitled, "My Life as a Bird Dropping"? Kinda doubt it.

MEETING CHUCK AND VEE

[Kinley / Roy]

wonder if incredulity is a tangible thing. I never thought
of it as such until Dr. Kurtz and I found and decoded
the recording. But in my mind I see incredulity as a thin
sheet of silly putty. Mine has been stretched and stretched and
stretched. I thought when I could read a newspaper through it, it
couldn't be stretched anymore.

Then it was stretched beyond that. Like a condom that is so
thin, none of the sensation of the act of intercourse is lost, it
seemed to almost not exist . . . . yet . . . . somehow it was still
there.

That is . . . . until I met Chuck and Vee . . . . and this former
microcosm of naked crazy people in Doe Run just became a
macrocosm. Like these people who had no clothes and no hair,
I had *no* incredulity left. I was simply all credulity. If you'd have
told me that Bigfoot and the Loch Ness Monster were sitting at the
table discussing the comet that wiped out the Dinosaurs, I'd have
been first in line to ask for their autograph.

Once I removed (or Sam removed) that damn itchy wool Italian
suit and we entered the gates at "New Eden" as they called it, (I
confess, the name cause me no small measure of consternation—
sounded like something Jim Jones or David Koresh would have
come up with.) I realized that Sam and his ladies were only a small
portion of a section of society of which I was completely unaware.

143

I counted two hundred wind turbines before I got bored, and I swear I was only halfway done. The roofs of all the buildings were covered in solar panels, and before I could get a word out, Sam filled me in, "If you'll notice, only the roofs have solar panels. And any area not needed for human activity is left completely natural. No trees have been removed solely for the purpose of solar panels, and only those under the immediate base of the wind turbines have been removed.

"Vee generates enough electricity for all of Madison, Iron, Reynolds and St. Francois Counties. The power company doubles their money by selling it to the public, and as part of their agreement to purchase at such a low rate, they are absolutely forbidden from informing anyone where this power comes from.

"Nearly all of the 'guests' here work on the maintenance of the equipment, the buildings, facilities, and grounds. Outside contractors are only used if the towers themselves need repair. We were afraid, a few years back, when a terrible storm came through that the towers might be damaged, but although we lost thousands of trees, the turbine towers withstood the storm unscathed."

As we entered the gates, I was herded off to the side to receive a special "initiation" while Marie, Constance, and Sam were allowed immediate access via retinal scan.

"Good morning, Roy!" the pleasant young lady greeted me. I was NOT accustomed to that name and it I didn't acknowledge her for a moment, as I gawked stupidly at the reception room. She repeated her greeting, "Good morning, ROY!" More assertive this time.

"Oh, hi. Still not used to my name yet." I felt like an idiot. Not only a naked idiot, but a naked idiot that didn't know my own name. Though once she stepped out from behind her secure reception area, and I realized she was naked as me and had enough piercings that she would NEVER be able to fly on a commercial flight, I didn't feel so naked, but still felt like an idiot . . . . an idiot with a growing sensation I quickly covered with my hands.

"Oh, don't worry about that!" she reassured me. "I see it all the time. I'm neither offended nor impressed." Amazingly (or not) her comment immediately killed the nascent erection I was trying so desperately to hide. "Follow me, please."

She seemed to have no interest in anything I might say, and so I followed like a puppy, though I wished I'd had the courage to walk beside her and at least make an attempt at witty banter, no matter how feebly . . . . but I didn't, and so I just followed her, admiring her perfect bottom every step of the way. I suddenly decided that there was only one perfect work of art in the universe, and that was the female body.

"It says here in your file . . . ." (I had a file???) . . . . that you've already received the intestinal cleaning, and I can obviously see that you've undergone the epilation. How many times have you been de-implanted?"

"Uh, uh . . . ." (what a stumble bum) . . . . "Just once . . . . in the mine."

"Oh, you've met Kateche?"

I nodded.

"He's my boyfriend." Lucky guy. "Okay, well, I've got one appointment available for you right now, and highly suggest you take advantage of it. We'll see about getting you on the schedule for additional treatments right away. It says here you have the potential to become an extremely valuable member of the cause, and you are to be given first priority . . . ."

Extremely valuable member of the cause???? What the Hell is she talking about ? I think I just nodded stupidly. Of course she couldn't see my stupid nod because I was walking behind her staring at her magnificent derriere.

"This way, please." She held the glass door for me as I suddenly had an attack of modesty. Strange . . . . it came out of nowhere, and held me like a handcuff. She took me by the wrist and gently, yet forcefully led me to the sheet covered table. At least I wouldn't have to undergo the rectal "exam" again.

She silently placed the electrodes to different locations on my head and body. "Why the body?" I asked.

"To release pent-up energy stored in nerve channels that cause a myriad of aches and pains."

"But I need all the energy I can get!" I whined once again, regretting my tone immediately.

145

"Not this, you don't. This is stored-up negative energy from past trauma. It needs to be eliminated in order for you to reach your true potential."

"OK. If you say so. You're the doctor. I'm just the patient."

"No, I'm just the receptionist. The doctor, if you actually want to use that term, is in Peru giving a seminar to other "doctors" on administering the de-implantation process." If she meant to comfort any of my fears with that statement, she failed miserably.

"Oh," was all I could get out before she flipped the switch.

*　　*　　*

Pictures! Pictures! Thousands! Hundreds of thousands! Pictures went through my mind like flipping the pages of a book. But unlike scanning the book, I was picking out all the recorded data in the pictures. I was really seeing it and recalling it . . . . not just giving it a casual, disinterested glance.

In another chapter I may be able to tell you all I saw, but for now, let me try to make you understand the relief that I felt. Seems my confidence level went up 500% . . . . and that was a relief in itself . . . .

If I hadn't had the second de-implantation, I cannot begin to imagine how I would have reacted upon meeting Chuck and Veronica. My guess is that I'd have been a blubbering idiot that had to be rushed to an Emergency Room.

Greeting me with outstretched arms were the two most beautiful people (male and female) I had ever seen in my life. No amount of exercise, no sit-up regimen, no plastic surgeon, no lifestyle lift, and no botox ever made more beautiful people. And not only were they as naked and hairless as I, they hugged me like I was the prodigal son.

And though I tried desperately, DESPERATELY, to suppress it, I felt a tingle in my penis that was causing it to twist upward of its own volition during the hug. I WANTED TO DIE, I was so embarrassed; especially in contact with Chuck.

Remember when I told you earlier I was all credulity . . . . how I'd believe anything. Turns out I lied. Veronica wrapped her fingers around my rapidly tumescing member and congratulated me.

"Sweet!!" she exclaimed as I so desperately wanted to disappear, yet thoroughly enjoyed her touch. I looked down at her hand and realized that my penis was three inches longer after I finished the de-implantation than it was when I went in. And that was flaccid.

Charles patted my back and with only a look of admiration and nary a trace of jealousy, said, "Well done, old son!" (Or so they say that's what happened. I really don't remember anything else until she removed her beautiful fingers from the biggest and most pleasant erection I'd ever enjoyed.)

MY LIFE AS A BIRD DROPPING

[Solan/Leo]

Didn't think you were going to have to read this chapter, did you?

Don't worry—It's short.

Spending your life looking forward to being bird shit is not as glamorous as it may sound. And no matter how much you would love for me to go into great detail describing the life of an insect, moving forward from egg to pupa to larva to bird dropping, I find it really detracts from the major point of my story. The best thing about being a bug is that the life cycles are short, and you can live many entire lifetimes in just a few seasons. I will, however, hit a few of the highlights.

One particular evening, I was buzzing around, minding my own business . . . . looking for food and sex . . . . just like any other evening, when this terrible screeching sound began to disorient me. No matter how I tried, I could not escape its soul-piercing scream.

While trying my best to fly away from its source, or at least gather some of my bearings, a leathery-sounding, haphazard wing-beat drew my attention. Didn't sound like any bird I'd ever been eaten by . . . .

Without completing the thought, I was once again snatched up and swallowed. As consciousness and life were both snatched from me for the umpteenth time, I marveled at the digestive tract of this beast . . . . entirely different than that of any bird who'd eaten

149

me in the past . . . . What? You can't accept that an insect can remember a past life? Exactly what the Hell do you think 'instinct' is?? You really need to get past your pre-conceived notions!!

I once found myself being attracted to this particular tree, and lifetime after lifetime, I kept returning to it, wondering, each time, what the attraction was. One particular evening, just before my next bird-shit-cycle, it dawned on me. One of my favorite predators, a particularly gorgeous bird; a tall, rakishly handsome creature with long, cobalt-blue tail feathers had excreted my remains along with the seed from which this tree grew! We were kindred spirits, this tree and I. My body had been the fertilizer that gave this tree its start!! Since my sense of time is completely indescribable in human terms, all I can say is that I returned to it over the course of so many lifetimes that it grew from a tiny, helpless seedling into a towering monster that shaded all the other trees within a hundred-foot radius. I suppose, in my current human form, (having some ability to describe to fellow humans) that it was in excess of a thousand years old.

Why did I just tell you that? To give you some comprehension of the number of lifecycles I endured as an insignificant bug. Just think how many stories I *didn't* bore you with!!

As I've said before, I have absolutely no way to tell you how long this had gone on, and whether someone at the Transmutation Station hit the wrong button, or felt I'd been punished and belittled enough, I suddenly, one day, woke up in a human body, and judging by the pink ribbon on my big toe, I was a girl . . . .

(Told you it was short . . . .)

MADISON COUNTY-NOW WHAT?

[Roy]

O nce I regained my senses after Veronica released her grip on my manhood, (or maybe I hadn't regained them at all) I managed to mutter, "Now what?"

"Relax and enjoy yourself," Veronica answered.

"Uh . . . . OK." I stupidly replied.

"Sam and Marie are at the pool, why don't you join them?" Charles gave me a verbal nudge.

"Enjoy your afternoon," Veronica added. "Then at dinner, we'll give an update and you'll get to introduce yourself."

"Update on what?" I asked, pretending that introducing myself in my unclothed state caused me no slight degree of alarm.

"You'll have to wait till this evening. I only give these updates in a group setting—not on an individual basis . . . . too time consuming that way." She paused for a moment as I stood there more or less dumbfounded, then added, "Go find Marie and Sam. They have someone they want to introduce you to."

As I made my way across the sun soaked field, still dotted by huge trees in spite of the storm a few years earlier, I gradually began to absorb the impact of my surroundings. Not only was this place self-sufficient, actually creating a surplus of energy, it was entirely compatible with the natural environment. It was a virtual garden of beauty. Trees soared in a sort of mystical majesty, flowers bloomed everywhere and bloomed out of season!! I wondered if this was the heaven promised to the hashishans[1] after they had assassinated their target. Was I being programmed to be an assassin as well? So far, no one had offered me any hash . . . . or a murder weapon, for that matter. Only my lack-of-implant kept me moving forward and not slipping into abject fear and remorse.

Besides, what the hell was I going to do? I had no car, no ID, no money, no hair, no clothes. If I thought for a moment of escaping, where on Earth would I go? I'd be in jail before I got five miles . . . . and if I tried to call Lois? . . . . Well, the options seemed to be worse and worse. The more solutions I posed, the worse the outcome seemed to be. The only answer seemed to be to stay where I was, with the people who had brought me . . . . and with the doubling of the length of my manhood, and the beautiful bodies that surrounded me . . . . what the fuck was I worrying about?? "Get over it, Kinley . . . . er . . . . I mean, 'Roy'" I reprimanded myself. "Will you just enjoy yourself for once???!!!"

When I got to the pool, my hosts had saved a recliner for me. "Got any sunblock, Marie?" I asked, fearing my first sunburn of the summer, even though it was September. I hadn't been out in the sun all season.

"You don't need any, Roy," she stated matter-of-factly.

"But I sunburn easily," I tried not to whine.

"In late September? You gotta be kidding me!" She made no effort to provide any sunblock from her bag.

"You don't need it, Roy," Constance tried consoling me. "You've been de-implanted twice . . . . sunburn's a thing of the past."

"Even on this pasty white skin?" I pleaded.

"Yes, even on your pasty white skin. Soak up a little Vitamin D. You'll feel better . . . . and I guarantee . . . . no sunburn."

---

[1] The word 'assassin' comes from 'hashishan', one who is high on hashish. It was an ancient technique of convincing someone under the influence of the drug to a kill a rival leader in exchange for a trip to The Land of Milk and Honey. After the assassination, the assassin was almost always killed, thus his trip to the promised land was guaranteed. This technique is still used today in terrorist suicide bombings

"How can that be?" Again I found myself with another shred of incredulity. "I've gotten a sunburn my entire life . . . . every single time I was out in the sun!"

"Well, if you really want one . . . ." Marie was setting me up for another of her sarcastic barbs . . . . "I can give you a blast of radiation. Will that make you feel better?"

I didn't reply; it seemed pointless to do so.

"Roy," Constance again interceded between her mother's sarcasm and my insecurity. "Sunburn is nothing more than old re-stimulated radiation poisoning. With your recent de-implantations, you'll be fine."

"You're telling me I've had past radiation poisonings?" Again, with the damn incredulity.

"Roy, shut the fuck up and enjoy the sun on your skin!" Marie demanded. "We won't mislead you. You're safe. You wanna know the mechanics of it? Fine! But do it on your time with your own research. We have classes available for you to take to assist you in comprehending you're newfound abilities and strengths. But for right now, we're trying to enjoy a nice relaxing day at the pool . . . . away from the normal stresses of Planet Earth. Can you just enjoy it with us? And quit worrying! I thought the last session would remove some of that . . . . guess we'll need to schedule another one."

I sat down on my lounge chair, somewhat sullenly, wondering how the rest of the day was going to go now that I'd gotten my required daily ass-chewing from Marie. As I contemplated recovering my dignity, I watched a beautiful woman swim toward me. Though she was facing down, no man ever had a derriere of that shape, and my eyes were glued to her as she approached the ladder, climbed out of the pool and walked directly toward me.

In a vision of indescribable loveliness, she strode toward me; heavy breasts swinging from side to side, flat belly descending down to a pair of fully engorged labia, begging me to kiss them. As I stood there in open-mouthed silence, she greeted me, "Hi, Roy. I'm Janey, your new septic system assistant."

My memory of what occurred after her introduction seems foggy at best; completely obliterated at worst, but I have a vague recollection of stepping on my tongue.

The next thing I remember is being at dinner and gradually becoming aware that I was expected to walk to the podium and introduce myself.

I don't think the words 'stage fright' even remotely begin to describe what I felt.

DAUGHTER OF EVENOR AND LEUCIPPE

[Leo]

For the sake of the continuity of the story, and trying desperately not to get bogged down in meaningless details, I will only relate incidents that affect the outcome of today, as I'm sure most of you have no interest in the mundane affairs of a wife and mother who lived 11,000 years ago. I supposed that means I spent a simply inconceivable number of lifetimes as an insect . . . . not to mention the time stuck to the "pole of apathy", which was even worse than the "pole of boredom".

My first few years in this life were fairly uneventful. My father was a farmer and hunter and part-time silversmith; my mother looked after the garden, raised thousands of flowers and house-kept our simple abode. I was an only child on a mountain where there were few children; so my parents were most often my only companions. I'd seen other people before . . . . on the days when we would go to the market, a journey we only made four times each year. Once when the short days began turning longer, once before our garden needed planting, then another after harvest, and finally on the winter solstice.

The village we visited had no name that I recall. It was simply called The Village. It wasn't until after I met and married my future husband that I knew of any village that had a name.

The morning of the day that transformed my life . . . . initially for the worst . . . . began almost like any other market-journey day. My father had packed the burro with our goods to sell, so that we may buy things for the coming growing season. Mother was packing jerked meats and roots for us to eat on this trip.

"Cleito!" my father called as he tightened up the cinch on our burro, Moses. "Cleito!" he shouted again before I reached him.

"Yes, father?" I asked.

"Cleito, my darling, we must talk before this journey. You're growing into a young woman now, and young men will begin to look at you in a different way." I didn't understand why he was telling me this, but I must confess, I'd been having thoughts about boys for some time now. They hadn't seemed to interest me, even on our last journey, but I had noticed one in particular . . . . a dark-headed lad with strong facial features and a chest that made me feel strange when I couldn't stop staring at his muscles. Before our last sojourn, I knew boys had that funny thing hanging between their legs . . . . even father had one . . . . but I'd never paid them any mind. I couldn't imagine having all that hanging between my legs and getting in the way. How did boys and men ever get anything done with all that flopping around?

The sudden flush in my cheeks must surely have given me away, but Father continued rambling, unaware of my condition, with his lecture, while my mind returned to the boy I recalled from our last journey.

I never told anyone of the river that ran down my inner thighs when I couldn't stop staring at the young man's penis on that trip. Mother must have known something was amiss, as she pulled me aside behind a building and wiped down my thighs. "It happens, honey. But you must wipe yourself clean. If not the sand and dirt will stick to your legs and you will be rubbed raw before we get home!" I was so embarrassed, I didn't even make the slightest protest.

I must have completely tuned out my father, thinking once again these thoughts that made my groin feel so strange. "Cleito!" He yelled this time. "You need to know this, young lady! The boys will want to take you away and make you spread your legs for them!"

As I was preparing myself to die of embarrassment, my mother, having overheard my father, hurriedly arrived on the scene.

"Evenor!" she shouted. This is a mother-daughter conversation, not father-daughter!" As she whisked me away from my father's presence, she turned with a stern face to him, and added, "I will take care of this and take care of it now!"

(Now in this modern day society, where clothing is the rule of law, teenagers are nearly always trying to discover what the other one has under their clothes. But in Cleito's time, there was no clothing, and no need for clothing in their warm climate. So though she already knew what a boy's anatomy looked like, she was having sexual feelings for the first time, and struggling to understand them.)

Mother did her best to explain, and though I had often seen her and Father involved in an act of affection, I hadn't begun to understand it until today. If this day had gone on like any other day, my little education might have done me some good. But today wasn't going to be an ordinary day.

We'd traveled for several hours, but the sun was hot and we paused to rest . . . . not only the burro, but rest ourselves as well. We found a little shade and some running water and Mother broke some meat and bread out of her basket to feed us.

*   *   *

The thunder of hooves brought us out of our afternoon nap, as ten or twelve men rode up to our little camp. The oldest one spoke, a man of about 40. He had grey hair and a grey beard, and rode a beautiful white stallion.

"Greetings, my friends!" he waved his arm in a grand gesture. "May we share your shade and your water?"

"Certainly, sir," my father answered. "Though it's hardly ours. We just stopped to rest and eat, and to give our weary burro a chance to do so as well."

"Well, I agree that it is not yours," the leader replied, his initial congeniality suddenly becoming acidic. "Actually, sir," he went on. "We demand payment for your use of my oasis!"

"We have very little, sir, but we'd be happy to share." I had never seen my father look so scared or so weak. I got a sick feeling in my stomach, as I painfully discovered that my father, a man I knew to be without fear, had indeed, this time, become fearful. If I'd known his fear was for me, I might have been more forgiving. However, at the time, I felt disgust, as I thought he only feared for himself.

"You have ample payment, Traveler! Worry not for your wife nor yourself. We'll gladly accept your young daughter as payment for your use and desecration of my oasis!"

"NO!" my mother screamed, running from behind me to throw herself at the mounted man. "Never! Take me if you must, but leave my daughter alone!"

"We take what is rightfully ours! You are the ones who trespassed on my oasis! Now you must pay what I deem is fair compensation! We take the girl!"

My father quickly stepped in front of me, and hissed, "Stay with your mother, Cleito!" He turned to the horsemen and for the first time in my life, I heard my father beg. And he was begging for my life, not his own. "Spare my daughter, good sir! Take my goods, ravish my wife, if you feel that is just compensation, but please do not harm my daughter!" He looked at my mother for forgiveness after his offer, and my mother acknowledged. One on one, my father would have fought. But outnumbered ten to one? And the opponents on horseback? She knew the best he could do was plead and barter for my safety.

The speaker turned his head as if to speak with his riders, but without warning, rammed his spear through my father's chest. The force with which he had struck caused the spear to exit out my father's lower back. Blood spurted from both wounds as my father fell to his knees. Mother and I huddled in fear and shame as we watched him breathe his last breath through bloody bubbles.

"I want the girl, not the old hag!" the murderer shouted to his men. She will make a fine wife for you, my son!" They all looked like brothers to me, so I knew not to whom he spoke. My mother was only 36, and far from an old hag. To me, she was the most beautiful woman I had ever met.

The brothers all dismounted, and one approached me, only to jerk me away from my mother's grip. I looked back at her in helplessness, as she once again screamed, "NO! TAKE ME! LEAVE MY DAUGHTER ALONE!"

"We'll take you all right," it was again the leader who spoke. "Boys!" he ordered, "Take turns on the mother, but only Aknon touches the girl." He stared at me with intense black eyes as I fell to my knees. "Take his penis in your mouth, girl! Show your obedience to him . . . . and to me!"

He forced his manhood into my face as a sudden flashback occurred to me. Suddenly I was skipped back thousands of years in the past: There I was, lying on the legs of the Evil One, seeing his mangled, nearly severed penis after I had killed him, and I realized that was how Cleo had immobilized him those many millennia ago.

I bit down. HARD!

He reeled back in pain, screaming like I'd never heard a man scream before, all the while clutching his hands over his groin and blood was spurting in all directions. I spat the disgusting thing out of my mouth and craved a cloth to clean myself with.

"For that, you bitch, your mother dies! And you will be shackled and properly punished!"

"NO!" I screamed. "I did it! Kill me! Leave my mother alone!"

As I stood there screaming, a rope from nowhere wrapped around my body and I was brutally dragged up to the old man's horse. The equine's eyes were wide with fear and his ears lay tightly against his skull. "Put no visible mark on the girl!" he ordered. "I see now the little bitch must be sold into slavery! She'll not harm another of MY sons!"

"I'm ruined, Father!" Aknon shrieked. "I'm ruined!"

"Yes, son, I'm afraid you are." From the look in Aknon's eyes, that wasn't what he wanted to hear. "I'm afraid you are, at that." In less than the blink of an eye, Aknon's father had murdered his second man of the day, beheading his son cleanly with a massive saber. Aknon's soon-to-be-lifeless eyes stared up at his father in disbelief. "A dead son is better than a son with no manhood," he justified himself to no one in particular.

"Boys, have your way with the mother! Take her often and take her repeatedly!" As the boys approached my mother he bellowed, "But wait!! We'll not lose another manhood today!! Or ever again!!" He dismounted from his steed, turned his saber around while walking toward her and hit her square in the mouth, breaking out almost all of her teeth. Blood gushed from her face as one of the sons approached her. How could they do this? It was far worse that any nightmare I'd ever had!

When he finished barking orders he tied the rope around my midsection to his horse. He dismounted and with leather ropes began to bind my hands. I thought my feet would be next, but such was not to be. At the small spring's edge lay a large stone . . . . a stone at which I knew I would soon be sacrificed. He jerked me over to the stone and tied my already bound hands to an exposed root. I was bent over the stone with my backside up in the air. Soon I heard hammering, and realized they were driving stakes in the ground to my left and to my right. Even the hammering couldn't mask my mother's whimpering. She no longer had the strength to scream.

Soon my feet were bound to the stakes they had driven and my legs were spread as far as they could go. I was completely helpless. "Touch not her womanhood!" he ordered. I want her to be a virgin when we sell her. You may take her ass as much and as often as you wish! I felt a thick substance dripping on to my backside, and one of them approached me from behind. When he began to force himself inside me, the pain was unbearable, and I screamed in agony as I desperately fought to keep him from violating me.

Out of nowhere, someone delivered a mind-numbing blow to the bottom of my foot, and I succumbed, letting him force himself inside my bottom. After a few moments, it seemed to be less painful, and by the time the second and third ones entered me, I ashamedly admit, I willingly allowed them. How could I be tolerating this rape while my mother and father surely lay dead somewhere behind me? I felt like the most horrible daughter in the world!

I soon lost track of time or the count. There must have been at least eleven of them, and upon their leader's orders, not one of them touched my vagina, but each one took his turn at my bottom. When they were all spent, I thought surely they would release me and clean me up. After all, they wanted to sell me as a slave!

To my utter dismay, when one of the boys asked his father about putting me on Aknon's horse, my heart sank when he answered, "Leave her there! The buzzards will take care of her!

She's already caused enough damage to our family! We'll not give her another opportunity!"

After watering their steeds, they laughed at my helplessness, but no one made any effort to free me. I was far beyond asking for help, so I made not even the slightest whimper as they mounted their equines and thundered off to the west.

* * *

An hour or so after my rapists had departed, I noticed the first buzzard. In my position, still tied over the stone, I couldn't see toward the sky, and this buzzard was on the ground in front of my face. Soon there was another . . . . and another . . . . and another. Would they eat me alive? Or would I die of the abject misery of dehydration while they patiently waited? Either way, I hoped it happened quickly. All I wanted now from this life was DEATH.

Abruptly, they all took flight and I gradually became aware of a hum and a slight breeze. The sun was almost set, and I hoped it meant my vision was fading as I died. Please, Gods, take my life. I had absolutely no reason to live.

I heard a thud on the ground behind me, as though something landed hard, but not so hard as a falling boulder might have sounded. I next noticed cool water running down my back and falling to the ground between my tied legs. There was a rustle of motion to my left as a figure approached. "Coming back to finish me off?" I asked, hoping they would.

I was answered by a beam of light that cut the leather strap tying my hands. My feet, hidden from my own view, were soon freed as well. Someone put a container of cool water in my hand. The container was like nothing I'd ever seen before, it was silver and shiny. I drank ravenously, and an unseen hand pulled the container away from my mouth. "Too much, too fast," said the voice in the last glimmer of twilight. You can have more soon . . . . but not now. You'll get sick."

Too late. I heaved it all back up. My rescuer placed the container back in my hand again, "Slow," he said. Take it easy. Plenty more where that came from!"

I raised my head to take advantage of the rapidly disappearing crepuscule and stared into the most beautiful pair of blue eyes I'd ever seen on a man. His strong chin and smooth face surprised me. All the men I knew had beards. Only boys had hairless faces. As my hand slipped out of his grip and accidently fell on his groin, I knew this was no boy. This was one of the Gods.

I passed out in his arms.

NUDE PUBLIC SPEAKING AND PLUMBING

[Roy]

We gathered for dinner at the Madison County complex. I had to admit, it was one of the finest dining experiences I'd ever had in my life, even if the wait staff was as nude as I was. They wore black bow-ties, both the men and women, to distinguish them from the rest of the group, I suppose.

As I was enjoying a cup of coffee and a splendid New York Style cheesecake, Veronica excused herself and proceeded toward the podium. I'd always found it hard not stare at a woman's derriere, but it was getting increasingly difficult. I discreetly turned my head from side to side, and with a sigh of relief, I realized that I was the only one trying to hide my staring. No one was being obscene or making cat calls like "normal" human males, but they made no bones about admiring an incredible work of art: Veronica's backside.

She introduced herself to any possible newcomers; me excluded I suppose. She began with some plans that they were trying to get put into action, and I was only half paying attention . . . . that is until I heard her call my *nom-de-septic-tank*.

"Roy, would you please come up here and introduce yourself?" Yep, she was talking to me. I stood up, and was amazed at how calm I felt. My heart should have been beating out of my chest . . . . public speaking was bad enough, but *nude public speaking?* That would surely give any man a heart attack! But again, I amazed myself. I began walking toward Veronica; at least a hundred pairs of eyes were staring at me; some from behind, some from the front, some from the side. My body was on complete display, and I didn't give a rat's ass! How could this be?? I'm beginning to enjoy the de-implanted state. It's pretty incredible!

"Introduce yourself, Mr. Roy," Veronica instructed as I took my place at the microphone, there being no podium to hide behind. I swallowed hard and cleared my throat as much as I could.

"Uh, hello," I stammered less than I expected to. "My name is Roy." Like Alcoholics Anonymous, first names only, I assumed. I didn't even know what new last name had been assigned to me, now that my former identity was lost to the wind. "I-I-I'm a friend of Marie and Sam and their lovely daughter, Constance." At least they might not crucify me if they realize I'm a friend of a friend? "I-I-I'm new here. This is my first visit." I was greeted with a moderate round of applause and phrases of welcome. She-e-e-w. I hadn't expected that, but it helped boost my confidence a little.

"I-I-I used to be a student." That seemed innocuous enough. Who hadn't been a student at some time? "I'm proud to be here today," I announced unconvincingly (to myself anyway), "to be a part of your wonderful group!" More applause induced more self-confidence.

"I'm going to be," the new-found confidence was allowing me to speak in a certainty that I'd never before experienced, "The new septic/sewer/plumbing guy around these parts!"

I was greeted with another round of applause. Sure, I thought, *nobody wants to play in human shit.* I'm sure they're glad I'm here. I looked over at Veronica, hoping she would excuse me, but no luck. It was obvious she was coaxing me on, but I didn't know how much it was safe to reveal about myself. Better too little than too much.

"Why don't you tell the folks a little about how you got here and why!" Veronica implored.

"The truth?" I whispered, covering the microphone with my hand.

"Sure, you're safe here, but only here . . . . not outside these gates," she answered quietly as she waved her arm toward the entrance.

164

"OK," I shrugged, then turned back toward the audience and hit the highlights of my story and the recording Professor Kurtz and I had found. When I finished, I was met with a standing ovation! What the Hell was going on here? What made this little tale be so important to these people?

Veronica thanked me with a nod and excused me. As I made my way back toward my table, sitting down next to the Goddess who had swam toward me earlier in the day, Veronica began to speak.

"I think most of you know what this means." They might, but I sure as hell didn't have a clue. "Roy," she went on, "has brought us a piece of the puzzle that we might never have otherwise located. We now have an actual recording of the events of our arrival on this planet, and the horrible misfortune that befell us shortly thereafter.

"This recording was made by none other than . . . . our beloved Leonidas!"

The crowd erupted into a roar, as I sat stupidly beside Janey, Sam, Marie, and Constance, who were now all on their feet clapping and cheering.

Who the Hell is this Leonidas?

CLEITO'S RECOVERY

[Leo]

When I awoke, except for God's little lanterns, a twinklin' on and off in the heavens, the sky was pitch black. Smoke curled up gently from a small fire of dried dung, which was a precious commodity in our arid environment. I looked dartingly around, in an effort to orient myself, as I awakened from what I was soon to realize was NOT just a horrific nightmare.

And I was alone.

As I contemplated shouting out for help, I realized that those who had raped and beaten me might be nearby. My earlier death wish had gradually reverted back to a natural urge to survive, and I remained silent as I contemplated my next move. I was a girl alone, a girl with ten vicious male enemies. Men who were certain I was now dead; men who would be furious to find me with breath still in my body.

Were my mother and father really dead? I eased the blanket off my body and stared at the ligature marks on my wrists and ankles. As the pain gradually began to seep back into me, my body began to ache all over. Not only were my limbs screaming in pain, I felt the lash marks on my backside, and my bottom throbbed from their repeated violations of my most precious orifice. Yes, surely they were dead. Had I been a man in this life, a vindictive rage might have boiled up inside me, but as a helpless girl, I only sobbed in grief, accepting my parents' death and trembling at the thought of my future . . . . if I even had a future. I hadn't yet learned that on this degraded planet, a woman's power lie in her ability to convince men to do her bidding.

After I'd been awake long enough for Orion to move halfway across the sky, I heard a rustle nearby . . . . like feet shuffling across the dry ground. Someone had left plenty of dung for me to fuel the fire, and I added some to the little blaze. Unlike wood, it wouldn't flare up, but it would provide a little more light for me to see who was approaching. My eyes rapidly searched around the campsite for any type of a weapon. I would gladly plunge a knife into my breast before I would let those bastards take me again! But no luck. Nothing sharper or heavier than a heap of goat dung.

When the firelight revealed his features, I recognized him. I knew not from when or where, but he was beautiful, and his countenance was one of care and concern. Not a shred of hatred or animosity was displayed in any of his expressions or body movements. Thick black hair curled around his ears and neck; a muscular chest provided a solid foundation for powerful arms and legs. And his manhood? I gasped sharply as I could not resist staring at his lovely penis. Neither my father, nor the boy who had caused the wetness between my legs on the last market visit had been endowed with a manhood like this creature!!

Unlike the other men I knew, his face was smooth as was his body. I'd always thought that men prided themselves on how much hair covered their body, and here was the most perfect man I had ever seen, and his body was smoother than mine. I suppose that in spite of my pain, I could not help but smile as he approached. He smiled in return, displaying yet another sign of his kindness. I found myself uncontrollably wanting this man . . . . a want I tried to deny in my current violated condition . . . . yet in that instant, I saw myself spending the rest of my natural born life with him.

I was so amazed at my own desire that I felt the only safe thing for me was to simply remain silent. It seems we smiled at each other for several minutes before he finally broke the ice. At first I couldn't understand him, and yet in a few phrases, his dialect evolved and became perfectly clear to me.

"Good evening, young lady," the words were understandable now. "Are you feeling better?"

"Y-yes," I stammered.

"That's good to know. Are you hungry? Thirsty?"

"Y-yes; and yes."

"That's a good sign!" He offered me water in a shiny container, and it suddenly dawned on me . . . . THIS WAS MY RESCUER!!

"Drink up, but drink slowly," he advised. That's when I remembered throwing up all over his feet earlier . . . . was that today? Yesterday? My sense of time was all off balance.

"It-it tastes good." My tone indicated more of a 'thank you' than a compliment on the water, but it did taste better than anything I'd ever drunk.

"It should, it's fortified with special plants and it's a little sweet to give your body a bit of a kick-start."

I huddled under my blanket, wanting to speak, but fearing my ignorance would make me less worthy of his attention, so we sat there in an awkward silence.

He eventually breached the awkwardness once again. "Do you have a name?" He kind of twisted his head around as if to look upward into my downcast eyes.

"Cl-Cl-Cleito," I somehow managed to mumble.

"Well, hello, Cleito. I'm very pleased to meet you. My name is Poseidon, but my friends call me 'Po', and if it's OK with you, I'd like to be your friend too.

"Are you going to tie me and beat me too?" I wished I hadn't asked it as soon the words were out of my mouth, but in my current state, they seemed to be the only words I had.

"No, ma'am. I'm here to help you . . . . that is, if you will permit me to do so. I got word that there was trouble for you and your folks, and I came to help . . . . but I arrived too late . . . . I'm sorry . . . . I could not save your parents."

I suddenly welled up with tears and tried to speak, but the words came out as nothing more than blubbering sounds; I was sobbing uncontrollably as I tried to speak and breathe with little success.

He hurried to my side and wrapped his arms around me. Some fearful instinct rose up inside me and demanded I push him away, yet I couldn't. His arms provided a comfort I didn't think I'd ever know again, as he gently kissed my neck and my cheek. "Go ahead and cry, Cleito, let your grief out . . . . don't hold it inside you," he encouraged.

The sobs came freely now . . . . I couldn't hold them inside if I'd wanted to, and I no longer wanted to. Mother and Father were gone. My life was changed forever, and the tears soon soaked the blanket I clutched to my face so desperately. He held me lovingly from behind and kissed my face and my hair again and again, as his body provided a bastion of relief to a girl without a friend in the world.

When my tears had finally exhausted themselves, I pushed his arms away, stood up and dropped the blanket. I'd never had anyone hold me like that . . . . maybe my mother did when I was little, but I couldn't recall. He stood up beside me, a good head taller than I, and I wrapped my arms around him. Like a little girl who's found her prince, I felt safer in that moment than ever before. He held me tightly in return, showering the top of my head with his kisses.

I suddenly felt the wetness returning to my loins and this time it was accompanied by a stirring in his penis. I held him tightly, but still it rose to life, tight against the skin of my belly. I turned my face upward to his and he kissed me long and hard on the lips, his tongue forcing my teeth to part and make contact with my own.

Where the words came from, I know not, but they left my lips of their own accord, "I want you inside me!" I whispered to him. I'd overheard my mother say this to my father, but until now, they just seemed silly to me.

In a move I discovered much later, was very outside his usual character, he refused, "No," I will satisfy your longing, and hope you might satisfy mine, but after what happened to you today . . . ." he looked up at the night sky, then changed his mind . . . . "yesterday, I mean . . . . I cannot violate your virginity.

"I will, however, with your permission, bathe you, clean you, and satisfy your longings this evening." He smiled a mischievous smile that would melt my heart for many years to come.

I nodded, "do as you please with me." His kindness opened a previously unknown willingness inside me. He asked me to lie on my back and fold my feet over my head, putting my womanhood on complete display. I willingly complied.

Without ado, he began rubbing a cream under my arms, all over my pubic mound and on down around my anus. It felt cooling to the heat that seemed to be trapped there this evening. After a few moments in this helpless position, he wet a cloth and began to wash me from head to toe. As he reached the areas where he had applied the salve, the hair that had grown the last few years simply wiped away with the cloth. I was now as smooth as he was, and I felt strangely liberated.

Now, after being consoled, comforted, fed and bathed and epilated, I felt newly rejuvenated; yet had an indescribable energy that my young body and mind had not before experienced. He lay me on my back and spread my legs wide as his lips and tongue began to caress my body so that it became excitedly aware of every nerve ending in my skin. Before long, my bottom was soaked from the juices flowing from my womanhood. When his tongue reached the folds between my legs, his thumb entered as well and parted my labia. A few more strokes of his tongue and his lips brought on ever increasing sensations, as my body writhed of its own accord under his spell. I reached for his manhood and tried to place it in my mouth but he pushed my hand away, apparently believing that my pleasure was not contingent on his.

I reached once again and found it, harder than any bone I'd ever touched, and placed it in my mouth. It immediately began spewing its creamy liquid into my mouth as I shuddered uncontrollably, in what I didn't recognize at the time, was my first orgasm. I didn't know what was happening, but I knew it was pure happiness!

His seed tasted salty and sweet, and the volume was so great I thought I might choke, but I soon swallowed it all down. I pulled his face to mine, craving to taste my loins on his face, as he licked his own seed from my chin.

So this was what all the fuss was about! I'd been a happy teenage girl when the sun rose yesterday. In less than 24 hours, I'd plummeted to the absolute depths of despair, and then rocketed to the stratosphere of happiness. A mere child yesterday . . . . an almost grown woman today.

Almost, I say, because I still wanted him inside me.

BACKHOE OPERATOR

[Roy]

s long as we were with Sam, we no longer had to put on clothes to drive, so after the pleasure, stress, and excitement of my speech, we headed back 'home' to Doe Run.

"Roy," Sam announced as we neared their farmstead, "Tomorrow, you and I need to go shopping for a backhoe and a truck and trailer to pull it with. I have to go back out on the road later in the week, and we need to get you set up before I depart."

"So," I asked, "do we dress at all anymore? Or can you manipulate people's perceptions so well that everyone sees what you want them to see?"

"No . . . . I *can* do that, but it takes too much energy and too much focus. It's relatively easy on a one on one basis, but to do it on a grand scale . . . . well, I wouldn't be able to concentrate on anything else."

"Where do you want to go?" I asked.

"We'll start at Luby Equipment and look for something a couple years old. Get the worst of the depreciation already off of it. Then we'll go start hunting for a used dump truck and trailer. You and Janey can use one of my farm trucks for the smaller stuff."

My foggy memory began to come back to me from earlier this afternoon. "Janey? . . . . my new assistant?"

"That's her! She's a handful and you will definitely have your hands full keeping her modest enough for Planet Earth. She has a tendency to, shall we say, ignore the textile rules? She's never been arrested, and never been molested because no one dares lay a hand on her, but it's really hard to keep clothes on her. She, uh, she, uh . . . ." He hesitated for a bit then asked me, "How's your credulity doing these days?"

"You can read a newspaper through it; but that's irrelevant, just go ahead and tell me. Hell, I'd believe any damn thing you said right now. And even if I didn't, I'd be proven wrong in a couple days, so what the fuck? Go ahead!"

He looked at me under a raised eyebrow, wondering whether to continue or not . . . . and I nodded approval as he fumbled for a starting point. "OK, you know that Marie, Constance and I are from Thera, a long-dead planet, right?"

"Yeah, I know that's what you say, and right now I'm doing my best to accept it, so go ahead. I mean, the de-implantations have helped me accept things I'd have thought were complete lunacy a couple weeks ago."

"OK, don't say I didn't warn you . . . . Janey is not from Thera. She's from a planet that was called Dune. Dune had a highly evolved civilzation . . . . and I don't mean a technology/debt-run-amok planet like Earth and Thera.

"Dune had a government that actually WORKED! They were, by nature, a very industrious people, yet with that industry, came a care and concern for the planet and the people that was unmatched on any planet that I ever knew about . . . ."

"How many habitable planets DO you know about?"

"I don't know, never did a count, but I'm guessing about 220-225. And that's not even a drop of water in the ocean."

"You're fuckin' kidding me!"

"Again with the incredulity? If you don't believe I'm telling you the truth, then don't listen. I will not lie to you. Lie to an enemy? Maybe. To a friend? Never. And believe it or not, you ARE my friend, and I am yours."

"OK, OK. Go on with your story about Dune. A couple more weeks and maybe a couple more 'liftings' and I'll be more capable of accepting these seemingly preposterous stories."

Again, the look under the raised eyebrow, "OK, but you need to let me finish."

I nodded in agreement.

"Dune was what we would assume on Earth to be Utopia. A benevolent government. A knowing society. By that, I mean one that understood the spiritual nature of biological life forms . . . . really understood . . . . not guessed at. Of course they were highly educated as well. There were no drugs on the planet, only nutrition-based treatments. They were technologically advanced, yet spiritually pure, unencumbered by evil. Now, I know you want to ask, how can there be good without evil? It seems like an unexplainable dichotomy that is necessary to civilization and mankind, and I'll give you a brief explanation: They realized that a spiritual being needs a game, no game equals no life. And so the game we play on earth is Good vs. Evil. That's the Earth game . . . . because the spiritual understanding here is so terribly poor.

"On Dune they had a *complete* understanding, evolved over hundreds of thousands of years. Knowing that a body was only animated by a spirit, and was more or less a pawn in the games of spirits, it was perfectly all right to kill a body. Just as a small boy kills his toy soldiers only to stand them back up again, the Dunists were perfectly capable of creating bodies and animating them. Nothing to it. They played the game, they killed each other, they created new bodies and created a new game. No big deal. Any five-year old Dunist could do it. The only crime in their society was the creating of mental anguish. And the only way to create the anguish was to make someone believe they would only ever have one body. If you can be killed over and over again, why would you worry about anything? No reason to!"

"And this killing of each other was Utopia?" This incredulity was never going to go away when I was constantly bombarded with these ridiculous considerations of these strange people!

"They were happy! They were the happiest people of any population that I have ever encountered . . . . and like I said . . . . there are at least 220 that I am aware of."

"But-but . . . ."

"No buts. Just listen. They tried, about a hundred years before the death of Thera, to teach Therans what they knew. Very, very few Therans . . . . maybe less than 1 % were capable of understanding what the Dunists were trying to teach. But you have to remember, 1% of 60 billion people is 600 million. Still a lot of folks.

"Then they ran into 'He-Whose-Name-Has-No-Vowels'" . . . .

"Huh?"

"Long story short, he was a being from another planet, who had set himself up as one of the Gods of Thera. There were many, but he had a tight rein over much of the planet for several thousand years. And he is a good part of the reason why Thera became so indebted to Nicha . . . . but I digress.

"This God/Alien/who knows what, we'll call him HWNHNV, managed to get himself into Dune because of their efforts to assist the Therans. Again, no good deed goes unpunished. It took him many tens of thousands of years to infiltrate and pollute this highly spiritually evolved society of Dune, but he was patient, and eventually managed to create EVIL into the population of Dune."

"Go on, go on," I pleaded.

"Well this conversation certainly drifted far from backhoes and dump trucks," Marie brought us back to reality as we pulled back onto the farm. "We're here."

I didn't know where we were, it certainly wasn't Sam and Marie's home. I stared out the window at a small, but well-built log cabin on the edge of a forest. "This is your new home, Roy." Marie announced.

"Where are we?" I desperately wanted Sam to continue his story.

"It's on the back side of our property. You're in a remote area, out of sight of the usual traffic and customers up at our house. You have your own entrance to the county road, and you can put your equipment in the barn there when it's not in use." Sam pointed to a new metal building about 100 feet from the cabin. "I'll be back to pick you up at 6:00 am. Sharp!"

"But I don't have any clothes! What will I wear tomorrow?"

No one said a word as we continued to stare at the cabin. The door soon opened, and a figure stepped out. Janey. Wearing the same thing she'd been wearing at the pool this afternoon . . . . that beautiful smile, and nothing more.

AHNEHON

※

[Leo/Cleito]

When I awoke the next morning, Poseidon was cooking a small animal on a spit. Later I would ask him why he spent so much time hiding his true identity and his magic from me, but he always answered that I must learn in increments. No good comes to anyone who must know everything all at once. The knowledge is too overwhelming and must be acquired in small doses. Otherwise, that which could create great benefit, could also create great harm.

After breakfast, he announced, "I must leave for a short time. You must wait for me. I will be back soon, I promise, but do not follow me."

"What is a 'short time'?" Was it minutes, hours, weeks?

"Count to 100, twenty times. I will be back before the twentieth count."

I just looked at him stupidly.

"You don't know what that means, do you?"

"No." I was ashamed of my ignorance.

"Don't worry. Watch the sun. When it rises over that dead tree, I shall return." He moved me to a location where the sun was on the horizon directly behind the tree. "Do not follow me."

I really wanted to obey him, and the thought of making him angry by my disobedience put a great fear in me. So I waited as patiently as a teenager can wait, fidgeting, worrying, trying to go after him, trying to sit still, and the sun kept rising.

It rose a third of the way up the tree trunk, and I waited.

It rose two thirds of the way up the tree trunk, and I waited.

It finally topped the tree and I stood up to look in the direction he had gone. No Poseidon. My patience had worn to its end. My heart pounded in my chest, the palms of my hands were wet with sweat, and I felt a deep, all-encompassing fear. Something must be terribly wrong.

I could follow his footprints for a while in the dust and sand. But soon the ground became a smooth rock and no prints were left behind. I followed what I thought was the only way he could have traveled, but there was no evidence of his passing. The sun was high overhead now, and thirst, slight at first, but gradually becoming more and more intense, only added to my fear . . . .

When I thought I might surrender to both the thirst and fear . . . . maybe just surrender to death even though I had been saved only yesterday . . . . I saw the ocean, but even I knew you can't drink ocean water. There was something floating on (or was it *above?*) the water . . . . something big . . . . shiny . . . . and humming . . . . that same hum I noticed when Poseidon had cut me loose from my tormenter's bindings.

I looked anxiously around to try to understand what this might be and where Poseidon might be, when I was suddenly grabbed from behind. NOT AGAIN! But alas, it was true. My captors had returned for me. I knew for certain when I heard their voices. I turned to fight, but was met with a fist to the face. I slumped helplessly to the ground.

"It's the girl, Father! You should let me have her for my wife!"

"Bah! Are you an idiot? After what she did to your brother? I should have let you kill her, but she'll be wife to no man!"

Another brother came to aid in my capture, and I was soon bound hand and foot, with a binding from my feet around my neck. I couldn't stand, or walk, let alone run. "Can we violate her once again, Father?" one of the sons asked; I couldn't tell which, as they all seemed pretty much the same to me.

I was completely helpless to stop them, as they rolled me onto my back to get access to my bottom. Oh, Poseidon, where are you? Please come save me!

One of the brothers held my feet tight against my ears while another forced his penis into my vagina. As my hymen ruptured, I screamed as blood flowed all over my bottom and all over my attacker. Without a word, the old man, Aknehon, grabbed his son by the hair and jerked him off me. "Only her ass!" he screamed.

"Why, what difference does it make if we're only going to kill her?" the son pleaded.

"Because she should know only pain . . . . no pleasure. You boys take her pussy and she will be pleasured. You must take her by the ass only!" I guess he didn't realize a woman can experience pleasure in either, but I was ashamed to admit that to myself after their attack on me two days earlier.

From nowhere, he came. One moment he was nowhere to be seen. The next he was there, wielding his saber of fire. I felt the wind from his magic blue blade; I felt heat from it also, and it even brightened the daytime sky. In just seconds I was surrounded by decapitated heads and bodies where my attackers once stood.

Poseidon used a small fire-saber and cut my bindings once again. "Are you OK? I waited too long, didn't I?" I wasn't sure what that meant, but it implied he'd been watching. "I'm sorry. I didn't want to use you for bait but I knew I had to. They smelled our fire last night and were watching us. I found their camp before daylight, and it was so close to my ship (that shiny thing was a ship?) that I had to get you to lead them away so that I could get inside. I'm so, so, sorry. I was sure I could get to you before they hurt you. Are you stabbed?" he pointed at my blood-soaked bottom.

"No," I assured him, "but you scared me to the point of death! I was afraid they had killed you!" I thought for a moment and then his words began to sink in. "You set me up?! Used me for bait?!" I launched into an attack, beating his chest with my small hands, and though I wanted to knee him in the groin, I wasn't mad enough to hurt the part of him I most wanted.

"I'm sorry, I'm sorry, I'm sorry. I had to make them come to you, but I had to get to my saber!" He looked at my blood-soaked posterior once again, and asked, "But why the blood?" He obviously didn't understand.

"I was a virgin until a few minutes ago. You knew that. You even said you wouldn't take my virginity last night!" It seemed as though I had the upper hand in knowledge on *this* subject. "Why didn't you? I'd much rather have had you than one of those bastards!"

"I'm so, so sorry! But your life is far more important to me than your virginity!"

"Stop changing the subject! I wanted YOU to take my virginity, not some beast I only wish to kill! I want to slap you right now!"

I couldn't count to 100, but I could count to ten. There should have been ten decapitated men lying on the ground around me! One, two, three, four, five, six, seven, eight, nine! I counted again. Nine, not ten, but nine. Nine sons and a father! He'd already killed son number one. That left nine sons.

"Count them Poseidon!" I demanded. "How many are there?"

"Nine," he answered guiltily. "By Cronus! One of them got away!"

I knew I needed him to be able to survive, and I felt myself falling hard for him, but right now I still wanted to kick him in his manhood. I don't care if he is magic!

My heart sank again. My life was still in jeopardy. We picked up each head, looking for a grey beard. No such luck. Each one had dark hair . . . . each one was young. Aknehon, the old bastard, had gotten clean away.

I was about to learn, I had met my tormenter long, long ago. And I would yet meet him many more times in the future.

LUBY EQUIPMENT

[Roy]

At the cabin, I crawled out of Sam's van as he reminded me once again, "Six A.M.! Be ready to leave!"

"But I don't have any clothes!" How the hell was I supposed to go to backhoe shopping with no clothes!

"Janey's got you covered," Marie advised.

"That's not at all reassuring," I grumbled, turning once again toward the naked woman standing in the doorway of the cabin. I couldn't imagine how Janey could have anything *covered*.

"Quit worrying, will you?" she admonished once again. "We won't put you in a compromising spot! I promise!" I turned back to her with a disapproving frown which she ignored. "You're one of us now. Part of the team. We've got your back!"

"I guess I'll have to take your word for it. What other choice do I have?" I'd found the courage to grumble, but little more than that. I still felt I was about halfway in prison.

"He needs to get laid," I heard Constance whisper to her mother before the van door slid shut.

"That's no shit," I mumbled to myself.

"C'mon in, Roy." Janey invited, "I've got steaks on the grill and beer iced down. Are you hungry?"

"You bet. But one question first, so I can relax . . . . Do you have something for me to wear tomorrow?

"Sure thing, babycakes, but we need to get some rules set down first."

"O . . . . K . . . . Don't know where you're headed with that intro, but I'll listen."

"I don't belong to ANYBODY but me. You got that?"

"Y-y-yeah . . . . Why are you telling me? I-uh-I-uh think you're beautiful . . . . but I have been around enough naked people for the last few days that, I-uh-uh-uh, have disabused myself of the notion that a woman who happens to be naked in front of me has any sexual desire for me . . . . I-I-I'll treat you the same way as I would any other woman in any other circumstance . . . . And besides, I not only had no idea I was coming to this cabin, I also had no idea you would be here either . . . ."

"O.K. I'm not sure how you treat other women, but you seem a decent sort so I'll give you the benefit of the doubt. Now, about the belonging part: I like to fuck. And I like to be fucked. I DON'T like being told who I can or cannot fuck. If you can abide by sentence number three, you might get to enjoy sentence numbers one and two. If you can't abide by three, then you're gonna be jerkin' off every night."

By the time I picked my jaw up off the floor and did my best to re-hinge it, she had decided I wasn't going to respond. I was trying, I swear, but it was like getting hit by a bomb. It took me some time to regain my bearings.

"I'm not one of these stupid Earth girls. Usually, I can't abide Earth girls. HWNHNV has fucked this planet up so bad that these people are worse than animals. At least animals don't get their entire memories erased between lives."

As I shook my head, trying to shake off the incredulity and simply absorb her statement as fact, I mumbled, "There's good old Hawaii-Nevada again."

"Huh?" Now she looked incredulous.

"Hawaii-Nevada. That's what I'm going to name this character. These initials and the long name Sam gave him, is too difficult to say. If we're gonna keep talking about this character, I'm calling him 'Hawaii-Nevada'. I know how to say that and it flows fairly easily off the tongue."

"O.K., I get it. Back to my point. I'll take care of you. I'll do my part of the cooking and cleaning. I won't let down my end of the bargain. But if I find somebody I want to fuck, I'm fucking him, and you don't have anything to say about. I DON'T BELONG TO YOU! Do you get it?"

I shook my head dumbly in agreement. "Yes. I get it." I didn't know where that left me in the sex equation, or if there even *was* a sex equation, but I knew where it left me in housekeeping.

"Good!" she smiled as she approached. When she was just inches away, my tumescing penis now pushing against her smooth, taut belly, she took my hands and placed them on her portentous breasts and forced her lips against mine.

"What about the steaks?" I managed to stammer.

"I'll go flip 'em now; I just wanted to give you a taste of what you might enjoy as long as you understand who I am. Go crack open a couple beers and meet me on the back patio." Her smile and her kiss were the rod and reel. I was the creek-bank fish: hooked . . . . I wondered if I could 'land' myself without screwing it up.

Until I learned all the parameters of this unusual (to say the least) relationship, I was going to do my best to keep my mouth shut and see how it all worked out. By the time I get accustomed to my new role in my new life, I may not be able to tolerate this relationship, but for now, it was the best thing on the horizon. Amazing how adaptable we humans can be.

When I arrived on the back patio, cold beers in hand, the steaks were done, and she was placing them on a round metal table with a purple tablecloth and daisies in a vase. Strange, I thought. Terribly late in the season for daisies. A rough wood roof structure provided us shelter from the late afternoon summer sun. I knew I was supposed to be immune to extremes of hot, cold and sunlight, but it still felt good to sit in the shade after being in the blazing sun most of the afternoon.

I had expected my erection to subside once Janey had pulled her sweet body away from mine, but it continued to throb, much to my embarrassment. Without any of the disdain I would expect in this situation, she acted as though being around an aroused, naked man was no more distasteful than a long pull on a glass of sweet iced tea on a hot summer afternoon.

While I felt the discomfort of awkward silence, Janey seemed perfectly content with the lack of conversation. The steaks were cooked to perfection (at least to my palate) and the cold beer went down easily in the afternoon heat.

In an effort to breach this silence and return to the wonderful sensation of Janey's lips on mine, I finally spoke. "Can you tell me anything about Dune?" After the words were out of my mouth, I couldn't imagine how that question would return us to sexual contact, but it was too late now.

"Roy," she answered with slight admonishment, "Let Sam tell you about Dune. I'm not a historian, I'm a sensualist."

"O.K." I felt silly again, but not for long. Without another word, she came to me, pushed the dishes toward the center of the table, and scooted my chair away, with me still sitting in it. She planted a firm kiss on my lips and her tongue forced itself inside my mouth. My still erect penis throbbed with delight.

She turned her back to me and spread her glutes apart as she sat down on my throbbing member. I guided it with my hand toward her glistening vagina, but she forced it away. "In my ass!" she demanded.

"What about lubrication?" I don't want to hurt you! Or myself for that matter.

"Silly Earthling," she giggled. I'm a Dunian woman. My ass needs no lubricant . . . . it makes better juices than any Earth woman's pussy." Again I was speechless. Everything I knew was wrong. No woman had ever talked to me like that! My penis slipped in with absolutely no resistance. A sphincter is supposed to resist.

After twenty minutes of the fiercest anal pounding I had ever seen, let alone participated in, we came to a shuddering climax, and she lifted her buttocks off my lap, and took me by surprise when she barked a sharp order. "Lick me clean!" she demanded. I hesitated, not imagining that I could ever do such a thing, when she barked again. "NOW! Before it all drips on the floor!"

I quickly dropped to my knees and lapped up my own semen dripping from her still, wide-open anus. While I had expected a foul taste and odor, I was surprised by the pleasing scent of hyacinths! And the taste! Indescribably wonderful!

With no hesitation after my tonguing of her backdoor, she turned quickly around and cleaned my penis and my testicles with her tongue, then kissed me with a wide open mouth. We laughingly traded bodily fluids back and forth between our mouths, and my penis quickly returned to its tumescent state. That had never happened before!

We made love two more times that night, when she shut me down. "You have to get up early tomorrow, and I have to fix your breakfast for you."

"What about my clothes? I still don't have any."

"I've got you covered. I laid something out for you to wear. You need a shirt, and overalls and work boots."

I started to ask about underwear, but knew that was a moot point, so I kept my mouth shut.

As much as I wanted to sleep with her, she retired to her own room, and I trudged, alone, to mine.

*   *   *

The next morning when I awoke to the alarm going off at 4:30, I cringed. As a college student, tutor, and assistant, I rarely rose before 6:00am, most of the time not till 7:00.

I slipped on the shirt and the overalls. I looked for socks but found none, so just pulled the shoes on over my bare feet. When I stumbled my sleepy-headed self toward the kitchen, I smelled bacon frying and the addicting aroma of coffee. Janey stood at the stove, wearing only the sweet smile that was her constant companion.

"Do you even own any clothes?" I asked, wondering if she planned on working with me in her birthday suit. How would that go over with the customers?

"I have some short-short overalls, and cut-off t-shirts. That's all I'll wear. It's enough to keep me from being arrested on this goofy planet, but don't expect me to wear them when we're not in public. And by the way, I don't get in the ditch. You have to do that."

"Fair enough. Can you run the backhoe?"

"Proficiently, and bobcat too. What about you?"

"Afraid you'll have to teach me."

"Hope you're a quick study."

"I can be."

"Good. You'll need to be. We don't have much time for you to learn." She set the plate of eggs, bacon, sausage, and biscuits in front of me, but before I was allowed to eat, she placed her breast in my mouth and made me lick just a bit. She quickly pulled away, and announced, "That's enough, your breakfast is getting cold and your dick is getting hard."

I realized the overalls weren't zipped and my penis was protruding out the zipper . . . . several inches further than it would have a few weeks ago, so I quickly tucked it in and pulled the zipper up.

As I finished the last of my coffee, Sam arrived in a tiny car I'd never seen before. "Good morning!" How did you sleep last night?"

Janey and I cast a knowing glance in each other's direction and I managed to say, "O.K., I guess." Sam grinned in understanding, yet a look of concern closely followed the grin. Janey waved goodbye, not approaching me for a kiss, and I realized that we were not lovers, just fuck buddies and roommates.

Sam, wearing a suit for the first time since I'd met him, pointed me toward the tiny car. "All electric, Roy. Batteries make 200 miles between charging, no matter what the big corporations say. Common knowledge says they only make about 45 miles per charge, but that's bullshit. It's just a way to keep the electric cars from going into widespread use.

"Just because we have to use fossil fuels now for some things, doesn't mean we have to use them for personal transportation," he added, thinking I needed further explanation, but I didn't.

"We're also putting a large number of acres in switch grass for bio fuel. It produces five and a half units of energy for each unit of energy consumed in its production. Did you get that? Five and half times!!" To say the least, he was excited about the proposition.

"If that's true, that's absolutely incredible, but I can't help but have an abundance of questions!"

"Like what?"

"How many acres do you own here?"

"Twenty-five hundred. But we're looking at buying ten-thousand in Kansas just to grow switch grass on."

"What else do you grow?"

"There's a variety of herbs that we cultivate, and sell to Spring Mountain Herbs."

"Then why the hell do you want me to be a backhoe operator putting in septic systems? Of all the projects you have in process, why do I have to play in the shit? I've got a college degree, for Chrissakes!"

"I'm sorry that you feel under-utilized, but everything we do has a specific end in mind. We need you to do this for a while, and after a certain something happens, then you'll be moved to an area more in line with your education and your abilities."

"A certain something?"

"Sorry that I can't tell you at this time, but it will all become obvious in time."

"What if I don't want to participate in your little escapade?"

"Your choice. You're free to go at any time. No one's holding a gun to your head, but if you want to stay with us . . . . and by that I mean ALL of us . . . . including the folks down in Madison County, we need you to help. So help or don't. It's your decision, but if you're going to be one of us, then BE one of us. Don't be a dilettante."

He had me there. Even though I really had no place else to go that wouldn't land me in the slammer, I had to admit, I really liked these people. They treated me very well in spite of Marie's sarcasm at my chronic indecision. I just had the best sex of my life last night, and maybe, just maybe I could help them save this planet from the stupid people living on it. And unbeknownst to me, there was still one very important piece of the puzzle that wasn't being shared; and it was a piece that concerned me . . . . and only me.

We drove onward through the morning rush hour traffic, Sam's little electric car easily dodging in and out of the ducking and diving vehicles. I was amazed at its pep. I thought only the internal combustion engine could manage that kind of acceleration.

"So," I decided to change the subject. "You were telling me about Dune. And old Hawaii-Nevada."

The look on Sam's face was one that must have been on mine for the last two weeks, so I decided to explain the moniker I'd given this psychotic deity.

"Well, if I can remember where we were . . . . oh yeah, I remember . . . . Before old Hawaii got his hands in the pie on Dune, sentient life there was probably the most idyllic anywhere in the Universe . . . . at least any part of the Universe known to me . . . ."

"That's a little conceited on your part, is it not? Thinking you could speak for the entire Universe?"

"OK, OK, I have to concede on that point. Two hundred and twenty planets with sentient life on them does not constitute knowledge of the entire Universe. I'll qualify the statement with 'any part of the Universe known to ME'."

"That's better." I had to maintain some type of control over my absorption of this unbelievable information.

"Dune was still the most spiritually advanced planet in MY Universe. And unfortunately, because of their contact with my planet, Thera, they too, were brought to their knees, but unlike Thera, Dune wasn't vaporized, it was exploded into billions of meteors . . . . meteors that would find their way to Earth. Part of our plan involves the rehabilitation of the remaining Dunists, which of course, Janey is one. They have been relocated all over the Universe in the bodies of all sorts of creatures, so that they could never again recreate their amazing civilization. With any luck, by saving Earth, we'll reunite the Dunists.

"I'm still not certain about my luck."

"Well, you could be dead like all the Therans."

"OK, OK. I *am* lucky, I *am* lucky."

"Glad we got that settled . . . . OK, Perhaps in Earthling terms, it's easier to tell you what Dune was NOT, not what it WAS. Dune had no:

1. Drugs
2. War
3. Witch doctors
4. Mental Illness
5. Homeless people
6. Clothes
7. Prisons
8. Murder

9. Infidelity

10. Jealousy

"OK, wait a minute, 'no infidelity'? Janey told me last night she has sex with whomever and whenever she pleases."

"I have to qualify that, because we're not talking about humans here. We're talking about Dunists in their native state, which is the state in which the Hyanthians were before they got so corrupted on Thera. We're talking about beings who are capable of enjoying each other's company without restrictions, without jealousy, without those base human emotions that cause so much difficulty on Earth."

"I can't imagine how that works . . . ."

"Of course you can't. You're from Earth. Maybe in another 100 DI's (de-implantations) or so?"

"But how did they raise their children with this laissez-faire attitude toward fidelity?"

"I guess we'll have to save the answer to that question for another time. Here's Luby!" I didn't get a chance to ask, but I still wanted to know about witch doctors.

I looked at the line of equipment and was amazed at its small numbers. "What happened to the big stock of equipment that these dealers used to keep on hand? I remember seeing 5 times this much equipment just a few years ago."

"What happened was the depression! The over stock went to China. Dealers that used to carry fifty backhoes on their lots now carry five or ten. No need for stock in a shrinking economy. There are so many used machines out there on the market that new ones are virtually impossible to sell, so they all got shipped to China."

"Then why are we buying a backhoe?"

"All will be revealed, Grasshopper. You must be patient. This is a well formulated plan, and you and this backhoe are instrumental to the plan. And I thank you in advance for your cooperation."

"OK, but I still want to hear how they managed a family with that attitude toward fidelity. The suspense is killing me."

"Don't worry. You won't die. And even if you do, you'll live through it." I had no idea that I already had.

I'm sorry to say that backhoes didn't interest me in the least.

THE SHIP

[Leo/Cleito]

When I finished my rant and had calmed down enough to be spoken to, Poseidon looked me in the eye and insisted, "Let's get you cleaned up."

"I can clean my own damn self, thank you very much," I said with perfect eighteen-year old sarcasm, as I walked over the smooth rock toward the ocean.

"Let's use fresh water and soap. I'm certain it will be highly pleasurable." He took my hand and against my will, pulled me toward his ship. I couldn't possibly see any way we could get to it as I now realized it wasn't floating *on* the water, but *above* it!

Light . . . . bright enough to be seen in daylight . . . . emitted from an opening in the ship that I hadn't before noticed, and Poseidon led me toward it. We were soon walking *on the light!* In seconds we were inside and my mouth hung open in awe. It was akin to being in the most beautiful home I had ever beheld. Stained woods, shiny hardware, and plush cushions on which to sit or lie down! I could not believe my eyes! I'd beheld nothing like this in my bucolic world of rough blankets, ornery burros, and blazing sun.

I immediately dropped to my knees, pleading for forgiveness. "Please, 'Lord of the Water', do not hurt me. I realize now that you are one of the Gods, and I am just a simple, stupid daughter of a shepherd and a farmer. I beg your forgiveness, Sir!"

"Stand up, Cleito. There is no need for you to be on your knees. I'm not here to harm you or demand your worship. I'm here to begin the re-civilization of your planet. For too long I have watched your people live like animals, struggling constantly for food and shelter, fighting, fighting, fighting. Fighting the harshness of weather, fighting to feed yourselves, fighting each other. And fighting each other I find the most horrible of all.

"I am here to start a new civilization. A civilization in which there is peace through understanding. Peace through knowledge. Peace through cooperation with all men."

I must admit, this was all a little much for an ignorant 18-year old to comprehend, but his message struck such a chord within my heart that I knew I must help him in any way I could. He'd been patient and kind to me thus far, and it would be some time before I realized that his future patience with me would far exceed that of Job (who hadn't even been heard of yet) who had to endure the torturous whimsy of HWNHNV, who hadn't yet been heard of either.

After I stopped staring at every little detail inside the ship, nearly all of which were fascinating to me, Poseidon led me to a small room and opened a door that I could see all the way through! He reached inside and turned something (I couldn't see what) and water began pouring out of the wall! It was a waterfall that was indoors! "Step in," he said.

"But it will be cold!" I protested

"Touch it with your hand." I put my arm forth, tentatively, expecting to be shocked by the water's chill, but it was pleasantly warm! "Go on. Step in. It won't hurt you."

I slipped the sandals off my feet and stepped into the glorious stream. The water soon ran red as it washed the blood off my body. "Hold your hand out, palm up." Poseidon took a small jar and pumped something out of it into my hand. "Rub it on your body." It smelled sweet, and I just wanted to hold it to my nose, but he took my hand and placed it on my chest and began a twirling motion. In a few more seconds, I had pumped the bottle several more times and had rubbed the sweet-smelling liquid all over my body and my hair. I'd never felt so clean in all my life!

When the sweetness was all washed off me, he reached in and turned off the flow of water, and handed me a cloth. "Dry yourself," he insisted.

"No. Join me and I will wash your back if you wash mine. My mother and I did this often, but we only had a pot and a dung fire to warm the water." Poseidon slipped off his sandals as well and stepped into the shower. He began to rub my neck and shoulders, and scrub the middle of my back, the part I cannot reach. I took him by the hips and turned him away from me. I filled my hand with the sweet smelling liquid and rubbed it across his shoulders, down his spine and around his buttocks. I reached between his legs and scrubbed his anus and lathered up his smooth testicles. When I bumped his penis, it was already standing up, and I felt a tingle between my legs as my lips engorged and opened. I wanted him inside me . . . . NOW!

I reached around his hips, and grasped tightly his erect member to turn him around. He placed his hands under my arms, and without effort, picked me up and plunged me down upon his erect phallus. I gasped as he entered me, but the pleasure was indescribable. I soon began writhing back and forth and up and down as my pleasure mounted and mounted and mounted. I soon screamed with a shudder as my passion overwhelmed me into a thrill I'd never before experienced. That thrill would soon make me Poseidon's willing thrall.

We made love three more times that night, and I spent my first night in a real bed. He was tireless in his enthusiasm for me, and the sensation he brought to me only fueled my desire. The softness of the bed was as heavenly as the hardness of his penis, and if this was all a dream, I didn't ever want to wake up.

MAKING DEALS

[Roy]

"**G**ood morning Gentlemen!" The voice seemed to come from thin air, but then he walked around the tracks of the dozer and came into view. "What can I help you with today?"

"Morning," Sam replied. I held back in a kind of stupid silence, like a boy going with his daddy to meet grown men. "Got any used backhoes for sale?"

"Got a repo in just last week, but you can get a 12-month warranty with a new one. Only 30 days on the repo."

"Let's look at the repo before we go any further." Sam turned to me and whispered, "They probably make more money on the repo than the new one anyway."

I didn't answer because I had no clue what to say. I was completely out of my element.

"This machine, new, lists for $62,589.00," the salesman announced, "but this one is 48-9."

"O.K." Sam answered. "How old is it?"

"Two years. The guy that bought it went bankrupt and we took it back."

"Lotta that bankruptcy stuff goin' around these days." Either Sam really was this nonchalant or he was an excellent actor.

"Yep, things are tough all over. Twelve years ago, we couldn't keep these things in stock. Now we don't even want the factory to send us more than five a year." He'd been honest; maybe too

195

honest for a salesman, but I could sense by Sam's body language that he appreciated the candor.

There was a protracted silence, a little too much for me, but I sensed the salesman was accustomed to it. He broke the ice with, "By the way, the name's Rob . . . . Rob Kaiser."

"Sam . . . . Sam Hiram . . . . and this is my associate Roy Johnson." Hmmm. Guess I had a new last name as well.

"You guys shoppin' around or are you buyin' today?" That was straightforward enough.

"Let me put it this way." Sam was laying his cards on the table, which surprised me. I thought he'd play them closer to his chest for a little while longer. "We're buying a backhoe today. We're gonna make it easy for you, now you just need to make it easy for us."

"What can I do to get your business?"

"Like I said, we're buying a backhoe . . . . and we really want it to be a Case. I like the new one, but I don't wanna pay sixty-two thousand dollars for it. I'll give you 50 grand and not a penny more."

Rob didn't reply, playing the old, 'he who speaks first, loses" game. The silence went on for several minutes, and I seemed to be the only one uncomfortably shifting my weight from foot to foot.

Finally Sam added one whispered word to his offer, a word I couldn't hear, and Rob started walking toward his building.

"What's happening?" I mouthed silently toward Sam. He just shrugged his shoulders.

Rob turned around as he got to the door and said, "For that price you have to pick it up!"

Sam and I grinned at each other, and for the first time, I felt a very tight bond with him. "What did you say to him?" Curiosity was killing this cat.

"Cash," he answered.

*   *   *

I'd never seen that much money in my life. I desperately wanted to ask him how he came upon that much cash and why he dared carry it with him, but I knew I had to hold my tongue until we got back to the midget car.

He opened his briefcase and handed the salesman five stacks of a hundred one hundred dollar bills, and then counted out another forty for the sales tax. "I might have a use for that in-floor safe after all these years," Rob grinned at Sam. "I don't often see cash."

"Completely off the credit train." Sam's answer was to-the-point and he had no intention of elaborating. "We'll be back next week to pick it up."

We shook hands and thanked each other. "Pleasure to meet you," and all that jazz. Sam handed me the paperwork, and we headed for the four-wheeled dwarf.

"O.K.," I said, "Curiosity is killing me? Where did you get that kind of money and why do you carry it? What if somebody mugged your or killed you for it?"

"First off, 'easier said than done.' Secondly, I have no use for credit and no use for banks. I do a little business with them, but no more than is necessary to be legal."

"But what about muggers, robbers, murderers . . . . ?"

"You've seen me alter another's perception. Shouldn't that answer your own question?"

He had me there. "Did you alter Rob's perception back there?"

"A little. I still want him to make a profit and remain in business. I wasn't stealing the backhoe and I didn't want him stealing my money. Simple enough?"

"I guess so." I still felt like I was on the outside looking in, and still not comprehending what I was seeing.

"C'mon," Sam changed the subject. "Let's go buy a truck."

We traveled to downtown St. Louis, and pulled into the Broadway Dump Trucks parking lot. Long story short, we were now the proud owners of a truck and a backhoe. "Trailer?" I asked as we pulled back out onto I-55.

"I've got one you can use," he answered.

Once we were headed south on the concrete ribbon, my overwhelming puzzlement got the best of me, and I was desperate to strike up the conversation we had halted upon arriving at Luby Equipment. "I simply cannot wrap my brains around this attitude toward fidelity of the Dunists. How on earth does that work? You mean to tell me no one ever got jealous and killed a spouse? It sounds beyond incredible!!"

"The simplest way for me to explain it is that their emotions are different than human emotions. Human emotions follow a pretty consistent track. Kind of like following a train. Once you start being human, or riding a train, you know there's pretty much only one place you're going to end up. Dunist emotions run on a similar track, but it has a different destination. I realize it's very difficult for you to grasp, but with subsequent D.I.'s it'll become more and more obvious to you.

"There are certain rules, seemingly self-perpetuating rules, that are mocked up by a society, and they run forward, generation to generation. They get tweaked along the way, and morality evolves, but humans think that their rules, their moral code, is the only one that's correct; which couldn't be further from the truth. It's just a code. It works . . . . not very well . . . . but it works to some extent. But it doesn't mean that another race, with a different emotional train track couldn't have a *different* set of rules, a different moral code. And that code could be just as workable or even far superior in workability than the human code. A moral code is not right or wrong. Actions can be right or wrong according to the code, and within the code. But comparing the two codes side by side, one could not say that one was right and the other wrong. One could judge, however, which society lived the best, which had the least fighting, the least drama, the best education, the best harmony . . . . is any of this making any sense to you?"

"Yes, but I am still human, which, by the way, brings up another question." In most cases, I preferred to drive by myself, but riding with Sam and pondering these questions reversed my usual trepidation of being driven by anyone else.

"What's that?"

"What's the difference between a human and a Hyanthian, or a Wyvern, or a Dunist, even?"

"Let me see if I can explain this accurately . . . . actually . . . . I don't think it's that difficult to understand. There is a very slight DNA difference between humans and Hyanthian bodies . . . . and though that difference is important, maybe that's not the place to start.

"There are basically two different factions of spiritual beings in the universe. Hyanthians and Wyverns. Unfortunately it seems that there can be no good without evil. The dichotomy conundrum is something I don't understand . . . . even to this day, so I'm not going to try to explain something I don't get.

"Hyanthians are encouragement, kindness, affection, intelligence, honesty, civility. Wyverns, on the other hand are force, ignorance, hate, jealousy and deceit. Now the first thing you must notice when I say these words, they are *not* descriptive. They are not adjectives. They are nouns. It might seem like a nuance too subtle to be of importance, but it definitely is *not*. I was not describing their characteristics, I am telling you what they ARE.

"Having slightly different DNA doesn't distinguish Hyanthians from humans or Wyverns from humans. The only *outward* difference between true Hyanthians from humans or Wyverns is the complete absence of hair on the Hyanthians, but the inward difference is night and day. You must understand that the theory of Evolution on Earth is completely backwards. Humans did not evolve from a common ape-like ancestor, they DEVOLVED from Hyanthians, and therefore, Dunists! Although other life forms have been evolving toward more and more sentience on Earth for millions of years, humans are a giant leap *backward* in the evolutionary line of Hyanthians."

"And," I asked, slowly putting two and two together, "is there any life form more highly evolved, even *more* sentient than the Hyanthians?" As soon as the words were out of my mouth, I knew the answer.

AMPHIBIANS

[Leo/Cleito]

When I awoke the next morning, my lover was nowhere to be seen. After I had searched his entire ship, the curiosity of the indoor water fall was drawing me back to it. I turned the handle he had turned yesterday, and fresh water began to tumble out of the wall. As I stepped into it, a shock ran through my body! It was ice cold! I put my mouth up to and drank, but I could not wash in this!

I twisted the handle a little more to the left and this time I was more cautious, just reaching my hand into the 'rain' that fell from the opening in the wall. Fearing it would still be cold, I got another shock. It burned! It was hotter than the hottest water we'd ever heated over a dung fire! I was beginning to understand. I could make it hot or cold by turning the handle!

After a few attempts, I got the water to be warm enough to stand in, and I stepped carefully into the stream. A-ah, how pleasant it was! I wish my mother and father could see this! That wish was followed by a deep sadness, as the reality of their demise suddenly slapped the pleasantness from my thoughts. I'd been so caught up in my own survival and this beautiful man who had saved me that for a short time, I'd forgotten all about them. I could only hope that the water could wash away my renewed sadness.

When I stepped from the magic rain, Poseidon had returned and was grinning from ear to ear, and he too was soaking wet. "May I join you my little flower?"

"I'm done," I said as I stared at the floor. I didn't want him to see that I'd been crying, but he easily saw through my pitiful attempt to hide my tears and bloodshot eyes.

"What's wrong, little one?"

"I was thinking of my mother and father. Wishing they could be here with us. I miss them so."

He wrapped his wet naked body around mine, and as my lips touched his powerful shoulder, he tasted of salt. "Were you swimming?" I asked.

"Yes . . . . you could say that, thus my need for a shower . . . . otherwise the salt gets all over everything. I'll be out in a minute."

I tried to entertain myself while he washed the briny water from his skin, but I couldn't keep my eyes off his gloriously male body. I found myself wanting him again, and realized my thighs were wet once again.

He stepped out and began to dry himself off. I tried to resist, but found I could not. I approached him on my knees and wrapped my small fingers around his penis. It quickly stood up and I was powerless to stop myself. I licked it from the top of its leaking single eye, all the way to his testicles and back to the top. "Please!" I begged. "Put it in me again!"

Like an enthusiastic lover, he did as I requested, and within seconds, I had another shuddering climax. When he had shot his seed into me, I begged him to take me again. I couldn't understand what had come over me! I was like a rutting animal! Just a few weeks ago, I was a mere child! At the time I had no way of understanding the relationship between grief and overwhelming sexual desire.

"No," he insisted. "I want you to meet my mother." I've been to see her. That's why I was covered in salt."

"What's her name?" I asked disinterestedly, thinking only of that wonderful joy between his legs, and not even contemplating why his mother and salt could be connected.

I was completely lost in my own reverie, being an eighteen year old who had just discovered the pleasures of sex. I wanted him every waking moment, it seemed, and some of the sleeping ones as well.

"Look!" he said as he pulled my reluctant body toward a window in the wall of the ship. Was I seeing what I thought I was? Could that be real, or had he somehow tricked me?

"Do you see that?" he asked. "Do you know what that means?"

"No," I admitted.

"We're in the ocean."

"I know that, silly."

"I didn't say 'on' the ocean. I said 'in'."

"Now you're just being ridiculous. No one can be IN the ocean."

"Look!" he insisted a second time as he grabbed my arm and pulled me once again to the window. The largest fish I had ever seen slowly swam past the opening. It was then I saw its massive teeth.

"If that's the ocean, then why does the water not come in through the window? Even wind comes through a window, why would the water not come through?" I was sure this was some type of magic trick he was playing on me.

A sudden look of recognition appeared on his face. I knew not what the recognition was, but he grabbed me by the arm once again.

"I will prove it to you! Silly girl!"

"No. I want you to put your thing in me again. It's fun! Now make it hard for me again and put it in me!"

"Later. I have to make you understand this!" And he dragged me to a door. If only our doors back home would have shut so tight, we could have kept out the ever howling-wind and its constant companion, the ever-drifting sand.

He opened the door and we stepped inside a small room. Everything inside it was wet and it smelled like the sea. He closed the door tightly behind us, and then I noticed a second door, on the opposite side of the tiny room from the first door. He began loosening some handles and the seawater began pouring into the closet-sized room. I began to panic, but he seemed as though he didn't have any other thought but to show me what was outside the door.

As the water reached my waist, he pushed open the outside door as seawater flooded the room. He swam out as I stood there, the saltwater burning my eyes and the inside of my chest. I could see him turn around and smile at me, waving me onward. I made a feeble attempt to follow him, but he quickly swam out of sight, and I felt a terrible pressure crushing my body.

In a futile attempt to mimic him, I took a deep breath, and with terrible pain, the sea water filled my lungs. As consciousness slipped rapidly and painfully away, the vision of Aknehon once again murdering my mother and father filled my rapidly fading conscousness.

Yet in the next moment, they were beside me, comforting me, and welcoming me once again into their arms. I knew they couldn't come back to life, so that only left one possibility . . . . I was dead yet again.

DUNISTS

[Roy]

"You're living with one," Sam confirmed what I already knew, as he made the exit onto Highway 67 south.

"So a Dunist is a step up from a Hyanthian?"

"A small step, but a step nonetheless."

"What's the difference?"

"It's the degree of spiritual purity."

"You mean to tell me that Janey has a higher level of spiritual purity than you? Or Marie?"

"Absolutely. Even you know from listening to the recording you brought with you, that the Theran Hyanthians wore clothing and had hair. All except Princess that is."

"Well why is that? Or do you even know?"

"It has to do with the amount of spiritual corruption imposed by the Wyverns. It's kind of like measuring a pollution level. Dunists are the purest spirits I've ever encountered. Next come Hyanthians, Humans and finally Wyverns. As a pure being, one descends from Dunist, down through the scale to Wyvern. And there are a myriad of tiny grades in each of the four major levels.

"We were created pure and have been going downhill ever since." That kind of slapped me in the face. I'd always thought people were born evil and had to be coerced into decency.

"But I thought you just said there were two basic factions of spirits, and now you've just mentioned four!"

"Sorry, I thought it easier to stick to basics, but it is a little confusing. There are two BASIC types, and human is not much more than a high-level Wyvern, and a Dunist is a high-level Hyanthian. Janey happens to be a lower-rung Dunist. Otherwise you'd never catch her on a planet like Earth. Upper echelon Dunists are about as likely to associate with humans as humans are likely to sleep with rattlesnakes." If he *didn't* mean that as a horrible insult, he'd failed miserably.

"Upper level Dunists had no desire to clear the implants from Human minds. They felt the association with humans was too risky. Their lives are incomprehensible to humans, so I won't try to explain them much further. It took a Hyanthian to take the risk of associating with humans, because Hyanthians still had something to gain, particularly after their primary planet, Thera, rendered completely uninhabitable because of the death of all its trees, had been vaporized. In fact, by the time of Thera's death, you couldn't tell a Hyanthian from a Human . . . . not even by the smell." That's when I remembered what the recording had said about Solan's grandfather and his sister Princess. They must have been upper-level Hyanthians.

"That's why Karpokula worked so hard to devise a method for removing the implants. She wasn't going to get any help from high-level Dunists who actually had the ability to help. She wasn't going to get any help from the Humans who were stuck down in the mud and didn't even know they were stuck in the mud, and she sure as the Seven Hells wasn't going to get any help from Wyverns who wanted EVERYONE stuck in the mud.

"Karpokula?" I asked with obvious confusion.

"Sorry. She was Cleo on the recording, and uses the name 'Cleo' on Earth these days. It gives her a name recognizable by society, but for many thousands of years, she was known as Karpokula. You'll meet her before long. Without her, there's no doubt that earth would go the way of Thera, or the U.S. would, at least. But now that humans have the capability of completely obliterating each other, don't think that same capability couldn't obliterate the entire planet."

"Nukes." I said, and Sam nodded in agreement.

As we approached the Bonne Terre exit, I asked if we could stop and get something to drink. "Got water in the cooler in the back seat," he replied.

"Well, can we take a leak then?" I still had a thirst for sweet drinks, but didn't want to admit it to Sam. When I returned to the car with a Coke, he didn't say a word, but I could read disapproval in his countenance. Little did I know that sugar was part of the Wyvern enslavement.

He tried his best to keep quiet, but he finally broke down and advised, "I suggest you read the history of sugar, rum, Coca-Cola and slavery in the Western Hemisphere. It's a real eye opener."

I nodded, but took a slug of my Coke anyway, in a sort of childish defiance, and he didn't mention it again. Little did I realize at the time that two more D.I.'s and my thirst for Coke, and sugar in general, would evaporate like a drop of water on hot asphalt in late July.

"So, is the fact that Janey is a Dunist the reason why she is so reluctant to put clothes on?"

"Yes. Clothing is part of the descent toward Wyvernism. And wearing clothes, to Dunists, is like willingly accepting to be enslaved." It all suddenly started to make sense. Adam and Eve were naked and unashamed.

"Dune was the Garden of Eden of the Universe . . . . until HWNHNV showed up."

THE PAINFUL RETURN

[Leo/Cleito]

I fell to the earth at my mother and father's feet, I was so grateful to see them once again. Mother held me in her arms as my father stroked my dry hair. I suppose it wasn't until I realized my hair was dry that I was certain I was actually dead.

"Hello, Cleito," my father welcomed me back into the fold. Mother only cooed as she gently massaged my temples. "We're so glad to see you here . . . . but," she added with great sadness in her eyes, "we cannot allow you to stay."

"Why?" I pleaded. "I miss you so. I want us to be a family again!" Neither of my parents said a word, and when I looked up at them to see why, they were looking behind me. I turned to look in the direction of their gaze when I noticed the strange woman for the first time.

She was very tall and very dark complexioned. She was adorned, as were my mother, father and myself, only in the skin in which she was born. She was mature, not a teenager like me, but not ancient. Her body showed the signs of much living, but yet that very experience made her appear very attractive to me. She beckoned me to come hither, but I clung tightly to my mother.

"You must go to her, Cleito," my father ordered, much to my dismay. "You are a woman now, and no longer a child. You have the future to worry about now, not the past. In fact, you carry with you the spawn of a God, and you will be the mother of a

Great City, and it will reign for thousands of years. The Gods have allowed me to see the future, and you are its Mother. We will meet again, but for now, you must go with Rhea." He pointed to the dark woman, and my mother tried her best to stifle her sobs.

"Go, child. Go now, before my heart hurts me further," my mother pled. It pained me so to see her in such grief, but Father pulled me away, and put my hand in Rhea's. There was at once, a comfort I hadn't felt since the days when mother bathed me as a child, and though I was torn between my parents and my father's vision of the future, Rhea's touch pulled me onward . . . . toward I knew not what.

I suddenly felt a terrible pressure on my chest and intense stinging in my eyes. I struggled for a breath that was not forthcoming. I tried again and again, as the pressure on my chest crushed me and then abated. Crushed and abated, crushed and abated. Finally, I threw up salt water out of my mouth and the breath came. My body was alive, covered with sand and salt, and I was back inside it.

My vision was blurry and I noticed two people standing over me, though I couldn't make out features. My hearing was intact in spite of my pitiful vision, and I heard a woman's voice. "Silly boy!" she exclaimed. "She can't breathe water like we can! She's human! If you kill her by accident, she will never bear your five pairs of twin sons! Your lineage holds great promise, and will, if the Wyvern's don't foul it, be the greatest civilization this planet has ever seen!"

"I'm sorry mother. I forget just how fragile they are. I didn't mean to hurt her. I love her!" Even though I couldn't see him, I knew Poseidon's voice. And he'd just told his mother he loved me.

"She's pregnant, Poseidon. Your first two sons, Atlas and Gades already grow within her! She will bear you four more pairs of twin boys . . . . if you remember that she is only human!"

I must have fallen immediately asleep after overhearing the conversation, for when I again awoke, I was nestled comfortably in Poseidon's wonderful bed, and the sand had been washed from my body. I went at once to the window when I realized the father of my unborn sons was not on board. What I beheld in that moment was enough to make me fall again into unconsciousness again, but I held my ground and stared out the window in gawp-jawed disbelief.

Under the water was an entire city. People swimming underwater and fantastic structures! No roads . . . . I supposed they were unnecessary. It was beautiful beyond belief! The brilliance of the colors was incredible. Never in my short life, had I seen much beside the endless tan of the desert, and the small green oases. Reds and blues only came on blankets and the occasional bird. But here colors in every hue were everywhere! People rode around on small machines that pulled them through the water, and for the first time in this life, I felt something I had no word for. I knew I could never live in this world. I could not breathe water like they could. I was restricted to land. And the feeling?

You know it as *envy*.

LEARNING TO LIVE WITH A DUNIST

[Roy]

"**S**trip!" a naked Janey demanded before I'd even gotten all the way out of Sam's midget car in front of my new home. I'm sure many men fantasize about their woman demanding this of them, but I must admit, it left me a little annoyed.

"Can you give me just a freakin' minute?! I'm trying to talk to Sam!"

"Janey and I will go pick up the truck and backhoe next Monday. You need to get busy with this!" Sam said as he handed me a newsprint-type booklet.

"What's this?" I asked

"DOT manual. You need to get your CDL."

"Great. One more thing I gotta learn how to do," I mumbled.

"You're a college boy, and a pretty smart one," Janey was actually encouraging me? Kinda caught me off guard.

"Thanks. I'm sure I can do it," I said, to reassure myself more than my companions.

"Looks like you got your weekend work cut out for you. Besides it keeps you from lying around doing nothing . . . . since you don't have a J-O-B." Sam grinned at me and I knew he was right. I needed something to occupy my time besides pumping him for information about the history of humanity . . . . a history that contradicted everything I knew . . . . and pumping Janey in an entirely different method.

I pinched the thickness of the booklet between my thumb and forefinger and grinned back at him, "I should be ready by Monday. This is nothing compared to some of the stuff I've studied."

"Don't underestimate how tough the state can be in enforcing this. The written test isn't too hard, but the pre-trip and the driving and parking might knock you to your knees."

I couldn't believe it could be that difficult, but I just nodded and he took off, his little car making almost no sound except for tires crunching the gravel beneath them.

I hadn't even gotten my head out of his passenger window when I felt hands at my chest loosening the straps of my overalls, and those same hands pulled them to the ground. I turned around with the turgidity of my member bulging its girth and length. Janey started unbuttoning my shirt and in seconds it lay on the ground. "Step out of them, Roy. I want you NOW!"

After our discussion on the ride home today, I had a new appreciation for this wonderful being who shared my roof but not my bed. I tried to tell her as much, but she pressed her lips to mine, and when I opened them, she bit my tongue, gently, but firmly and backed toward the front porch as I tried not to trip over the pants around my ankles.

Before she released her powerful grip on my tongue, she wrapped her right hand around my now throbbing member, and knelt on the front porch steps. "I need you now, Roy. Now! Still holding onto me with her right hand, she laid her head on the top step and with her left hand reached around and pulled her glutes open as far as she could with just one hand.

I guided my throbbing erection toward her glistening pussy, but she quickly guided me higher, and ordered, "NO! You know what I want!" So instead I pushed into her warm welcoming rectum, and she sighed in absolute pleasure before screaming with her first of five consecutive orgasms.

When I'd finished, she stood up abruptly, handed me a damp cloth, and wiped herself clean. She then reached into a cooler that I hadn't noticed sitting on the porch. She pulled a cold Michelob out of the ice and handed it to me.

"You're supper's ready to go on the grill!" she grinned from ear to ear. I suppose that meant I'd made her happy. She'd certainly done that for me, and I wondered if she might sleep with me tonight. Only time would tell.

"After talking with Sam today, I have a new understanding of who you are." I seemed to stumble over my words whenever I talked to her. Sex was great. Verbal communication, not quite so much.

"And?"

"I understand Dunists a little better than I did. You are still a mystery to me, but I want to understand."

"Sorry, Roy, but the only way you'll 'get' me is to undergo more D.I.s. When you've been elevated to Grade V Hyanthian, you'll get me. Otherwise, 'trying' to understand is as far as you'll get. I can't explain it any further, because it would be like trying to explain rocket science to an aborigine who didn't even have a written language."

I knew she hadn't said it to insult me, but I couldn't help but feel a little slap of insult, nonetheless. When she saw the look on my face, she apologized again. "I didn't mean to be rude. It's just that you are not yet at that level that you could begin to comprehend. I'm glad that you and Sam talk like you do, but the talks aren't enough. You HAVE to get as many implants lifted as possible. It was a cycle of implanting that occurred over many thousands of millennia, and a couple of liftings won't make it comprehensible to you. It might take ten, it might take a thousand. I have no way of knowing."

While I tried to find some type of a response to her perception of my insignificance, she smiled and looked me in the eye. "Don't worry; you're still an excellent fucker, even if you are still human." I was even more at a loss for words, when it suddenly occurred that she wasn't capable of lying. Maybe she wasn't even capable of using a euphemism. Hell, maybe she didn't even know the definition of a euphemism!

"Thank you, I think," was all I could think to say.

"Don't look so glum, Roy-be old chum. I still like you. That hasn't changed. You're just human. Don't apologize for it, but by the same token, don't expect me to apologize for being Dunist." I wished at that moment that I was a Dunist as well. Maybe some day in the future?

We went to the back patio and she placed some pre-pressed burger patties on the grill. We had her special grilled potatoes and onions with the burgers and a couple more Michelobs. "This weather won't last much longer," I tried to make ordinary human conversation.

"No, but you're gonna be amazed at how well your body can take the cold this winter." I'd already had a taste of that in the mine, but long term exposure of a naked body to the cold? I had my doubts.

I guess she could see the apprehension in my face, because she looked me in the eye, and said, "You're a human, still. And a Missouri human on top of that. You'll just have to find out for yourself."

She was right about that.

MOTHER OF CIVILIZATION

[Leo/Cleito]

find it more than just a little ironic, that I, who never thought of himself as anything other than *male* would find myself in the life of the Mother of the Civilization whose reputation had survived the ages. I suppose, when one thinks about it, after spending many lifetimes as a multitude of insects, being a female human isn't really that far-fetched.

But to a "modern" human reading this, I'm sure it's nearly unfathomable. I wish I could help you bridge between facts and your pre-conceived notions, but that's something you'll have to do on your own.

Atlas and Gades were the first of five pairs of twin sons I bore Poseidon. When they were just toddlers we began building the great city of Atlantis. In a time when manual labor and the beginnings of metal tools were the only way humans moved earth and water, Poseidon's magic transformed a watery world into a spiral of land and water, land and water. Our city was soon the trading and education center of the world; and for the first time since my grandfather, my sister and our small party left a disintegrating Thera, I was part of a thriving civilization . . . . a thriving civilization of excellent swimmers.

There is one thing I do need to add here, as I'm sure you wonder about the stalker who had hunted me for many lifetimes. Ten years after Atlas and Gades were born, I gave birth to my final pair of twins, Azaes, and Diaprepes. Shortly after their birth, a wrinkled, strange old man began to appear wherever I happened to be. He looked familiar, though at first, I just caught a glimpse of him here and there. But when the youngest twins turned nine, I often found him staring at me, a malevolent look in his countenance. He knew me, but I did not recognize him. I often noticed Poseidon whispering to our youngest sons shortly after the stalker first appeared, but even after my prying questions, my husband refused to discuss his private father-son conversations with me.

I plunged into my memory as deep as my safety defenses would allow me, but I could not place the old man's face. Poseidon, however, would never forget, and I must admit, his secrecy pained me so. But on the morning of my 38th birthday, all would be revealed.

As I awoke from my slumbers on that morning, contemplating the coming of old age, Azaes and Diaprepes were hiding and giggling outside my bedroom door. I knew they must have some birthday surprise planned for their mother, orchestrated, of course, by their father, so I pretended to be asleep and enjoyed the cool morning air and soft silk sheets.

Finally, their excitement no longer containable, they burst through the bedroom door carrying a platter so huge it took both of them to control it. Upon it was a large silk napkin covering something . . . . I couldn't imagine what . . . . and a thousand thoughts ran through my mind. I'd never seen anyone's breakfast in that shape or form. What on earth could it be?

They soon began arguing over who was going to get to pull the napkin back, but I interrupted and said, "Do it together, boys!"

In unison, they jerked the cloth toward themselves, and there sat the most gruesome sight I had beheld in twenty years. The white hair was matted with blood; the lifeless eyes stared into nothingness, and blood was nearly spilling over the side of the platter on to the marble floor.

"Happy Birthday!" they shouted in unison.

Still dumbstruck by the sight, all I could muster was, "What is it? Had my family gone crazy over night? Was my husband teaching our young sons to be murderers?

Poseidon entered the room, wearing only his enigmatic smile, and said softly, "Look closely, Cleito. Surely you remember him."

Diaprepes, hesitantly using one finger to push hair out of the eyes of the abomination, made it all evident. It was the head of Aknehon. "We killed him, Mama!" the boys shouted with male pride.

I'd been responsible for this evil spirit's death once again. It wouldn't be the last time we'd meet . . . . and he was a master at carrying a grudge . . . . even into the next life, and the next, and the next, ... ad nauseum. For the first time, I discovered that killing your enemy was only a temporary solution.

*   *   *

The only thing I have to add to this tale is about *orichalcum*.

It is NOT, as has been said many, many times, a metal similar to gold and copper. It was not mined in the mountains near Atlantis.

It came from within the physical body of Poseidon . . . . and he passed it on to all our children and therefore, passed it on to all our descendants. I can only say it is the metal of the Gods. It glows red with a slight orange tint, and it is absolutely magic! It does not reflect light, it *is* light. Without it, Atlantis would never have been brought into existence. And without it, the Collectors would have had no interest in Earth or in Humans . . . . but that is a story I must save for another day.

My story as Cleito ends here, as the rest of the history of Atlantis resides with my sons and grandsons, not with me. If you find them and they choose to tell it, that's up to them. But for now, I'll leave the rest of the speculation to you.

STUPIDITY

[Roy]

Have you ever begun a new career after spending your life in an entirely different direction? I realize I was only in my late twenties at the time, so I can only imagine how you 50-year-olds felt trying to create a new life after the Great Depression that began in 2008.

I spent the weekend studying the little manual for truck drivers, and I was soon frustrated beyond belief. Janey had actually dressed on Saturday morning, and was helping Constance teach the migrant worker children who worked for Sam and Marie.

Long before she got home, I had thrown the booklet down in disgust and decided to go for a walk in the woods. The season was quickly morphing into autumn now; many of the hickories and walnuts had already dropped their leaves. The maples, sassafras, and gums were brilliant in their color. Occasionally a few of the oaks complemented the others with scarlet or a deep purple.

As I'd become more and more accustomed to daily nudity, I hadn't bothered to put on anything for my walk except socks and hiking boots. I took a nice walking stick, but other than that, I was unarmed when I saw it.

I stood there in a gawp-jawed disbelief, a state I seemed to occupy almost continuously these last few weeks. Once again, my belief that nothing more could shock me got thrown to the wind when I saw it. It wasn't black, like I'd expected; more of a rusty brown. It was gaunt-looking, and that look made me feel like I could personally be on the menu.

The bear appeared to be three feet tall at the shoulder and maybe four feet at the hip. It didn't look like any black bear I'd ever seen . . . . in a cage or on TV. Fortunately for me, it was as scared of me as I was of it, and it quickly lost itself in heavy brush.

Just as I was once again deciding it was safe to take a breath, I detected another movement above and behind me. I turned slowly to avoid any sudden motion and until it flicked its tail, I didn't even see it.

Fifteen feet above my head, on the heavy branch of an ancient oak, sat the cat. A tawny tail flitted from side to side as its owner eyed me. I wondered if, as it stared at me, that it saw cuts of meat, like in the old cartoons. I was beginning to believe that I wasn't going to need to worry about getting my CDL. I'd *be* lunch before the day was out.

As I stood there gripped by the stupidity of indecision, my choice was made for me. I heard a loud swoosh in a giant tree above me, and the largest bird I had ever seen took flight from the high branches. His wing-span was ten feet if it was an inch! As my heart thumped, threatening to beat right out of my chest, the cat jumped, just missing a deer that had been hiding in an autumn olive thicket. They both sprinted off in the same direction the bear had gone, and my heart decided it might stay in my chest just a little longer.

It didn't take me but half a second to decide I'd be better off heading back toward the house. I was too excited to try to study any stupid shit about big trucks, so I turned on the TV, but there was no signal. I fumbled around through a stack of DVD's when I found something interesting. It was labeled "Leo/Solan", and I put it in the player. It seemed to be a video observation of some guy going about his ordinary life. It was a difficult life, I must admit, from what little I saw before I dozed off, but couldn't imagine how anyone could find this the slightest bit entertaining.

I awoke to the sound of a shutting door, and realized Janey was home. "You been sleepin' all day, Roy-Boy?" She sounded pissed.

"No, not all day," I admitted sheepishly. "I studied till I couldn't take it anymore and went for a walk in the woods. Didn't know if I was going to get eaten or not before I got back home." I had called it 'home'. I guess I was getting accustomed to being here.

"How many D.I.s you had?" It seemed like a ridiculous question to ask as a response to what I'd just said, but I answered anyway.

"Two."

"Aw, you got nothin' to be worried about, then. You're out of the food chain."

"Huh?" Nothing seems to make sense anymore.

"After two D.I.s, you're not in the food chain any longer . . . . they know you won't harm them . . . . you're revered with near God-like status by the animals"

"What . . . . you mean they can sense that?"

"Sure, didn't you know that?"

"I guess not," was the best I could come up with.

"You're still in the 'Human' classification, but you're two levels above the average. It may not seem like it yet, but you're so advanced beyond *homo sap* that you have *almost* nothing to fear from animals. I say 'almost' as you're not quite yet bulletproof."

"And you are, I suppose?" I tried the mask the sarcasm, but didn't do very well at it.

"Nearly. I'm not sayin' my body doesn't get battered, but I heal pretty fast. Once you can withstand sub-zero temperatures without wrapping yourself in clothes, a little bat from a bear paw doesn't seem that traumatic."

"O.K." I said, resignedly accepting her statement, but not yet buying it completely. "Let's change the subject. I need help with this stupid book."

"Well, don't you sound like the professional scholar!" she exclaimed mockingly. "What do you need? . . . . Never mind. I know what you need. Put your shoes back on; we're going out to look at one of Sam's trucks . . . . and bring your book."

We hopped in a golf cart she had driven to the school, and we headed over to Sam's house about half a mile away. "What's he been doing today?" I asked her.

"He went to Kansas to try to close the deal on the ranch; the one he's going to grow switchgrass on."

"Is he gonna buy it?"

"Yes, I think so. Veronica got him a grant from the Federal Government. It took a year and half, even with her connections, so the Feds are going to put up half the money for the purchase, and half the money to plant the crop."

"How many acres?"

"I think it's about eight thousand."

"Wow!" was all I could think to say.

We pulled up in his barnyard and his semi-truck and trailer sat beside one of the larger buildings. Marie came out to bring us some iced tea, and we chatted a few minutes before Janey made me crawl under the truck.

She pointed out all the things I couldn't quite grasp from reading words on a piece of paper and two-dimensional drawings. In a matter of seconds, the things that seemed so impossible to grasp earlier in the day became clearly evident. I knew enough about cars and pickup trucks that I had a rudimentary knowledge, but becoming intimately familiar with the details of a big truck cleared up the overwhelming confusion I had had trying to read the book.

"You can't learn anything from just reading words on paper. I teach this to the kids at Constance's school every day. You've got to get out and touch it with your hands, build it, if it doesn't already exist, even if your first model is nothing but clay. Nobody ever studied only a book and was magically able to go out perform. That's why universities have labs . . . . you knothead!"

I deserved that. If anyone should have known that, it would be me. No one had ever put it in those words before, and I realized I had made a major personal leap in my future ability to study.

"When you gonna teach me to drive?"

"After Sam and I get back with the truck and backhoe. If you think there's any way I'm putting' a rookie in Sam's road tractor, you better think again, there, Roy-Boy. You can practice in the dump truck . . . . unloaded of course."

I had to laugh at myself. A few hours ago, I was so frustrated I didn't think I'd ever learn how to drive a big truck. Now, like a teenager craving a driver's license, the two-day wait for my dump truck to show up was going to seem an eternity.

Stupid? Not any longer!

THE BROTHERS' DISCUSSION

"**P**oseidon?" his brother asked, "have you seen what's going on down there?"

"Yes, Zeus. I hoped it wouldn't happen, but you know how the humans are. Cleito was such a prize, I thought surely our offspring would transcend the common frailties of the race."

"It's because their lives are so short! No wonder they descend into the lower depths of depravity! When each new generation is born, with memories of the last life nearly completely erased, they forget the extremes that we all went to in order to build a civilized society on this planet!"

"Well, you know that was the deal we had to make with HWNHNV. You remember, he nuked the Dinosaurs to clear the path for the humans, but we had to agree to their short life-span. It's in the contract."

"You, think, Poseidon, that I don't remember that? We haggled over it for what, five thousand years?"

"Five thousand, two hundred eighty seven years, six months, and fourteen days."

"What, you don't have it down to minutes and seconds?" Zeus asked with his usual sarcasm.

"Don't be such a smartass, Zeus."

"Well, I really hate to say this, Poseidon, but I think it's time we take them out. The corruption and degradation of your amazing creation is beyond redemption. It's time to take them out and start over again."

"Well, we can't all be the father of Athena, Zeus. If my offspring were more like your daughter, maybe we wouldn't even have to consider this. You're an enigma inside yourself. You swallowed her mother to keep her from bearing the child you feared too powerful, and yet you want to kill my offspring because they are so mortal. Sometimes it' is all I can do to restrain myself from strangling you!"

"Calm down, brother, calm down. I know you don't want your entire mortal line wiped out. But I don't see another option.

"Why is it that the one who pisses you off in the first place is the one who tells you to calm down!? I swear you get more like HWNHNV every single day!"

"Well, I'm the senior brother and I say they need to go."

"You're not the *older* brother!"

"I said, 'senior', as in 'more important; more powerful."

"To the Seventh Hell with you! I can't stop you. Mother already said she agreed with you. She always did like you better! Do what you have to do, but don't ever, ever, ever talk to me again! I'm gonna go find my own Goddamned planet! You can have this piece of shit, because all you wanna do is kiss the ass of He Whose Name Has No Vowels!"

"Go ahead, get mad. But we still have to abide by the contract and you know it."

"Maybe you have to, but I don't. I'm off to find my own place. You and HWNHNV can have this one! I say screw you both!"

That was the last they ever spoke. Poseidon retreated to his underwater home and changed his name to Neptune, to deny any familial relation. Zeus supercharged the earth's crust beneath Atlantis and the stone began to liquefy and ooze off into the ocean. Almost all of Poseidon's entire human bloodline was obliterated by the destruction of Atlantis, and he moved under the polar ice cap to sulk.

After nearly twenty-five hundred years of sulking and feeling sorry for himself, the not-so-newly christened Neptune decided to exact his revenge on the brother who had betrayed him. This revenge, though *hot*, would be served *cold*. He turned all his long-dormant heat generators toward the polar ice cap.

HWNHNV took credit for the flood, saying he was destroying a decadent society, but in reality it was Neptune's revenge on Zeus that forced Noah to build a boat. HWNHNV does get credit, however, for warning him. After all, he still had to have someone to torment. Poseidon departed Earth in a remorseful rage shortly after the polar ice caps melted and hasn't been seen on Earth since.

Unbeknownst to Poseidon, Zeus had a tender spot in his heart for Poseidon's line, and because it wasn't *technically* in violation of the contract with HWNHNV, Zeus let the great-grandchildren of Diaprepes live, on one condition. They would be given webbed hands, the sonar ability of dolphins, a fluke instead of feet. . . . . and they would never again set foot on dry land.

SWITCH GRASS

[Roy]

"We're the proud owners of eight thousand acres of Kansas Prairie!" Sam announced, as he took off his little car like a big man takes off his shirt. In spite of the fact that no redneck American boy in his diesel-guzzling, four wheel drive, F-350 would be caught dead in a mini-mobile, you can be sure his grandkids will, because it will be all they can afford to drive.

"And somebody needs his truck-driving lesson this week, doesn't he," Sam chided like one might do to a child. I can't say it sat well with me.

"I can't imagine who that might be," I answered in mock sincerity.

"I took him over to look at your truck so he could get accustomed to the pre-trip inspection," Janey actually *defended* me. It nearly brought a tear to my eye! I was growing quite fond of this perpetually nude dynamo, even though I knew she would never be mine. It wouldn't be long before I discovered just how much "not-mine" she was. But what I didn't know that morning certainly wasn't hurting me.

"You didn't let him drive it, did you?"

"Of course not. He's not ready for that yet."

"Good" He then quickly changed the subject, "You ready to go pick up this rig, Janey?" Sam asked. It really was happening! I was going to become a septic system installer. Woo-Hoo! I could hardly contain my depression.

"Cheer up, Roy. This is only temporary. When you get Leo handled, then you can utilize your full potential. Until that time, you need to do what needs to be done. You gonna be OK with that?" Sam was the coach and I was the reluctant player, performing in the position I didn't want. "By the way, I got something for you on my way back."

"Leo? Is this the same Leo I saw on the video?" He didn't answer and handed me a brown envelope, about half the size of a regular sheet of paper. I couldn't imagine what it could contain. I opened it slowly, glancing back and forth between Sam's face and the envelope. In it were a single piece of paper and something plastic, like a credit card?

The paper was the birth certificate of a boy born in 1986 to a Rose and Jim Johnson. "What's this got to do with me?" I asked him.

"Look deeper!" he admonished.

I got my fingers around the plastic card and pulled it out. Did he get me a credit card? Cool! . . . . Shit! It was a driver's license. Roy Johnson's driver's license, with my photo on it.

"Does this mean I don't have to take the test?" I asked hopefully.

"Not on your life. This is your new identity. I know you're capable of driving a car, but you still need to take this test to drive a truck. Don't want you killing anybody because you don't know what you're doing!"

"How did you get this?" *Boy, these guys must be good!*

"Veronica," was all he said.

"Care to elaborate?"

"Not really. You still need 'plausible deniability'. Let's just say she has been watching for some time and knows how the planet runs. We sort of have to act like the CIA without the assassinations, the drug-dealing, and third world political puppet regimes."

I just made an ugly face and kept my mouth shut.

"You,' he added, "can't get a CDL without an adequate identity. Now that that has been taken care of for you, all you need to do is pass all the tests!"

Janey came back out of the cabin wearing bib-overall shorts and a tiny tube top. They were *very* short and she made no effort to button up the sides. I guess she wouldn't get arrested, and customer service would be a breeze once the guys got a glimpse of her in those overalls.

"Get back to your book!" Janey instructed like a school teacher. I really dislike this position of being low man on the totem pole. I hate being an amateur, and here, after all this time in the field of my choosing, I'm in an entirely new one, and once again the most ignorant guy on the premises. I'll be glad to get the feeling of competence once again . . . . even if it is only competence in the field of shit.

The pair turned to get in the midget-mobile once again, but right before Sam sat down, he said, "Yes . . . . that same Leo." I started to say something else, but he waved me off.

"Gotta go!"

Yeah, yeah. *Gotta go, gotta go, while I sit here and study to be a truck driver.* Huh! And that Leo guy? He didn't look like much. Why the Hell was he so damned important?

Before I picked up the manual again, I looked at some other paperwork Sam had brought back. *Switchgrass!* Now that interested me!

OK, so it took three years for it to really get growing. But 540% more energy produced than that required to grow and harvest it? What would the boys at ADM and Ciba-Geigy have to say about that? Would we be having wars over corn and switchgrass like we have wars over oil? Maybe not—if de-implanting humans really works. If not, I can just see it now. Government mandates to rip out the switchgrass and plant corn, after billions in political donations from Monsanto . . . . Humans never change. I started to empathize with Janey's dislike of us. What did Sam say? *Upper level Dunists won't have anything to do with humans.* I guess I'm beginning to understand why. I wonder if that meant I was actually progressing.

Then I saw the rest of the plan. Now I was really getting fired up! Not only would he be growing switchgrass, but there were plans to install eighty windmill generators, complete with solar panels mounted on the towers. They were high enough off the ground that they wouldn't shade the switchgrass, and they were controlled by a sensor that followed the sun so that they were always at maximum exposure to the sun! Hell, it was almost like having your own personal oil well, back in the seventies when oil was still produced in the good old USA!

It was quite a task for me to put aside my excitement and go back to my truck-driving manual, but I managed it somehow. After two more grueling hours of reading and 'practice-test-taking' I put the booklet aside and turned on the DVD.

There was that goofy Leo, getting up, day after day at 3:30 am. Working his ass off, coaxing employees, dealing with difficult contractors, making payroll, and going home to a wife who acted like she wanted him dead. Day after day, week after week, month after month. What the fuck is wrong with this guy?

Where is his enjoyment of life? Why is he doing this, over and over and over again? It didn't make any sense to me. I was watching him in his house (I have no idea how they shot this video without him knowing). He came home to his wife, attempted to have a pleasant conversation with her, and in minutes she was provoking a fight. And this wasn't an isolated incident. I hit fast-forward—rewind—fast forward again—rewind again. There it was, just like a mid-afternoon soap opera. Again and again, repeating the same conversation (or lack of it) over and over and over.

And then it hit me! I was no better than him. Lois had treated me that way every day for as long as I could remember. I couldn't criticize this Leo character without criticizing myself. Except I was a whole lot lazier. I didn't work nearly as hard as this slave.

"He must be *awfully* important to them," I muttered to myself.

Just as I was putting the DVD back in its case, I saw another one; this case was labeled, "Hank", but I was in no mood to watch any more boring lives on DVD. I slipped on a pair of hiking boots and grabbed a baseball bat. I needed to take another nude walk, as Janey had insisted that I needed to get *very* accustomed to it, and I needed a change of scenery. Even though she swore I was out of the food chain, I still felt better with a baseball bat.

My walk was almost as boring as watching Leo's life. No bears, no mountain lions, no Piasa birds bothered to show their faces. Just a couple hawks and an owl. Seemed kind of funny for an owl to be out at this time of the day.

I should have watched the DVD. When I saw it later, I realized that Leo and Hank were polar opposites. Hank's life was as exciting as Leo's was boring . . . but I wouldn't have traded places with him either.

Yes, for my entrée I'd like a plate of excitement and a side order of enthusiasm. But by all means, hold the meth addiction. I find it highly unsettling.

A MICRO-ORGANISM'S LIFE

[Leo]

"Not this one again!" I heard the voice moan. I can't be certain I actually heard it. After all, I have no ears. I think I just sensed it. Call it ESP for lack of a better term. I suppose I'm back at the Transmutation Station.

"Oh, yeah, he's back! After the Atlantis debacle, his orders state 'ten thousand years as an amoeba, and then possibly promotion to grasshopper'."

"Why don't they just leave him as an amoeba? He'd cause a hell of a lot less trouble that way!"

"Because they still like a *game*, same as the rest of us. If he's a permanent amoeba, where's the game?"

The next thing I became aware of was the flexibility of my body. Cool! I could make it do anything I wanted! I loved surrounding another organism and 'swallowing' it. Oh my Gods, if the boys back home could see me now!

I'd stepped in it again. Atlantis was such a walloping success, it had gotten the attention of HWNHNV and gotten me set back four hundred million years on the evolutionary chain once I was returned to the Transmutation Station. You know how much he hates success! That's why I was assigned to be an amoeba.

After eating a few little creatures, I ran backward in my memory banks to remember what the implanters had said. "Ten thousand lifetimes? Or was it ten thousand years?

Shit! It was clears as a bell. 'Ten thousand years'. By the time I got back to being human, Atlantis was nothing but a memory, and an occluded memory at that.

BACK TO THE MINE

❦

[Roy]

About four in the afternoon, I saw a cloud of dust rising up off Sam's long driveway. Too much dust for one vehicle, so I knew it must be Sam and Janey. I made my way out of the woods and walked up toward Sam's barn lot. I guess the D.I.'s must be working, because though my entire garb consisted only of a pair of socks and hiking boots, I didn't seem the least bit worried . . . . or ashamed. Shame was something that was peculiar to humans and lower level Hyanthians. The Dunists, I later discovered, didn't even have a word for it.

Sam had attached his equipment trailer behind his road tractor, and was towing the backhoe on it. Janey was driving "my" new dump truck behind him, and when she bailed out, she was missing the short-short bibs and the tube top. There was a time when I might have said something about her lack of attire, but those days were rapidly disappearing.

"Tomorrow," Sam announced as I helped him undo the binders that held the backhoe securely to the trailer, "Janey will teach you how to do the pre-trip inspection and then take you driving." I didn't answer as we undid the chains, so apparently he assumed (correctly-I might add) that I wasn't particularly excited about this upcoming concatenation of events.

"Tonight, however . . . ." he picked up the conversation that I'd let drop to the ground, "We're going back to the mine. I want to show you the next project I would like you to supervise . . . .

237

that is if you're up to it . . . ." I know he was trying to encourage my participation in his plan, but the thought of being the 'Doctor of Shit' still had me pretty depressed.

"O.K.," I reluctantly agreed. Which, by definition, isn't really an agreement at all, is it?

"Cheer up, Roy-Boy," Janey chided. "Marie's barbecuing on the back patio, and if you promise to at least feign enthusiasm, I'll let you have some pussy tonight." Her ear-to-ear grin was irresistible, and though I tried my best to hide it, I smiled along with her. Frankly, I don't think she was 'letting' me have anything. But women of all races (even Dunists) can pretend that they're doing something altruistic, solely for the benefit of their man. Funny . . . . that was the first time I'd ever had that thought . . . . was it the result of the D.I.'s? Playing the game was gradually becoming fun for me . . . . for the first time ever. It suddenly occurred to me that I had always abhorred the game.

"Make it early . . . . either right after supper . . . . or late," Sam reminded. "Roy and I are going to the mine tonight."

"We'll make it late," Janey replied. "I'll help Marie with the clean-up while you guys go to the mine. Come straight home when you're finished!" She mockingly demanded, staring at me with her hands on her hips, trying unsuccessfully to hide her perpetual insouciance.

Marie was in the sombrero-like shade of the back patio; the three-story Victorian completely blocking the still-hot October sun. The heavenly aroma of charcoal and grilling beef wafted around the corner of the house as the three of us turned the corner. Sam went inside and soon returned without his jeans, shirt and work boots; carrying a cooler full of Michelob long necks.

After he set it down, I grabbed two, opened them and handed one to Janey. "You know you can't get drunk anymore," she said before she took the first swallow. "The first D.I. eliminates that."

"I still like the taste," I replied after taking a long draw at the bottle.

"Me too," she said. "Nothing wrong with that. Still a hundred times better than soda."

"Don't start, Janey." Though human women often gesture with their hair, Marie was perfectly capable of facially expressing her emotions in spite of being completely bald. From this lack of conversation, I gathered that Janey undertook frequent rants on the diet of humans, particularly those in the U.S. I looked from one to the other and decided this was a really good time to just keep my mouth shut.

"Roy," Sam said my name to change the subject. "Tonight I'm going to show you something that will rock your world."

"What?" I asked. "Are you afraid you haven't yet made your point? That you haven't 'rocked my world' already? C'mon, Sam. Give me a break for Chrissakes! My world has been rocked so hard it's upside down and the people are falling off of it! A little 'normal' wouldn't hurt me a bit!"

The three of them just laughed at me. I could feel my face reddening like a pepper in August, when Janey attempted to sooth my ire. "Roy, honey. You ain't never gonna be 'normal' again. Even if you tried, you'd soon find it so boring that you'd be begging for more 'world-rocking'!"

At that moment, I didn't want to admit it, but I knew she was right. In spite of my seemingly continual gawp-jawed incredulity, life had become infinitely more interesting now that I was a member of this clan. I doubted I would ever be able to return to being a 'normal' human again. As I thought about it, the very idea became more and more abhorrent to me. Why on Earth would *anyone* want to be a 'normal' human? It was like asking for a life-long prison sentence! I suppose that's what happens when one gets a taste of being truly free. No wonder high-level Dunists wouldn't associate with humans.

After a perfectly cooked rib-eye and sliced potatoes grilled in butter and seasoning, not to mention a few more cold Michelobs, Sam and I loaded ourselves in the micro-mini-mobile and headed to the mine. It was the first time I'd really paid attention to how quiet this little car really was.

"Doesn't this thing have a gasoline engine as backup?"

"No, I already told you that, and it's also part of what I'm going to show you tonight. This little beast is battery powered and it charges off a perpetual motion motor that generates three times as much energy as it consumes." *Did he actually say, 'perpetual motion motor'?*

239

"Oh, bullshit. Everybody knows there's no such thing as a perpetual motion motor! They've been trying to invent one for years and it doesn't work. It always ends up consuming more energy than it creates."

"Have I lied to you yet?" he raised an eyebrow at me.

"As a matter of fact you have . . . . when you picked me up at the truck stop."

"O.K., I deserved that. But what about since then?"

"Not that I know of . . . ." I left it open-ended intentionally. He could have lied to me a hundred times; a thousand times, even. How could I possibly verify something that took place thousands of years ago on another planet? Hell, everything he'd been telling me could be the fabrication of a sick mind . . . . I had to admit it, however, that everything he said did make sense in some twisted, perverted sort of way . . . . at least perverted according to Earth-think.

When we arrived at the mine, I couldn't help but ask, "Why do we have to climb down this ridiculous ladder? Couldn't the aliens, with all their technology build a damn elevator?"

"Quitcherbitchin' . . . . and besides, you need the exercise. You're gonna be sittin' on your ass a lot these next few months."

As we descended once again down the vertical shaft, the soft glow of light grew brighter and brighter as we neared the bottom. And once again, I heard that familiar faint hum I'd heard the first time I was down here. It could have been any number of things, so I paid it little heed. We traveled what seemed like the length of two football fields before we came to the lighted area. The rest of the mine looked as though it hadn't been touched in decades, but here there was sign of recent human—oops, I mean Hyanthian, activity.

Sam led me down a series of corridors as the hum grew louder and louder. It was never uncomfortable to be near the sound, it was simply the hum of motion . . . . of bearings rolling, I thought . . . . incorrectly . . . . I discovered much later. We finally arrived at another vast room, at least a hundred feet in diameter, and in the center of it was a large, round, table-like affair that nearly filled the entire space. Around that table was a ring. The ring was stationary, but the table rotated inside the ring.

Spaced at regular intervals around the ring and the table were large dark objects. I couldn't tell what they were, but some were rectangular and some were 'banana' shaped.

"What in the world is this?" Nothing in my frame of reference could help me identify this monstrosity.

"It's that perpetual motion motor. You remember? The one you said doesn't exist?"

"Aw, c'mon, Sam. Stop pullin' my leg! What is this, really?"

"I'm tellin' you the truth. I know you're from Missouri, so I have to "show" you, so come over here and watch, and see if you can wrap your noggin around this."

We went over to a bank of boxes of electrical equipment, none of which made any sense to me, but he seemed to know what he was doing. He pulled a lever down and the rotating table began to slow.

"What? Did you cut the power to it?" I asked a little too smart-assedly, even for me.

"No. I used the electricity it generates to apply the electric brake to the hub. The only way it can be stopped is by mechanically braking the rotation." To my dismay, the lights in the room began to dim, and as the table came to a complete stop, we were left in absolute blackness. I turned around to look down the corridor, and it, too was blacker than the darkest night I'd ever seen above ground.

"This electronic field generated by the motor is what blocked the cell phone service in Doe Run for years. AT&T finally found a way to block the interference, but they had to put a tower directly on top of the mine for the blocker to work."

"O.K. I think I'm convinced. Can we turn the lights back on now?"

"Only if the solar powered generator kicks on. You don't want to stop this motor in the dead of night. You'd be down here in the dark till morning."

"It's near dark now, isn't it?" My heart was thumping louder with each passing second.

"Yep. Better flip the switch to the solar panels," he said dryly, as though he wasn't the least bit concerned. I wish I could have shared his nonchalance.

In the now-abject silence of the mine (except for dripping water), I heard a slight hum . . . . *hopefully that was the solar generator kicking on* . . . . said the pounding in my ears.

Slowly . . . . ever so agonizingly slowly . . . . the big table began to turn. I couldn't imagine that something as small as a solar generator, powered by a rapidly setting sun, was going to create enough power to get the big table with its massive dark weights bearing down upon it, spinning quickly enough to turn on its own before tomorrow's sunrise.

I waited in the inky blackness, fearing to even turn my head as the little electric motor-powered by the solar generator—struggled to force the big table to turn—but turn it did. A snail's pace at first, then faster, and faster and faster. Once it regained momentum, Sam flipped off the switch to the solar generator and the lights soon came back on all over the mine. Inky blackness gradually became re-illuminated by bright white LED light.

"So what does this do?" I asked, still not completely convinced that this was the real McCoy.

"It turns a gigantic generator stationed in the next level below us. The generator supplies all the electricity in here . . . . it's only a one way flow—out—it doesn't flow back in . . . . that's to keep us entirely clandestine.

"It then puts massive amounts of electricity on the line. Ameren insisted at first that they know the source of the power, but Veronica has a contact within the state legislature, because of the blackmail she had on Number Four[2] . . . . but that's another story.

"We got around their 'need to know' through a little legal maneuvering, so they know we're generating, they just don't know *how*."

"Well, isn't that level below us full of water?"

"Generators short out under water, silly. Haven't you ever heard of a pump?"

---

[2]   "Number Four" was the number assigned to the Farmington State Mental Hospital. Each of the state's facilities was assigned a number. The locals referred to the hospital as "Number Four".

"Yes, but the volume of energy required to run the pump large enough to keep this from flooding surely uses everything you can generate!"

"Oh ye of little faith! The pumps don't use 10% of what this generator puts out. And we recoup most of that by putting a series of turbines in the discharge line, and one large one where it dumps back out into the St. Francois River."

I know I just stood there looking like a moron, so he went on try to clear up my confusion.

"I know you're not from around here, but when I was a boy, the St. Francois River had water in it nearly all year long. There are a series of caves under the river; they go east toward Farmington and collapse there every once in a while. To the west of Farmington, the rock has cracked and the water from the river makes its way to the mine.

"When the mine and the caves are all filled up with water, the St. Francois flows on its merry way. But when Cleo got here, and decided the mine was the perfect location to set up, the first thing she had to do was pump the water level down. Once the level was sufficiently pumped down, they began shipping the magnets in late at night. They mostly only worked in mid-summer when the water level was already at its lowest point, and they didn't have to use as much electricity to pump as they would have in the winter.

"It took them eight summers to get the perpetual motion generator built and in service. Fortunately, in the fall of '98, just before the November rains flooded everything once again, they got all the adjustments made and got it on line.

"If you pay close attention (since you live here now), in the summer, the river dries up completely. That's because the flow isn't sufficient to keep up with the pumps. Once the flow increases and the caves fill up with water, our pumps have to work harder, but because the water filters through so many underground fissures before it gets to the mine, the seepage rate is still far slower than the capacity of the pumps."

"O.K., I think I get it. But what was the point of bringing me down here tonight. Did you forget about what I've got waiting for me when I get back to the cabin?"

"Not on you life, buddy, not on your life. But once you finish your career as a turd jockey, I want this you to start building these all over the planet."

Maybe I had a reason to live after all . . .

UN SAN GIGA

[Ancient Sumer]
[Leo]

Like a fully grown and fully armed Athena, who was birthed from the brow of Jove, I, arrived this time, fully grown, and fully-furred from the hand of Aruru. Not from inside her body, like Athena, but from a damp lump of clay into which she breathed life. I bet the boys back at the Transmutation Station are rolling on the floor in laughter.

Man from mud. Little did I know at the time the impact that phrase would have on the next five thousand years . . . . If it wasn't for Cleo and Veronica, I'd still believe it true. Ashes to ashes, dust to dust. What bullshit! For bodies maybe, but certainly not the soul. I'd been everything from an amoeba to the mother of a great civilization. Man from mud. The joke's on you, mankind.

My name is Enkidu. This life was given to me for one purpose . . . . to be a dichotomy within myself for the company of the son of a God named Gilgamesh. How can a man be his own dichotomy . . . . yet on this planet, how can he not?

The beginning of my life is like a childhood fantasy, except for my frightening appearance. I was friend to the stag and stallion; wolf and bear; goat and cow; hare and hound. We had no fear of each other, though I can't say the same for hare and wolf, or bear and goat. Ah the conundrum of being a participant in the food chain!

245

My life was harmony, like a beautiful song sung in all its varying parts . . . . until one day while filling my water bag, I ran into the trapper. I didn't notice him at first, though the sudden departure of my friends surely should have alerted me. He crouched, like me, across the pool from which I drank, and the hatred in his face would have warned a more cautious man.

But I was a babe in the woods; I knew no spite, no evil, no treachery. But soon, I would learn. And it was to be a painful lesson indeed.

*   *   *

A week later I was awakened by a strange noise in my camp. A more cautious man would have already been awake; another lesson I would soon learn. She was the first human woman I had seen, and her eyes cast in me a new dichotomy . . . . I was overcome with a powerful desire; a desire that fear should have overtaken . . . . but it did not. The fear was present all right, thus the dichotomy. But it was too weak. Few wish for stronger fear, but I wish, in retrospect, that it had been stronger that day.

She soon loosened the belt from her robe and it fell to the ground. Her smooth hairless skin, in stark contrast to my bear-like covering, aroused a sensation new to this body. As I tried to rise from my bedding, she pushed me back upon it and began planting kisses all over my hirsute face.

"My name is Shamhat," she announced in a husky whisper. "I am here to bring you great pleasure."

With her kisses came ancient memories; memories of pleasure, fidelity and trust. Memories that bled through, in spite of electronic memory erasure and new implants. Some things always bleed through. Thus the phrase, 'Déjà vu'.

Yet, I was soon to discover, that pleasure, without fidelity and trust, is not pleasure at all, but the most horrible kind of pain, lying in wait to run its paralyzing spear through your heart.

We made love for six days; day and night, night and day. And through that time, I never noticed my friends had abandoned me. But after day seven, I prayed for death. And Death refused to come.

"You see yon trapper across the lake?" she asked me on that fateful morning.

"Yes. I see him and have seen him before."

"He sent me here."

"You did not come of your own accord?"

"I was paid, you simpleton."

"But why? Do you not love me?"

Her mocking laugh was worse than the spear of death. For though I felt great pain, I had no wound, and Death would not come.

"Ah, ye child; ye innocent. It's my place to teach those like you the way of this world. Were it not for the Gullibles like you, Harlots like me could not make our way. It's a sad world, but place no blame on me, for I did not make this painful world."

"But yet you contribute to it?"

"Do blame the trapper and Lord Gilgamesh, but not me. For they are the ones who planned this betrayal. I am but their tool."

"But a tool only too willing to perform her evil deed!" I cried in agony.

"The trapper could not make great riches with you and the animals as confederates. His traps lay empty because of you and your interference. Now that your friends have been betrayed by you, much as you have been betrayed by me, his traps will always be full, for your former friends fear you now, more than they ever feared him."

"But Lord Gilgamesh? I was created by Aruru to be his near-equal, his friend, his balance (yes, even his dichotomy) for his power is too great alone! And now he has orchestrated my betrayal!"

"Only wickedness survives on Earth, Enkidu. It is written in the handbook."

"Handbook? There is a handbook for Earth?"

"Of course, but humans are not allowed to see it. There are rules, but you must discover them on your own. For some it takes a few days, for others a lifetime, though I doubt, a Yeti, a Sasquatch, a Grassman, or whatever you call yourself, you will ever learn them. For though you are a near-human, you will lie forever in that limbo between man and beast, never being either, never trusted by either, always an outcast. Always an *outcast*."

It was true. My friends no longer allowed my approach. A great distance was always kept from me. My true friends now viewed me as enemy . . . . as I now viewed woman. Of murder and betrayal, betrayal is the greater sin. Murder is only a result of the betrayal.

What greater power is there than to know the rules of the game when no one else does? Ignorance of the rules constitutes the slings and arrows of life. It's easy to walk on water if you know where the rocks are!

NOT QUITE A TURD JOCKEY

[Roy]

The next week was pretty boring. Not much worth writing down. Janey and I went over the pre-trip inspection, over and over and over it. She never ceased to amaze me, because she never hesitated to crawl under the truck and trailer to show me a brake pad or a pitman arm or a drag link. And not just because she crawled under the truck on her back, but because she was nude the entire time. Not once had I met an Earth woman who wouldn't think that was the ultimate in humiliation.

Sam did insist that she wear something at least semi-modest (by American standards) when she rode with me to take the driving test. As reluctant as she was, she complied with his wishes. A male examiner might have easily passed me while drawn into her overt sexuality, but I've met some of them that reek of 'Gestapo'; or we might have gotten a female examiner who would have flunked me the moment she saw Janey. She put on a pair of jeans and a t-shirt, though friendly headlights heaved a soft "Hello" to everyone she met. Oh well, what could I do?

I passed the test with no further ado, because Janey was nothing, if not a thorough teacher. She made sure I understood every term in the book; she went over the pre-trip exam with me to the point of ridiculous redundancy (at least to me it seemed that way); and she made me drive every back road until I got enough practice to be able to shift gears properly. That took some time!

Then she took me to the highway and made me drive to St. Louis in the worst of rush hour. No doubt she was a strict task master, but to this day, I applaud her for putting me through the ringer. "No point in being a dilettante!" was her oft-repeated warning. "If you're going to do something, be the best you can be . . . . never be a namby-pamby!"

Many a time I couldn't see the point in her obsession with my perfection of the driving skill. *This is just a temporary thing*, I kept telling myself, but she had other plans, and they didn't all include driving. After I'd succeeded in obtaining my license and started learning how to operate the backhoe, I began to understand her insistence on perfection. It wasn't about one particular skill, it was about learning to discipline yourself to be consistent enough to acquire that skill . . . . and maybe hundreds of others!

The day I got my Class A license, we were on our way back to Doe Run, when I noticed a change in her demeanor. I didn't want to say anything about it for fear I'd lose what respect I seemed to have gained by getting this license. When I first met her, she treated me like some annoyance she'd been saddled with; an annoyance she sometimes used for her own personal pleasure, but an annoyance nonetheless. I wasn't her lover, I was just her fucker. 'Lover' implies some affection, but fucker is just that . . . . nothing more. "Make me cum, now go away."

That evening, after we made a pot of stew, as it was now getting too chilly to cook outside (not that *we* couldn't take it, but the food cooled off too quickly) she approached me with a delicate touch, far less mechanical than in previous encounters. "Make love to me tonight, Roy," she cooed like an inamorata, not a mere fucking machine. 'Love' was a word she'd not used with me before.

I suppose we spent hours in bed that evening. It's hard for me to fully remember everything that occurred. But afterward, she seemed, for the first time since I'd met her, to be in the mood to talk about herself. I could only guess that my licensing had earned me a respect I hadn't previously deserved. Funny how we all want to be respected without earning that respect. It seems to be the scourge of the modern society; maybe all of humankind.

Though she hadn't yet actually opened up about her past on this evening, I sensed a willingness, a wantingness in her that I'd never felt before. I thought the best way to bridge that space between willing and doing was to ask a question. I'd never had the courage to attempt it before, but tonight she was different, so I just blurted it out.

"How did you meet Sam and Marie?" I tried to break the ice with the most innocuous question I could think of, but my execution of the question was incompetent at best.

"Oh! The answer to that could be so long we might never get to the part you can understand!" But the implication was that she might reveal part of the mystery.

"Well, try me. What's the worst that can happen?"

"You could bolt for the door and never speak to me again."

"Well, that's not likely, unless you tell me you're a zombie and you're going to eat my brains right after sex."

She smiled a sheepish sort of a smile; not her usual ear to ear grins of satisfaction. "Not recently," she replied . . . . "but I have been known to." It was my own damned fault. I asked the question. It's all on me if I don't like the answer.

"I guess I should start when Sam, Marie, Toni, (oh, you haven't met Toni yet?) and their entourage escaped the disintegrating Thera and arrived at Dune. And that goddamned HWNHNV followed them . . . ."

I just stared; politely, but I was still staring, nonetheless.

"You see," she continued, "in the disguise of "goodness" he lays the traps that people, societies, civilizations and even entire planets fall into. I know there's a different definition of "Good" on Earth than the one to which I was accustomed. To a Dunist, 'good' means *enlightened*. It seems to me that on Earth, it means running around bandaging every wound, pouring out sympathy, and generally doing for others what they should be doing for themselves.

"Now I don't mean that a person shouldn't help others, but the best help you can give someone is the wherewithal to help himself. Anything else only aggravates the problem. Sure, an injured person needs treatment, and on Earth that usually means 'medical' treatment.

"But what if you could teach a human how to patch up his own fragile body with his own mind, much like a mechanic fixes a car?

What if he understood that this body that he now possesses (and doesn't actually *possess him*) was one of thousands that he had owned and would be one of thousands he had yet to own? Wouldn't that be the 'goodest' thing you could do for another?

"And what if you could make that body's tolerance for heat and cold and pain and trauma a hundred, a thousand times, even, greater than what it is now? Wouldn't that be the ultimate act in 'goodness'?"

"Yes, but what if you made that person so strong and powerful that he became a Super Hitler, or a Super Stalin?" Being all powerful might be a great concept but it made me shudder to think of the possible consequences of it getting in the wrong hands.

"It'll never happen."

"Why? How can you possibly believe that?"

"In order to be truly powerful—*truly powerful*—one must first be truly kind—truly benevolent—and that characteristic only comes with *enlightenment*. An ignorant being will never be kind. It's his ignorance that keeps him locked in the chains of fear and hatred."

"How do you know that? I mean, is this one of the unwritten rules of the Universe or something? And if it is, how would *you* come to know that?"

"Ah, my little Earthling . . . ." She wasn't really being condescending, but if I'd had any hair, it would have stood up on the back of my neck.

"If these are the rules of the Universe, then why does Hawaii-Nevada get away with this shit? I mean, after all, if you are the creator . . . . why would your Universal Rules work in contrast to your own character?"

"Oh . . . . I see. I'm sorry, but you are making an erroneous assumption that so many humans make!" She grinned, like one who's in on the joke. I, sadly, was not.

"Well don't hold me in suspense! What do I have wrong?"

"Well the short answer to that question is, 'Everything', but I don't think that's what you wanted to hear."

"Yeah, well it's a little vague as a starting point," I grumbled in sarcasm. "Can you find some little detail that I could grasp and build from there?" I'm sure you all have been in a situation where you're the only one NOT in on the joke . . . . It's damned uncomfortable, and I could feel my blood pressure spiking.

"HWNHNV is NOT God . . . . NOT the creator of the Universe . . . . Is that detail small enough?" I felt like she'd dumped twenty tons of bricks on my head. Now I have never been a Bible-Thumper, and I hate proselytizing with a passion, but I always felt there was some force bigger than me in the Universe. A God I could understand and that could understand me . . . .

"Brush up on your Old Testament, my friend. Now that you've had a couple D.I.s, your ability to grasp what you read has surely vastly improved. Now the King James Version, even though it's been seriously prostituted, is probably the best you're going to find. Stay away from these new versions, especially the NIV, because they lose so much in their milque-toast translations to make it acceptable to a totally *unenlightened* populace that it's a crime that they even call it the Bible.

"The optimum version you could get that would provide you with the greatest understanding would be a Greek Bible translated from Aramaic, but by the time you learned Greek, I could have you completely de-implanted and you could be a Grade V Dunist, and you'd already understand the whole of the Universe anyway! So don't bother with that . . . . just read a little Old Testament, and you get a good idea of who this HWNHNV really is. If you're looking for true Omnipotence from him, you're looking in the wrong direction. How he and Jesus got hooked up into the same Bible just blows me away. They couldn't be more opposite . . . . just another good example of what an abject mess humans really are."

"I resemble that remark," I said sheepishly.

"Yes, you do." I know she couldn't help it. Dunists tell the truth; they don't sugar-coat. I would later find out they didn't even have a word in their language for "euphemism", so I just accepted her insult, knowing full-well there wasn't any animosity in it.

"Well, I still don't get it. If HWNHNV is not kind and benevolent, then how the hell is he so powerful?"

"He's not. It only seems that way because of your ignorance. Have you ever *known* something; I mean known something with such certainty that no one could ever bullshit you into believing otherwise?"

253

"I guess, maybe . . . . I don't know . . . ."

"Well that answer, in itself, is very scary! OK, let's try this: Are you certain that the Earth will rotate and that the sun will 'rise' tomorrow?"

"Yes. I guess that's the one thing I could say I have certainty on."

"OK. Now let's go one step farther . . . . I have just erased your entire memory, and you are born on Earth *not knowing nothing*. Now, with that blank slate of a mind, I tell you that the only way the sun rises if you lick my pussy every evening at sunset, or I will refuse to let it come up tomorrow."

I smiled. She knew I couldn't resist. "OK, you've got my attention now . . . ."

"And the one time you forget, or refuse to obey my command, I smite you down and kill you, and then I look for a new pussy-licking slave and tell him the same thing."

"I guess the sun didn't rise for me the next morning . . . ."

"And that will be stuck deep in the recesses of your soul, lifetime after lifetime after lifetime. Now you are bathed in ignorance and in complete certainty that your erroneous belief is the absolute truth . . . . and that's all he does. He and his minions provide false information and declare its absolute truth, and somewhere way back in the past, you *were* actually killed for your failure to comply; and that failure, and your subsequent failure to live, create a false certainty for you for all of time, until another false certainty, or perhaps if you're extremely lucky, a *genuine* certainty comes along and kicks the old one to the curb . . . .

"And that's all he does. He's not powerful at all. He's just devious. And not a very brave deviant at that. You will soon learn that the chains that hold you in place are entirely of your own construction and that only you can break them . . . . and in actuality, you don't even have to *break* them . . . . all you have to do is stop continuously creating them."

"I can't-I can't-I can't . . . . I can't believe that. If it's that simple, why can't I break them now?"

"Because the implant tells you that you can't, and that the consequences for doing so, or even attempting to do so, are not just life-crushing, but *soul-crushing*. The only way to truly enslave a being is to convince him to enslave himself. In the last half of the twentieth century they called that slavery "Credit Cards."

Well, I guess that's one chain that's broken. Roy Johnson possesses no credit cards; and Kinley Thorsen has vanished into thin air . . .

MEETING GILGAMESH

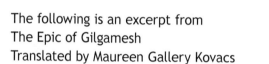

The following is an excerpt from
The Epic of Gilgamesh
Translated by Maureen Gallery Kovacs
Electronic edition by Wolf Carnahan, 1998

Enkidu spoke to the harlot:
"Come, Shamhat, take me away with you to the sacred Holy Temple, the residence of Anu and Ishtar, the place of Gilgamesh who is wise to perfection, but who struts his power over the people like a wild bull. I will challenge him!

Let me shout out in Uruk (land of Gilgamesh): I am the mighty one!

Lead me in and I will change the order of things; he whose strength is mightiest is the one born in the wilderness!"

The harlot replied,

"Come, let us go, so he may see your face.

I will lead you to Gilgamesh—I know where he will be.

Look about, Enkidu, inside the haven of Uruk, where the people show off in skirted finery, where every day is a day for some festival, where the lyre and drum play continually.

Where harlots stand about prettily, exuding voluptuousness, full of laughter,

And on the couch of night the sheets are spread!

Enkidu, you do not know how to live,

I will show you Gilgamesh, a man of extreme feelings!"

Look at him, gaze at his face he is a handsome youth with freshness!
His entire body exudes voluptuousness
He has mightier strength than you,
Without sleeping day or night!
Enkidu, it is your wrong thoughts you must change!
It is Gilgamesh whom Shamhat loves,
And Anu, Enlil, and La have enlarged his mind.
Even before you came from the mountain,
Gilgamesh in Uruk had dreams about you"
And for the second time in less than ten days, I had sealed my own fate.

SEPTIC

[Roy]

I had a lot of trouble with the word septic. I thought it had something to do with shit. But it's really about bacteria. We use "anti-septics" to prevent infections in our bodies, but when it comes to our waste, we need the "infection".

When a human (or *any* body for that matter) body becomes septic, it means that it's overrun with bacteria that is attacking the body. When it comes to sewers, "septic" refers to the bacteria that break down the solids in the waste system. In this case the bacteria are attacking your poop.

But enough bathroom humor. I spent the next six months installing septic tanks and drain fields with an almost constantly naked female co-worker. I, however, managed to remain clothed for my customers. I can say in retrospect, that it turned out well that my septic assignment was temporary. With the coming economic depression, the septic system business became so cutthroat that many of my competitors went out of business like Janey and I did.

During the first three of those six months, I was not allowed to visit Sam and Marie. I kept asking why; they kept insisting I'd find out in due time. But during my downtime, I was expected to review all the recordings of this loser named Leo.

I can say this now, because the situation has changed so much, its former animosity nearly unrecognizable, but I could not fathom, for the life of me, why I had to watch this fool. He seemed a reasonably intelligent sort of a Joe, but his life was a constant turmoil. As he once described it to me, it was like the bet between two bar patrons about taking a swallow from a cup of tobacco spit.

It seems that one bet the other $100 that he wouldn't take a sip from the spittoon. His buddy said, "I'll take your hundred dollars and tipped up the spittoon. But instead of taking one small sip, he swallowed the entire contents of the filthy cuspidor.

"OK, I give," said the bettor. "Was it so good that you couldn't resist drinking the whole thing?" he asked sarcastically.

"Nope," gulped the drinker. "It was all one big long string. Once I started I couldn't stop till I got to the bottom."

I'll bet it came back up as one long string as well . . . . but now I'm making myself sick, and probably you as well. But Leo didn't drink from a spittoon, he was drinking from a tank like the ones at the fuel-tank farm on I-40 between Greensboro and Winston-Salem, North Carolina.

"I couldn't get out!" he later admitted to me. "Between the responsibility to my children, my employees, my customers and my vendors, not to mention a wife that wanted to destroy me, I was in a trap from which there was no escape . . . . until 9/11 offered me a way out." I'll let him explain that himself, but I needed to add a little context to this chapter.

When he introduced himself that morning, I recognized him from Veronica's, but I hadn't ever spoken to him, nor had Janey. And though I was well aware that she told me she belonged to no one, I couldn't help the heartache I felt when she removed the last of her skimpy clothing the day we installed his septic tanks. I knew she was going to sleep with him, but I had no idea he would try to pawn her off on this "Billy" character when he was done with her.

When we went back to install Leo's drain field, I knew I had lost her, and though I was partially de-implanted, I still felt my heart breaking. But I can't say she didn't warn me.

He seemed a nice enough sort of guy, and against every fiber of my being, I made no claim to her, so when he asked her out, I faked a smile and let her go. I knew if I'd tried to stop her I could very well be looking for a new place to live. And if I allowed (ha- like any human can "allow" a Dunist to do anything) her to go, then we would still be friends. If I tried to stop her, it would only blow up in my face.

I knew I would never be satisfied with a human woman again. Janey had seen to that. The Kardashians had destroyed an entire generation of women, a destruction that could only be repaired with an Apocalypse. I knew there were other women who were members of Veronica's club that had been started on the de-implantation process, so maybe I wasn't completely ruined.

That was my last septic tank. I'd done what I was supposed to do. I'd fulfilled my contract. It had cost me the best thing that had ever happened to me, but it was time to move on. When I talked to Marie and Sam the night of Janey and Leo's first and only date, we agreed it was best for me to move to Veronica's for a while. There was plenty of room and plenty of work for a guy like me in the compound, and I would be close to the machine. Total de-implantation, here I come.

"One more thing before you go," Marie added, and suddenly headed the conversation in a direction I'd never have imagined. "Just so you completely understand . . . . we need to take you to your grave . . . ."

"MY WHAT?"

"Your grave, Roy. Or Kinley's grave actually."

I think I hit my head on the table when I passed out.

BECOMING MY OWN WORST ENEMY

[Leo/Enkidu]

I admit I was corrupted by the finery of Uruk-Haven. Everywhere I looked I saw voluptuous women, only barely clothed in the finest of colors. Handsome young men vied for the attention of the ladies. The scent of cooking meats, the glitter of precious metals, and the sounds of joyful music all filled my senses.

And it was here I was invited to attend Gilgamesh on his quest to murder the God Humbaba and cut down the Cedar Forest; two acts that would set in motion my own dwindling spiral for the next four thousand years.

I can't say if the constant repeating of one's personal goals was the rule of the day, or whether it was simply the endless braggadocio of the arrogant Gilgamesh. In retrospect, and in full memory of at least 30,000 years of my past lives, I don't think I've ever met a more despicable individual in all my lives. I started to say "human", but chose "individual", for I'm still not sure he was a human.

"I am a God, I am the King of Uruk," he announced, over and over and over ad nauseum. And after he initiated the ruin of my life, and after he had killed the Bull of Heaven, much to Ishtar's outrage, his full-of-himself-ness knew no bounds. I imagine, that after the destruction he caused, if he has any conscience at all, he's been living as a cedar tree for the last 3500 years. He just might be a fence post on an Ozark farm as we speak. That's a good job for him . . . . at least the damage he can cause is minimal . . . . as a fence post.

He decided, through the urging of the Gods that he must murder Humbaba the Terrible and cut down the Cedar Forest guarded by His Terribleness. Sometimes I believe the Gods are as petty as politicians.

And since I was cast from mud to be Yin to his Yang, or vice versa, I was to support him whether I wanted to or not. My four legged and winged friends run from me, and fly from me in horror since Shamhat stole my purity. Even she was in love with Gilgamesh, so where did that leave me, a hair-being? No animal would ever trust me again. No woman would ever love this thing that would one day be called Yeti. What choice did I have but to travel with Gilgamesh and put into motion the awful slaughter of a truly enlightened being and his precious Cedar Forest, which was the basis of all enlightenment?

One lesson would not be lost on me. No matter how terrible the personal consequences, we always have a choice. And sometimes, not often, but on rare occasions, DEATH is the correct choice.

*   *   *

We traveled for two weeks to reach the Cedar Forest. The land was hot, dry and dusty. Our throats were often parched as we rationed our water carefully. (If Gilgamesh was a God, why did he need to drink the water I so desperately needed?)

We camped on the open desert at night, and Gilgamesh never tired of expounding to me his greatness and all the magnificent things he would accomplish. By the third night, I had placed small pebbles in my ear canals to muffle the endless ramblings of his professed amazing-ness. I doubt he even noticed.

On the fifteenth day we arrived at the gate to the Cedar Forest, where we encountered the huge Humbaba. He was a mountain of a creature, towering at least two feet over the head of Gilgamesh, and Gilgy was a big man.

"Who goes there?" he shouted.

"It is Gilgamesh and Enkidu," my fellow traveler answered. "We have come to kill you and cut down the Cedar Forest as proof of my strength and power. I have defeated every man I've ever fought. I killed the Bull of Heaven, and I am here to kill you as well."

"Many have tried and all have died," Humbaba sneeringly replied.

"But I am King Gilgamesh, Lord Gilgamesh, and with my companion Enkidu, we will slay you and your forest!"

"I don't like this!" I hissed at Gilgamesh. "Why do we have to kill him and cut down the forest? Is this really necessary?"

"I must prove my power to the people, the creature, and my father as well!" He was angry that I dared question him, but the whole "Daddy" thing explained volumes of his character. Prove to Daddy that you are great . . . . no matter the cost.

At Gilgamesh's urging, I gathered what dead wood I could find, and set fire to the great doors that guarded the Cedar Forest. In the dry climate, they were soon engulfed in flames.

I admired Humbaba's bravery. He charged through the burning doors in an effort to bring the fight to us as well as protect the forest from our destruction. With swords flailing, he and Gilgamesh went after each other. Despite being the smaller man, Gilgamesh was holding his own. With a nod from him, I slunk through the burning doors and found the Cedar of all Cedars.

She was a magnificent matriarch, with a diameter in excess of fifteen feet, and she towered three hundred feet over all the other cedars in the forest. She was the mother tree, the tree that had provided the breath of life to all other creatures for thousands of years.

One look at her, and I knew I would never be physically able to do what was expected of me . . . . cut her down. I could hack away at her for the rest of my natural life and never bring this giant down . . . . nor should I. Torn between my awe and respect for this mother of life, and my duty to aid Gilgamesh, I was soon paralyzed in depression and collapsed beneath her . . . . letting the Fates decide my future . . . . and decide they did.

After an hour of fighting, it suddenly grew quiet outside the gates. I entertained the idea of arising and peering outside to see how the fight ended, but decided instead to remain and await my fate.

I didn't have to wait long. The form of Gilgamesh soon paraded toward me, with sword in his right hand and the massive head of Humbaba in his left. "Why have you not cut down the tree?" he demanded.

"Surely we do not need to cut down the tree!" I protested weakly.

Humbaba was placed here to guard the forest, and now that I have killed him, we must destroy the forest!"

"But why?"

"To protect it from the humans! The forest, particularly the Mother Tree, contains the secrets of the Universe, the very essence of life itself. Now that Humbaba, the creature whom no man could kill, has been slain, we must destroy the forest to keep the humans from obtaining these secrets. Only a God-King, like your own Gilgamesh, should know these secrets. The people must never know. It is the only way I can maintain my power over them. If knowledge is available to everyone, then I am not a God-King, and I MUST be the God-King!"

I probably coined a new word on the spot; I don't think it had ever been heard before: Megalomaniac.

I was dealing with a raving lunatic, and I had been a party to the worst catastrophe to befall the human race since the drowning of Atlantis. I wanted to crawl in a hole and die.

I won't bore you with the endless whining that was attributed to me in the epic poem. Apparently I was quite the whine-bag, as my conscience, becoming so burdened with the realization of the atrocity I had committed and was about to continue, wanted to end this life of mine. I protest the whimpering I was blamed with, but maybe that's my conscience just creating another justification.

"Get your axe and cut down the smaller trees!" Gilgamesh shouted to rouse me from my coma. "Pile them at the base of the Mother Tree! If we can't cut her down, we'll burn her to the ground!"

Reluctantly, I did as I was told, and after much sweat, I had cut 50 small trees and stacked them around her trunk, and if wasn't for the spectacle of the fire, I'd never have looked up again, my depression was so great. If you've ever thrown a dead cedar on a campfire, you have some slight idea of the towering inferno the Mother Tree soon became.

Within a couple minutes, the flames shot higher and higher. As they reached the upper branches where there was still much greenery, the smoke blotted out the sun, and temporarily cooled us in its shade.

But then that smoke burst into flame, and the three hundred feet of the tree was tripled by the height of the flame shooting into the air. I'm sure they could see it in Uruk in broad daylight.

I fell to the ground in a blubbering mass as regret paralyzed my body. I had committed a crime against my planet and against my race so severe that only a Gilgamesh could be more evil than I.

If you insist on reading about my blubbering, paralyzing, whiny regret, you can certainly read the rest of the Epic of Gilgamesh. I find it repulsive. I will leave you with this:

Gilgamesh performed one act of kindness to me before he returned to Uruk. Sick of listening to my regret, he pierced me through the heart and tossed my limp body on that raging inferno.

Finally, the arrogant God-King had done something nice for me.

KINLEY THORSEN

1985-2009

Marie and I made the trip by ourselves. She obviously felt that if I didn't see it for myself, I'd never be able to let go of my past identity.

We pulled into the narrow border town of Texarkana, making our way down State Line Boulevard that separated Texas from Arkansas. A few miles out of town she turned south with a familiarity that seemed unreal to me. I knew this area because I'd grown up here. My family's roots were deep in east Texas. We didn't have a GPS, and she never once asked for directions or checked any written notes or maps. How on Earth could she know the location of my family cemetery? I soon answered my own question in the first three words . . . . "on Earth". Marie wasn't bound by Earthly considerations.

When we arrived at the half-acre burial ground, the new headstone stuck out like an albino at a Zulu family reunion. The pink Missouri granite, exported to East Texas by the Doe Run Monument Company, was painfully obvious among the weathered white marble stones of my ancestors.

"Is the grave empty?" I asked in all hopefulness.

"No."

"Then what happened, did you get a body from the morgue or from the motel fire or something and bury it here?"

"No, Roy."

"OK, Marie, you're startin' to freak me out here. What the Hell is going on?"

"Kinley Thorsen is buried in this grave, Roy. Not you. Your *body* is buried here."

"Oh, bullshit. I'm standing right beside you. I see you plain as day; are you telling me you can't see me?"

"Oh, sure I can see you. You're not a figment of my imagination." She half smiled.

"Then stop bein' so damn cryptic and tell me what the fuck you are talkin' about!"

There was a significant pause as she looked out over the East Texas countryside, in some ways very similar to southern Missouri. "Do you remember when your car exploded at the motel fire?"

"Of course. That's most of the reason I am standing here with you today." My sarcasm wasn't well masked.

"A piece of shrapnel from your car flew across the field and struck you in the head. You died at the truck stop."

"Stop talkin' bullshit, Marie! I know good and goddamned well I got in that truck and rode to Doe Run with your husband!"

"Yes *you* did. No doubt about it. But your body died on the lot of that truck stop. The shrapnel hit you in the back of the head and your body died so quickly that you didn't even notice. Sam felt so guilty about being responsible for your death that he invited you to get in the truck and come to Doe Run so we could remedy the situation."

"You know," I shouted loudly enough that people in Houston could have heard me, "ever since I met you people, you have stretched my credulity to Jupiter and back with one fantastically unbelievable story after another. And I'm simply not buyin' this one!

"I was not dead when I got in that truck. I was not dead when I arrived in Doe Run! And I'm not dead now!"

"That's true, you're not. YOU are not dead. You cannot die . . . . but bodies can, and bodies die every day. And your body died in that truck stop."

"Then what about that zip drive? I remember having it in my pocket the entire drive to Doe Run!"

"Do you remember when Sam made the State Trooper believe (and you as well if I recall correctly) that we were all dressed when he stopped the van last month?"

"Oh, you're bullshittin' me again!"

"No sir. He took the zip drive from your dead body and created a replica for you to "hold" on to during your trip to our place."

"So are you telling me I'm just a damn ghost?" De-implanted or not, I was really pissed.

"Not anymore," she answered.

"OK, fine! Fuck it then. Just tell me the whole goddamn story and I'll believe it like the gullible sap that I am!"

"You're not gullible, Roy." In spite of my wrath, Marie never lost her equanimity. "I realize how difficult this is for you to grasp, but surely you know we are no longer bound by the "everybody knows-rules" of Earth."

"You mean like "everybody knows that when you're dead, you stay dead?"

"Yes, like that one. Sam procured enough skin cells from your body and brought them back, along with *you*, to Doe Run and we created a new body for you."

"Whaddya mean, 'along with me'? Didn't you just say he left me laying in the lot at the truck stop?"

"Your body, Roy, only your body. You are not your body. It's just a possession . . . . like a car."

"When people lose a car, they get another one. When people lose a body, that's it, they're dead!"

"Just an Earth rule, Roy. It doesn't mean that the whole of the universe must abide by an Earth rule. It's necessary for enslavement of the human race. I really thought you'd been de-implanted well enough to realize that."

"Well, I guess not!" I snapped, sarcasm dripping from my words. As I struggled to regain my composure, I asked, with the antagonism still dripping from me, "Then what happened?"

"In six weeks we had a new body grown for you, and on your first trip to the mine and your first de-implanting, you entered it and took control of it."

"So you mean to tell me I didn't have a body for six whole weeks?"

271

"Yes. Are you not under the impression we went to the mine the day after you arrived in Doe Run?"

"That's the way I remember it."

"I'm sorry, Roy, but we had to do it . . . . or let you go . . . . and we needed you . . . ."

"Sorry for what? Did you do something to me that I can't remember?"

"I need to tell you because I don't want any more secrets between us. You are one of us now and you need to know the full truth."

"OK, stop with the fucking mind game and tell me what the hell you are talking about!"

"You arrived at our home as a spirit only. Your body lay dead in parking lot. But you did not know that 'you', Kinley Thorsen, had died. You were completely unaware. Unlike humans, who can only barely see faint outlines of the beings without bodies, Sam and I had no trouble seeing you, in full bodily form, as you see yourself.

"We needed time to grow your new body so we put you to sleep."

"Well how do you put a ghost to sleep?" This just didn't make any sense.

"With an electronic wave. It puts you in a pleasant dream that seems as though it only lasts a few minutes, but it replays again and again. It causes you no harm, but only fills the time with pleasant memories."

"Why did you have to put me to sleep?" My hostility seemed suddenly abated as I recalled fishing with my brother when we were just kids. Was that the dream they played in my 'head'? If you don't really have a head, where does a dream exist?

"Your clothing would have disclosed the situation. You wouldn't have been able to put on any other clothing than that you perceived yourself wearing at your time of death. A couple of days and you would have realized you were dead. We couldn't risk your reaction. Like I said before, we need you."

"So is this body, that was grown in weeks, instead of years, going to suddenly fail on me? And am I a clone?"

"Only your body is a clone, Roy. You are still you. Whether it lasts ten years or a hundred is up to you now."

So Kinley Thorsen really was dead. And I was stuck with his DNA. In a murder trial, that could become a real problem.

Fortunately, when they tried to pin Dr. Kurtz's death on me from the DNA found on an envelope in his paper shredder, Kinley was already dead and buried, the body identified by DNA and dental records. It was important that I stay out of trouble from now on.

SHAMHAT'S CHILDREN

Seven months after Enkidu was burned in the pyre of the Cedar Forest, Shamhat gave birth to twins, a boy and a girl. When they were presented to her to suckle, she shoved them away. "Take them away and kill them! I want no children, especially not children of Enkidu!"

The midwife took them away and stroked their dark hair. Having recently given birth herself, her breasts were enlarged with milk, and she suckled the hirsute twins at her own breast, allowing them to live.

When Aruru heard of the birth of the hairy children, she went to find Shamhat. "What have you done with Enkidu's children?" she demanded.

"I sent them away to be killed, you foolish woman! I want no part of children, especially not ones that look like apes!"

Aruru showed no mercy. With the same energy that brought life to a ball of mud, she sucked the life from Shamhat and cursed her to walk barren and loveless for all eternity. The harlot's lifeless body slumped to the floor and evaporated as dust.

Then Aruru went to find Enkidu's children. When she found them with the midwife, she instructed her to obey this command:

"When the children no longer need to nurse at your breast, you must send them to the East. I will arrange passage for them with a traveling band of merchants who roam from Un San Giga to China and back. I do not want them killed, but I wish never again to be reminded of Enkidu.

When they arrived in the Himalayas, they were well equipped to survive in the cold . . . . and the rumors of the Yeti were born.

SATURNINE

[Roy]

"**D**o you know what that word means?"

I must not have been paying any attention. "What word is that?"

"Man, Roy, you must have been lost in some deep thought there. You haven't responded to anything I've said for several miles."

"Oh . . . . oh, sorry. I was just thinking about Janey . . . . that and seeing my tombstone. Kind of a rough day, don't you think?"

"I'm sure it is. Willfully letting her go and then finding out you're a dead man is probably a little tough to take. But then I was dead for years; if not for Veronica, I still would be. It's really not such a bad thing. There was no DNA testing when I died, so there's really no trace of me. Your case is a little different, however. I'm sure you have a DNA trail somewhere."

"Oh, well, forget that. What was the word you were asking me about?"

"Saturnine."

"Well, I know it has something to do with being gloomy," I answered just as we pulled into the parking lot at Harry's Gas and Convenience Store. "Are you implying that I'm 'saturnine'?

Completely ignoring me, she asked, "OK. Now, to the best of my knowledge, you've never actually stopped in here before?"

"That's right. This is the first time."

"OK, now go in this store and look at the people, thinking about that word."

Marie stayed in the car and let me go in alone. I walked over to the cooler and got us a couple bottles of water. There were six people in the store in addition to me; one cashier, a young couple with 80% of their visible skin covered in tattoos, an obese woman standing in front of the deli, one tired cook behind the glass, an old man with a long beard checking lottery numbers, and one huge young man hiding behind a heavy dark beard and heavy dark glasses, standing at the checkout counter paying for diesel fuel, a can of Skoal and a twelve pack of Budweiser.

I spoke to no one but the cashier. She wasn't hostile, but she wasn't friendly either. The others only spoke in mumbles or whispers . . . . if they spoke at all. The irony is that they probably all know each other.

When I got back in the car with Marie, she looked at me with a raised eyebrow and asked, "Well? Whaddya think?"

"Looks pretty saturnine to me."

"Now," she added, "Let's expound on the definition of that word a little. Where there is light, Saturn brings darkness. Where there is warmth, Saturn brings cold. Where there is joy, Saturn brings sadness, where there is life, Saturn brings death, where there is luck, Saturn brings dire consequences.

"Now, 'Saturnine' also applies to the absorption of lead into the body, as the ancients believed Saturn to be made of lead."

"Oh my God!" I yelled loud enough for people to hear through the rolled-up windows. "And Doe Run and Park Hills and Bonne Terre were all lead mining towns."

"Now, Roy, think about that darkness, cold, sadness, death, and bad luck that I mentioned earlier. Make the connection between these attitudes and the lead mines." She let me think on that for a while before she added, "The lead has been leaching into the water supply for well over a hundred years. Even the so-called 'safe' levels aren't really safe when you consume it every day over a lifetime."

"And that's why so much of this place looks so down in the dumps? But how did you and Sam escape this lead poisoning"

"When we were living on the Calvin farm, we drank nothing but rain water out of the cisterns. Can't say I was fond of it, but the prevailing winds blew the lead dust away from their farm. And there was never any reason for there to be mining under their farm anyway, because the lead played out a mile and half east of their place. When we drilled our well, there was no evidence of lead residue in the tests we had done."

"And that's why you have to use migrant labor on the farm instead of hiring locals!"

"Sure. We'd be glad to give jobs to local people, but if we did, we'd go broke . . . . not because we'd have to pay them more money, as our migrants are well-paid, but it's because they're so saturated with lead, that we couldn't possibly use them. Their attitudes are so surly, we'd be better off closing the doors and going to work in the city . . . . if we were just human . . . ." She added with a grin.

"But . . . . there's another consequence of all this saturninity. (I know spell check is gonna tell you that isn't a word, but just run with it.) These people, in spite of their disillusionment, depression and irritability from the lead poisoning still often make an attempt to escape from it. And what do you think that escape is?"

"Meth?"

"Yep, you got it. In an effort to combat a chemical poisoning that is ruining their lives, what do they do? They resort to another chemical poison. It gives an intense high, followed by another lingering depression. Lead poisoning isn't the only reason for meth addiction, but it's a significant one. St. Francois and Jefferson counties have some of the worst meth use rates in the country . . . . and look what's in Jefferson county."

"I remember seeing the big smoke stack from I-55. Is that where the smelter is?"

"Yep. Now, do you also realize that this meth stuff was invented by Nazis and that Hitler was a user?"

"Are you serious?"

"Absolutely. His doctor, Theodore Morell, gave him daily injections, and actually that was probably the downfall of the Third Reich. You've got a drug addict at the helm of the greatest war machine the world had ever seen. It couldn't end any other way."

"So, do you guys have some kind of plan in place to halt this meth use?"

"Well," she said, "education, understanding, and implant removal will prevent future generations from becoming users. The problem is the current users. If they don't make an effort to get off the shit of their own accord, no amount of treatment will make a nickel's worth of difference."

"So what's the solution?"

She hesitated a little too long this time, and I was afraid I already knew the answer. It wasn't going to be popular and it certainly wouldn't be pretty. Her response caught me completely off guard. "Are you familiar with the Opium Wars?" she asked.

"Vaguely."

"Well, I suggest you get Sam to tell you about them some time or maybe just do your own research. But I ask you this: 'What do you do when diseased rats infect your food supply and your population?'"

"Call an exterminator?"

"So, have you answered your question by answering mine?"

I suppose I had.

THE HOT GATES AND THE POLE

[Leo]

After my funeral pyre over aromatic cedar wood, in an effort to make restitution for my failure, I spent the next 300 years as a Sequoia. The boys at the Transmutation Station were glad to send me back as a plant. I'd be much less trouble, and as a tree, the cycle would be long. That thousand years as an insect had me back at the station nearly every 36 hours, and the amoeba? I was back twice a day! That was exhausting for both me and the Station boys.

I was prepared to spend three to five thousand years as that majestic Sequoia, but a bolt of lightning shortened my life by more than ninety percent. At three hundred I was only a sapling compared to the big boys in the forest.

But this paragraph is about the Hot Gates, or at least the part which hasn't before been told. If you want to understand most of the details without getting bogged down in a boring history lesson, let me suggest Frank Miller's 300, or the movie by the same name starring Gerard Butler. I think he did a great job of playing me. I really didn't remember being that brave. And except for our conjugal visit, both the graphic novel and the movie tell the tale better than I could.

The part that they didn't tell you was that the wives of our brave-but-hopelessly—outnumbered band paid us a visit our last night on this Earth. We knew the morrow would bring our demise, and our lovemaking in the face of imminent death instilled a passion in both the men and women that I had forgotten and repressed until my reunion with Cleo in the garden of Veronica. Her visit to the Hot Gates was the catalyst that kept her looking for me for the next three thousand years while I languished in an ignorant apathy.

We gave our lives that next morning as our women hastened back toward Sparta so that my friend Themistocles could herald in a new age of freedom for mankind.

Because these stories have been so well told over the centuries by better historians than I, there is no need for me to elaborate. However, I must tell you what occurred after life as Leonidas . . . . and my next trip to the Transmutation Station.

*　　*　　*

"This guy has got to be stopped! Sending him back as a bug only slowed him down. Sending him back as a rape victim only strengthened him! Even being a Goddamned tree didn't stop him! Send the son-of-a-bitch to the Pole. Maybe a thousand years on the pole will break him!"

Think flag pole, zero degrees Fahrenheit, and a little boy's tongue . . . .

There's not much to tell about ten centuries years stuck to the pole with an electronic beam. The words 'boredom' and 'apathy can't begin to describe the depression into which I sunk. And the worst? I couldn't even die.

When I was finally released, I was sent to what is now eastern Turkey (though I had no clue as to my whereabouts at that time). It took me some time to get my bearings, but I knew I was extremely small, though I was able to leap 100 times the length of my body. Guess I'm not human!

I was hatched into a great forest, and though the trees were close together, they seemed to be nothing but spars; no leaves and no branches. And then my whole world shook and shivered; it was then I realized I could feel its motion! I'd never before been able to feel the Earth move . . . . unless during an earthquake . . . . but this motion seemed to be constant! What kind of a planet is this?

When I eventually ran into another inhabitant of this strange world, it all became abundantly clear who and what I am.

My world is the back of a wharf rat, and I am a flea.

My name is Bubon, and my plague would soon become world-famous.

THE TREATMENT PROGRAM

[Roy]

'm sure you know that most drug treatment programs are a failure. They must be repeated again and again if they have any hope of success. Lindsey Lohan is the spokes-child for the failure of drug and alcohol treatment programs, and she may be in the headlines again as you read this . . . . if she hasn't yet killed herself.

"Would you consider supervising a treatment pogram?" Marie asked.

"You mean PRO-gram?"

"No, I didn't. I am a master of the language you know," she smiled smugly.

"Are you saying what I think you are saying?"

"Well, I'm not talking about Nazi death camps, but I am talking about a pogram to remove the addict from the society. We're not targeting any group based on race, religion, creed, ethnicity, blah, blah, blah. We're only talking about the addict."

"O . . . . K . . . . I'll bite. How does this work?"

"First of all, it can't be done on-planet."

"Are you actually talking about LEAVING the planet?"

"Yes. The only way we have any hope of treating these people is to totally remove them from the influence. Even neutral ocean waters aren't sufficient, as there is still the possibility of interference. We have to get them off the planet. Now, unlike Mao, we're not going to dig trenches and have mass executions, but I'm also not saying we're having NO executions. Unfortunately, there will be a few."

"You're serious about that too, aren't you?"

"Roy, one of the things you may have to set aside is the belief that all people are entitled to the same rights."

"But that's what this country was supposedly based on: Equal Rights!"

"And look at the condition of the country! Would you, in good conscience, grant the same rights to Hitler or Pol Pot as you would Mother Theresa?"

"Well of course not!"

"Then didn't you just prove my point? That all people should not be entitled to the same rights?"

"OK, but how the hell do you decide who is entitled to what rights?"

"It requires educated judgment. And it is *not* an art, it's a science, and a very exact science, it is. And if you wish to supervise the program (or pogram), you must learn the science."

She allowed a minute for that to soak into my thick skull. "I guess it's better than being the Doctor of Shit, but I was hoping to work on the magnet motors or the swtichgrass program."

"We all have to go where we're needed most."

"OK, OK, I'm not arguing any more. I'll do it . . . . So now what happens?" I really wanted to supervise Sam's energy program but it seems that I have to do what I'm asked whether I really want to or not.

"While Constance and Janey train you, I'll be getting people signed up."

That's when she showed me the flyer. I couldn't believe my eyes.

Free Meth
During Free Treatment Program
Quit in 30 Days Guaranteed!

When I could get the hinge of my jaw to work again, I voiced my first request. "I don't want Janey training me, Marie. Constance is fine, but it'll be too distracting to me to be around Janey when I'm trying to learn a new skill."

"I get it; Constance can handle it."

"Then what about the 'few' executions? How do we explain those who don't return?"

"OK, just a little more information and then we gotta go, I have work to do. Most of these people are (or were) decent humans. Only a very small percentage of them are Wyverns. After the basic biological withdrawal from the physical portion of the addiction, the mental part is conducted via a de-implantation cycle. And as you know, the Wyverns won't survive it."

"Then how do we explain the fact that they don't return?"

"Have you ever seen the movie, 'The Forgotten'?"

"I don't recall."

"'I don't recall!'" she mocked. "OK, smartass, then sit down and watch it. That will explain everything. Except we're not forgetting children. We're forgetting Wyvern dope heads."

"OK, one more thing. Are you really gonna start cooking meth for the addicts?"

"Oh, hell no. It's a legal prescription drug in the US. It's still manufactured by medical laboratories and available by prescription."

"And how are you going to get a prescription, let alone the volume you'll need."

"Actually, we don't need that much, they'll only get enough to get them on the ship, after that, we'll start the detox program. And our source? Veronica will make the arrangements. She has the leverage we need.

I needed to learn more about this Veronica person. It sounds like she works the fucked-up system to our advantage, but for now, I'm turning the reins back over to Leo. I'm leaving the solar system.

THE CARTERETS

t's now time for me (Leo) to remind you where we left off in the last volume.

Rasputin has escaped from his electronic handcuffs and has struck Cleo in the head. She is lying motionless in a pool of her own blood on the floor of our small craft after it lost power and was forced to set down on a small islet in the South Pacific. Homer and the two Rasputin thugs are nowhere to be seen. Hundreds of hungry cannibals are banging on the side of our ship, while Billy and I both feel paralyzed and incapable of resolving the situation.

But first I need to explain to you a little about our location and why the people have resorted to cannibalism.

The Carterets are a group of islands in the South Pacific, and are part of Papua, New Guinea. In the last few years, as the ice caps melt and ocean levels rise, the Carterets are the first victims of Global Warming. Originally only a foot and half above sea level, they are now becoming inundated with salt water and their small farming plots are, one by one, becoming poisoned with salt.

Many residents are trying to locate their families to the large island of Bougainville, but are having difficulty finding land. Others refuse to leave at all, and will either have to be removed in an emergency evacuation or they will simply starve or drown.

The island on which we landed was a small atoll outside the jurisdiction of Papua New Guinea, and was still an uncharted island in 2010, when we landed there. Their tiny island farms had been completely inundated with salt water and as a result they ended up killing and eating all the animals on the island. Just a few weeks before we landed there, they had begun a Donner-Party-like existence. Unlike the Donners, who held out hope of a rescue and didn't begin to eat each other unless the eat-ee had already died, these islanders had devised a lottery, and like Owen Coffin,[3] the short straw meant you were on the menu.

*   *   *

I touched Cleo's carotid artery and found no pulse. Had this Wyvern psychopath killed the woman who had waited for me for 3500 years? I looked around for a weapon, for if there was anyone who deserved to be murdered more than my so-called brother, Rasputin was that one.

But nary a weapon did I see. What I did see, however, were stars when Rasputin kicked me in the head while I felt for Cleo's pulse. I, too, went down, all the while wondering what had happened to Homer.

Once I was down, I realized that although the blow knocked me to the floor, I didn't really feel any pain. Was this a result of being de-implanted? Rasputin, however, was expecting me to stay down, so I made no effort to arise. While lying on top of Cleo, my face touching hers, I felt a strange sensation. At first I couldn't make out what it was, and my first thought was that it was a bug on my cheek.

It was excruciating, lying still while a bug ran across my face . . . . until I realized it wasn't going anywhere. The motion was continuous, but it wasn't moving across my face; it was only in one location on my cheek. And then I realized there was a regular rhythm to it . . . . and the rhythm kept repeating.

---

3   Owen Coffin was a young man who went to sea on a whaling vessel in the 19th century. He and his fellow sailors were left stranded on a small whale-boat, and when starvation became reality, the sailors elected to draw straws. The short straw meant you would be the one the others killed and ate. Owen drew the short straw. One should also give a listen to Mountain's song "Nantucket Sleighride" written by the late, great, Felix Papplardi, which is dedicated to Owen.

Finally it dawned on me that it was Morse Code. Cleo was batting her eyelashes against my cheek! Eventually getting my dumb head out of my ass, I realized what she was saying: "I'm OK. Don't move."

I admit I felt pretty stupid that she'd been repeating it over and over until I got it. So that she knew I'd finally cognited, I blinked back: "Got it."

After kicking me to the floor, Rasputin once again yelled at Billy, "Get us the Hell out of here and I'll see that you're handsomely paid for rescuing me!"

"Well, Mr. Rasputin," Billy answered with a sarcasm peculiar to Missouri working-class folk, "I can't fly the damned thing, and even if I could, it won't run until the solar panels recharge the batteries. The sun ain't out to recharge them, and even if all those things weren't goin' on, I'll be damned if I'll ever fly you anywhere. I'll gladly die before I ever help a son-of-a-bitch the likes of you!"

Rasputin swung at Billy, expecting to knock him to the floor as well, but his blow was met with a face as hard as concrete and Rasputin's hand shattered like a windshield hit with a BB. He was screaming in pain when Cleo pushed me off her and rose to meet the old Wyvern.

"You're not winning this time, you old shit!" she flatly announced.

"I always win, you stupid woman! If you can't fly this thing, then let us out!"

"You sure that's what you want?" she asked. I elbowed her in the ribs. What was she thinking?

"Let me out now!" he demanded.

"I'm taking you back to justice . . . . Hyanthian justice."

"You let me out now! If you don't, I'll smash your instruments and you'll never get off this island!"

"What do you think, Leo?" she asked with a smirk that only I could see.

"I'd say let him go. If the batteries don't charge, we're stuck here, and we can't radio for help."

"OK, OK, I acquiesce. Billy, open the hatch and let him out."

The moment he was out the door, he turned to Cleo and said, "You stupid bitch! I've got a GPS beacon implanted in my skull, and your ship was jamming the signal. Now that I'm out, I can send a signal to my staff in China and I'll be picked up in less than an hour, and your stupid ass will be blown into tiny pieces!"

"Yep! You're right! I am a stupid bitch!" she confessed with that same smirk as she closed the hatch. "I'm the stupid bitch!" Turning toward me, she asked, "Where's Homer?"

"Right here," he announced as he turned the corner. "When we lost power, the electronic restraints all failed and that's how they got loose. I got a needle in the necks of the two goons from Washington and got them knocked out. I knew you were faking it, so I just bided my time."

"Let's get those two out as well," she ordered. Billy, Homer and I dragged them to the hatch and dropped them to the ground. I looked for Rasputin but I couldn't find him. There was a heated commotion in the mass of brown bodies about 100 feet from the ship that was suddenly disrupted when we opened the door and kicked the other two men to the ground. Several of the natives ran toward them, shouting a word I couldn't understand.

"What are they saying?" I asked, turning toward my inamorata.

"Dinner," she answered matter-of-factly.

I guess Cleo was getting her justice, just not the kind she had had in mind.

"When we get a chance," she added, "we're coming back to rescue these people."

"We'd better hurry, then," Homer exclaimed. "Another couple weeks, and there won't be anybody here to rescue . . . ."

"Just wondering," Billy asked. Can the last two people eat each other at the same time, until there's nothing left but a head and a torso?"

"You've been alone too long," I mumbled.

TOTAL FAILURE

T wo hours after the Carterets had devoured their human victims and they were resting in the shade of a rock overhang, the cloud cover finally broke and old Sol peeked through an opening. There were no trees left on the island, so rock outcroppings offered the only remaining protection from the oppressive South Pacific sun. It wouldn't be long now before the entire island was inundated, but cannibalism would surely destroy the population before the remaining land disappeared below the sea.

By dark the batteries had charged enough and we were finally able to lift off. "It's a good thing we brought something to feed those starving people," Billy grinned. I sure wasn't looking forward to being on the menu!"

When the radio would function again, Cleo called back to Madison County to check in with Veronica and give her an update on our status.

"I'm going to call Toni to bring the Galaxy Hopper here to pick them up," Cleo announced to Vee over the radio. "She'll have to blue-flash them and put them in the cargo hold until we can get them de-implanted and educated. But having these folks on our team will be invaluable. We can set them up on Bougainville and train them start removing implants on their own people."

"No can do!" came Veronica's voice back into our ship the second Cleo let go of the microphone button. "Marie has sent

Roy to an outpost in the Enigma Galaxy with a full load of meth-addicts. We've got no ship to transport anyone."

"Dammit!" Cleo exclaimed. "I know that was on the timetable, but we've got a situation here! I've got an island full of people that are going to drown if we don't get them removed!"

"Should we contact the US Navy?" I stupidly asked.

"Oh, Hell, No! Then we lose them forever! If the Navy gets hold of them, we'll never see them again!" She keyed the microphone again and asked, "When will they be back?"

"About two weeks."

"There may not be any left alive in two weeks! Can you call them back?"

"Sure, but that isn't going to help. It takes two weeks for the ship to get back, even if I call it back right now!"

"Is that the only ship you've got?" I asked, hoping not to annoy her again.

"Well, like Rumsfeld said when he got so much grief about un-armored Humvees, 'You go to war with what you've got, not with what you wish you had.' This has been a shoestring operation from the get-go, but it was the only option we had. If we got this planet de-implanted and got our loan paid off, we could have financed other projects and other ships, but these two are all we've got!"

"We've got bigger problems than a drowning island!" Veronica's voice came over the radio, and it was the first time I'd ever heard 'worry' in her voice, and now I was really scared.

"What's wrong?" Cleo asked.

"We've got the US Marines at the gate and choppers flying overhead. Not to mention being buzzed by F-16's"

"You know what that means!" Cleo was furious.

"I sure do," Veronica replied. "The President has betrayed us!"

"And after I rescued his entire family . . . . that son-of-a-bitch!"

"I wonder what went wrong!"

"Not enough DI's, I suppose. Either that or he's a fucking Wyvern! But that simply can't be; after all, he made it through the epilation! I assume he has no idea that we captured Rasputin and fed him to the cannibals?"

"You did what?" Now even Veronica couldn't believe her ears.

"Fed him to the cannibals," Cleo repeated nonchalantly.

"I don't know what we're going to do, but you sure as Hell can't come back here!" Veronica warned.

"How many people are in the compound?"

"Over two hundred."

"Shit, I can't transport that many . . . . ten maybe but not two hundred."

"That leaves me no choice but to blue-flash and leave by our vehicles!"

"Take as few vehicles as possible. Your only hope is to retreat to the mine. Camouflage the vehicles and get everyone to the mine. There are plenty of resources there to last till the Hopper gets back. No one who had a car at the resort will ever be safe again. We may have to abort the entire operation."

"No, Cleo." Even over the radio there was doubt about the determination in Veronica's voice. "I won't give up. We're just going to have to find another approach . . . . after we retreat to safety."

"Where's Sam and Marie?"

"Sam is in Kansas, supervising wind turbine construction. Marie and Constance are at the farm in Doe Run."

"Then they're safe?"

"Let's hope so. We need to have contacts in the area. And since they had no licensed vehicle at the resort, they should be all right." Veronica paused for a moment. "I'm sorry Cleo. I thought we were well on our way . . . ."

"Not your fault, Vee. I'm not sure this damned planet is worth saving. I've found Leo. You've got Chuck. Maybe we should just cash in our chips and get off this piece of shit planet and just let it go the way of Thera!"

"And let the Wyverns win again?"

"Maybe they already have, Vee. Maybe they already have."

*   *   *

Things had been looking up for the human race. For the first time since they'd been genetically engineered here hundreds of thousands of years ago, the humans were about to escape the chains of slavery that had been shackled to them upon their creation.

But freedom is a scary thing . . . . and most of the race lives in secret fear . . . . fear of what they themselves might do with real freedom.

And when that freedom was within their grasp, that same fear reared its ugly head and threatened to re-shackle the race and the planet into an eternity of slavery . . . . a slavery enforced by the President of the "free-est" nation on the planet.

Can a handful of Hyanthians and one crazy Dunist rescue Earth from itself and escape the fate of Thera?

Find out in Volume III of
Earth——The Salvage Game:
Poisoned Planet!